Same Old Truths

a novel by

DELORA DENNIS

Other Works by Delora Dennis

Code for Karma

To My Mom,

Who Always Said I Should Write a Book

SAME OLD TRUTHS

1

Bombs and Banana Bread

Settle down! It's still early. You don't want him to find you bleeding.

Every time Kay heard the approach of a car her stomach lurched and she'd jump up to look out the window. This last time she had failed to scoot her chair out far enough and scraped the tops of her thighs on the underside of the table. Trying to enjoy her first cup of coffee of the day was proving to be a lost cause.

As she rubbed her stinging thighs, she peered out over her weedy, unkempt lawn and felt a pang of embarrassment. Why hadn't she spent a little of her Saturday "policing the area," as her dad used to say, instead of sleeping in? It wasn't right to make her neighbors suffer just because she'd lost interest in keeping up any display of neighborhood pride.

I hope he doesn't notice.

Kay didn't want to admit it, but she was excited to see him. And way, way down in the furthest reaches of her heart, she secretly hoped he was feeling the same about her. After all, it only stood to reason that two people who had shared a life and two daughters, must surely miss each other from time to time.

But as the time grew closer to his arrival, she

couldn't help feeling a familiar dread and apprehension. It was only natural given all the bombs he'd dropped on her over the years.

Come on, Kay.   Give the guy a chance.

Still, she couldn't shake the foreboding that gnawed at her insides. She was tempted to pacify her anxiety with a healthy slice from the fresh loaf of banana bread sitting in her bread box. Instead, she averted carb overload by running to the mirror to check her face one more time.

Her dark hair (which he used to refer to as "light-black" just to make her laugh) was arranged in thick, soft curls which spilled across the tops of her slim shoulders. She'd been careful not to use too much make up, lest he think she'd purposely dolled-up just for him.

Presentable.

A quick breath into her cupped hand suggested a couple of Tic-Tacs might be in order. She was rooting around in her purse for the mints when the knock at the door finally came.

The two of them stood there on opposing sides of the threshold, looking at each other, not knowing quite what to do next. Dave made the first move with a tentative step forward, arms opened in invitation, causing Kay to reflexively step back in a slight recoil. She was embarrassed (and surprised) at her involuntary rejection of his friendly gesture, but tried to cover it up with an enthusiastic, "come in." She hoped he couldn't pick up on her nervousness/excitement (or her bad breath).

"Have a seat," Kay said, breezily motioning toward the dining room table, flinging the two breath mints she was holding across the room. The sight and sound of those little white pellets ricocheting off her hard Mexican tile in fifteen different directions was just too comical. As gracefully as she could, Kay chased and picked up the errant mints, letting out a little cough to stifle the giggle trying to bubble up out of her throat.

"Can I get you a cup of coffee?" she asked.

"Sure, that would be great," Dave said, looking at her contorting face with that expression of annoyance she had come to know so well during their marriage. He took a seat and fidgeted trying to find a comfortable position which was neither too formal or too familiar.

Kay poured him a cup, freshened her own and discretely popped the mints in her mouth. Immediately she felt hair and other unwanted particles on her tongue. With a tight-lipped smile she slid into her chair. Their eyes met for the briefest of moments, triggering an involuntary heart flutter. The big green, puppy dog eyes, rimmed with thick dark lashes had always been his best feature...next to a dazzling Kennedy-esque smile and full head of ash brown hair.

Damn. He's still got it.

But he wasn't able to hold her gaze for more than a nanosecond. Kay couldn't decide if his lack of eye contact was due to guilt or because the sight of her repelled him. Regardless, she took advantage of the moment to discreetly pinch the floor debris off the

3

tip of her tongue.

Once he had given his eyes the appropriate interval of rest, he looked back at her and smiled as he glided the palm of his hand across the surface of the table. "I can't believe you still have this old table. Does the leaf still give you problems?"

She laughed. "Oh yeah. Mom almost lost a finger last Thanksgiving."

He laughed too and nodded. Then his face turned wistful. "Look at us. Sitting here having coffee. Just like the old days."

Her heart responded again, but this time it was sadness, not arousal, that caused the sensation in her chest. She was touched by his nostalgia.

He does miss us. We really were good together.

Dave let out a melancholy sigh and then launched into a series of nervous, rapid-fire, small talk questions. How are the girls? How are they doing in school? How do they feel about his move back?

Reluctantly, Kay allowed him to lead her away from Memory Lane. She was attempting to answer his questions when her attention got pulled toward something weird happening with his face. It was his turn to respond but his lips weren't in sync with what she was hearing. It was if she had just walked into the middle of a foreign movie. After a moment of trying to make sense of it, it suddenly became clear. It was a countdown.

Ten…nine…eight…

"Yeah, we thought it was time to come home since Sandy's mom is not in the best of health," he began.

seven…six…five…

"Of course, the idea of being nearer to the girls and giving Little Dave a chance to have a relationship with his sisters was very important too," he continued, making sure Kay knew the girls had also been factored into the decision.

four…three…two…

"As luck would have it, I was offered a job here that I just couldn't pass up."

One…

"The only crappy thing is, salaries being what they are here, I've had to take a big cut in pay."

DETONATE

"So, unfortunately, your child support is going to have to take a cut."

KA-BOOM!

The mushroom cloud in her head billowed with every pound of her pulse.

Why can't my intuition be right about lottery numbers, instead of this crap?

"So, exactly how big a cut are we talking about?" Kay asked, when she was finally able to speak.

He looked her dead-square in the eye. There was a long, uneasy pause. It reminded her of a scene right out of Gunsmoke with Sheriff Matt Dillon standing in the street in front of the saloon facing off against some gunslinger moments before he calls out, "draw!"

"Half," he finally fired off.

Ah hah! Now the real reason for his request to come see her had revealed itself and it had nothing to do with working out a new visitation schedule (or seeing her because he missed her).

Hell, we could have easily taken care of this over the phone.

There was a small (make that teeny) part of her that was impressed with his courage to give her this news in person. It was a far cry from the weasel that had put their five year old daughter on the phone to tell her he was moving out of state and taking his girlfriend, Sandy, with him.

My poor little Cory.

Kay remembered her daughter's confused, apologetic, "He won't come to the phone, Mommy," when she had asked repeatedly to speak to him. Maybe he had grown up a little in the last seven years.

Despite his cool, poker-faced delivery, Kay knew he was steeling himself against a potentially-explosive reaction. But she refused to give him the satisfaction.

Two can play that game. I'll see your cool and raise you a no-big-deal.

"I don't understand," she said. "Why aren't you going through legal channels to modify the order?"

Dave scooted his chair closer to the table. "I thought about it, but I just couldn't see racking up big bills - for both of us - when I knew you and I could work something out on our own." He gave Kay the kind of smile she hadn't seen since they were married.

He wants to work something out with me.

This was music to Kay's ears. Her goal of having a workable relationship with Dave had, up to this point, remained frustratingly elusive. During their years together they had always made such a good team, so she'd never been able to understand why he'd repeatedly rejected her attempts to build a new, post-divorce alliance. Now that he'd finally opened the door, she was determined to make the most of it. This was her chance to finally move forward.

"Well," Kay began, holding on to *her* poker-face, "I'd be willing to take the cut, if you were willing to help me with the kids. I'm talking about driving them to appointments, picking them up from school when they're sick, participating in their school activities and whatever else might come up."

"Absolutely!" Dave responded. "That's why I've come back."

Dave was clearly relieved and Kay felt encouraged to continue. "I'm also going to expect you to help with extras like their school uniforms and supplies. And since I'm carrying them on my health insurance, I think it's only fair that you split their co-pays with me." She couldn't believe how fast these demands were coming out of her mouth.

"Not a problem" Dave said.

"Oh, and as far as the girls' visitation with you is concerned, you should know Cory has made the decision not to go." Kay was happy to drop a little bomb of her own.

"And just why in the hell is that?" Dave said. Kay had hit her target.

"Well, I think she's just trying to exert her independence. You know how teenagers are."

"She's not a teenager," Dave snapped back. "She's only twelve."

"You know what I mean. She'll be thirteen soon and she knows twelve is the age she can no longer be forced to see you."

"Forced? I've *never* forced her to spend time with me. I don't understand it. We've always had great times together. Just ask her."

Kay didn't have to ask her. Over the last seven years she had listened to both girls' constant complaints about their miserable visits with their dad. Summer visits were "miserable" because they had to endure Sandy's nasty attitude toward them and

Dave's unwillingness to do anything to about it. And their scheduled weekend visits, when Dave flew in to see them, were "miserable" because Sandy accompanied Dave *every single time*. It was clear to both girls Sandy's mom was the true focus of the visit and not them. They always stayed at Sandy's brother's house and had to sleep on the floor. They felt unwelcome and uncomfortable.

According to the girls, on the rare occasion when they were alone with Dave, he'd revert to his old self and the three of them would have a wonderful time. Unfortunately, those times were few and far between. Cory's impassioned pleas to Dave to come alone, "just once," were always met with, "it's not gonna happen."

So now it was "not gonna happen" for Dave. Kay had tried to persuade Cory to change her mind, if only to keep Mariah, her younger daughter, from having to go to her dad's by herself. Cory would not be moved.

As if he was reading her mind, Dave quickly changed the subject. "How is Mariah doing with you-know-what?" he asked, pointing downward to his butt.

You've got to be kidding.

Kay wanted to lean in close to him and say in her best kindergarten teacher voice, "Come on, Dave. Use your words."

In this case the word was encopresis. That was the official medical term for "pooping in your pants." The pediatrician told Kay it was an involuntary reaction to stress and she saw it quite commonly in children of divorced parents. Of course, when Kay tried to explain this to Dave, his angry response was, "that doctor's only telling you what you want to hear."

"Interestingly enough, she hasn't had a single episode since she got back from her summer visit with you," Kay responded, trying to keep the smugness out of her voice.

"It doesn't happen at school?" Dave asked.

"Not so far," Kay happily reported.

"She doesn't have problems when she's here at home?" Dave said, his voice getting louder.

"My laundry indicates she doesn't." Kay was beginning to feel a little defensive.

"So she can control it when she wants to," he said. He sounded like a prosecuting attorney.

"Dave, if you're implying she does it on purpose, you're dead wrong. Why would she purposely humiliate herself?"

"I don't know. I just find it interesting that the only time it seems to happen is when she's with me."

Wow, Sherlock. You find it interesting too?

To avoid the heated confrontation threatening to erupt, Kay thought she'd better wind things up.

"Well, the good news is the doctor says it's likely she'll outgrow it. As for Cory, I wouldn't worry. She'll come around. You know her. She can't stand being left out."

Dave took the hint and took one last sip of coffee before getting up and making his way toward the door. "I hope you're right," he said. "I'm going to give her a call. I think I can change her mind."

Knock yourself out. Kay knew it was going to be a wasted effort.

"If it's ok with you, I'll pick them up Friday evening, right after I get off work. Is Sunday at noon an ok time to bring them back?"

"Sure," Kay said, resisting an urge to put her foot on his ass and launch him out the door. "I know the girls are happy to have you home," Kay lied.

Kay stood in the doorway and watched as he made his way back to his truck. He stopped unexpectedly and turned back to Kay with a concerned expression on his face. "Do you have someone to help you with the yard?"

Kay leaned slightly forward. "No. Not really."

"Bummer," he said. And with that he turned and went on his way. "I'll call you next week with the arrangements for the child support," he called over his shoulder.

Kay shut the door and let out a long, exasperated sigh. She realized moving forward might prove to be more difficult than she'd first thought. But she wasn't about to let those nagging doubts creep back in. All she needed was a big piece of banana bread to keep them at bay...at least for the mean time.

2

D.U.I.

(Driving Under Iffiness)

"Why are you such a pushover?" Kay's sister, Leslie, shouted at her over the phone. "You mean to tell me you just accepted what he said without any questions?" Kay could feel the sting of Leslie's disapproval. "Don't you think you should run it past an attorney?"

Kay's skepticism was just as strong as her sister's, but she, nevertheless, felt compelled to defend herself for giving in to Dave so easily. "I really don't think there's any need to involve an attorney. It's a friendly agreement between the two of us," Kay said, aware of how pathetic she sounded.

"Look. He's promised to help me with all the extra-curriculars. You know how much I complain about spending most of my life with a car stuck to my butt. Anyway, he doesn't have the same problem getting away from work that I do. That in itself is worth what he's deducting from my support."

"Bullshit!" Leslie responded, never being one to hold back what she was really thinking…especially when it came to Dave. "You need that money. Anyway, I don't trust him. He's always known how to push your buttons to get what he wants."

"C'mon, Les," Kay said, trying to appeal to

Leslie's levelheaded side. "Think about it. He's been gone for seven years. He's only been able to see the girls for eight weeks a summer and they're growing up without him. For Dave to be willing to take a big cut in pay just so he can move back home, tells me he really wants to be in their lives." Kay hoped Leslie would buy the logic of her explanation. Hell, she was trying to believe it herself.

Leslie scoffed. "They've moved back for Sandy and Sandy alone. You told me yourself her mother is sick and she wants to be near her and her brother."

"I know," Kay said. She was embarrassed to have her words thrown back at her. "But if it means the girls are going to have their dad back, who cares what the reason is?"

"Well, I just hope it turns out the way you want it to. Anyway, that's not why I called. I wanted to remind you not to forget the networking luncheon this Friday. I hope you're planning to come. The guest speaker is going to give a presentation on social networking."

Crap.

Kay tried to quickly come up with a valid excuse for begging off. "Oh, I meant to call you about that. We're going to be short-staffed on Friday and I have to cover the phones over lunch." This was partially true. Ruth, the receptionist where Kay worked had asked her to fill in while she ran an errand; it wasn't during the lunch hour. "But, I have every intention of making it next month."

"Aw, that's too bad," Leslie said, not really that

disappointed. "I just thought you'd get a lot out of the presentation. Didn't you tell me Ed is looking to take his marketing in a new direction?"

"Yeah. But I'm not sure if Twitter and Facebook are a good fit. Anyway, if you think about it, save me some handouts. I'd better get going. I'll talk to you soon." Kay ended the phone call, wondering why she'd been born with the "weenie gene" while Leslie got the "take-no-prisoners gene."

"Was that Aunt Les?" Cory asked, bounding down the stairs, almost knocking Kay over at the bottom. "I wanted to say hi."

"Yes it was. She's really excited that your dad is back." Kay hoped telling these little lies wasn't going to become a habit.

"Gimme a break, Mom," Cory said, clearly not buying what Kay was trying to sell. "She can't stand Dad. Never has…never will."

"Cory, this isn't about your Dad. It's about you girls. You know Aunt Leslie only wants the best for you."

"Whatever." Cory said in the universal snarky teenage refrain. "Anyway, the best thing for me is to not have to spend weekends at Dad's house." Kay could sense the power Cory felt speaking those words. It made Kay feel proud and sad at the same time.

She really is maturing.

"Why do you have to be so mean?" Mariah asked, following her sister into the room. "Aren't you glad we're going to get to see Dad more often?

"Shut up, Stupid," Cory barked at her little sister.

"Cory!" Kay snapped backed." *Ok, maybe I've overestimated the maturity thing.* Cory truly fit the definition of "Tween."

"She bugs, Mom," Cory whined. "Anyway, if it was just Dad, it would be great. But we have to see *her*, too," she said. "Mom, it's hard to believe, but Sandy's gotten even meaner since Little Dave was born. And Dad never does anything about it"

"Oh, Honey. Sandy is a new mom. It's only natural she's a little over-protective." The instant the words left her mouth, she knew she'd probably insulted Cory's intelligence.

"Over-protective of Dad you mean," Cory said. "She thinks she owns him. You know she's always hated sharing him with us. And now that Dave Jr. is in the picture she's ten times worse. Believe me, I'll never be missed."

"Well, I told Dad about your decision and he wasn't happy about it at all. I'm sure he's going to want to talk to you before this weekend. Are you ready to have that conversation?"

"Can't you talk to him for me?" Cory said. She sounded like a five year old.

"Absolutely not! If you really believe you're old enough to make the decision not to see him, then you're old enough to discuss it with him like an adult."

Cory's back straightened into a defiant posture. "Fine! I will. But you know he's going to try to lay a big guilt trip on me."

"Well, then you're going to have to decide if you'd rather spend the weekend here feeling guilty, or feeling miserable at your Dad's house," Kay said, falling back on the tried and true parenting technique of presenting the girls with choices. Not only was it a great little teaching tool, it had the bonus of letting her off the hook for making unpopular decisions. Sometimes watching Dr. Phil actually paid off.

"I wanna go," Mariah said, with sincere enthusiasm. "I haven't seen Little Dave in a long time, and I've really missed him."

"Yeah…he's about your speed," Cory said. The jealousy in her voice wasn't completely disguised.

"That's enough," Kay said. "You girls have gotta get a move on. You're going to miss the bus. And I have to get to work."

* * *

Kay had a 40-minute commute to work which she never minded. Her route took her in the opposite direction of rush-hour traffic and the low-stress drive gave her an opportunity to relax and prepare herself for the day. The return trip was the same, only in reverse. She had time to unwind before she had to take on the excitement/disappointment/frustration or whatever else the girls were anxious to report about what went on in school that day.

This morning, Kay was trying to get her head together before her 9:30 a.m. pre-arrangement appointment. Of all of her duties as an apprentice funeral director, "making arrangements" was probably her favorite. The process could be tedious and complicated and Kay took great pride in making it as stress-free as possible for "her families."

But rather than focusing on her meeting, her train of thought kept being derailed with concerns about how her and the girls' lives were going to change now that Dave was back in town.

No doubt, the cut in child support was going to have an impact on her finances. Kay had to admit she was spoiled by the cushion the extra $850 a month provided. But when it came to the well-being of her girls, no amount of money could compensate for Dave's absence. It certainly didn't ease the weight of responsibility that came with being a single parent. His willingness to play an active role meant some of this weight would be lifted off her shoulders. She wasn't lying when she told her sister his hands-on help was worth the deduction.

Then there was Cory. Her decision to remain behind on Dave's visiting weekends had stirred up a real hornets' nest. Kay still wasn't sure which side of the issue she was on.

On the one hand, she was proud (and a little envious) Cory was exercising her power to say no. Up to this point, Dave had had his way in practically everything, which included saying "no" to what she regarded as reasonable requests.

On the other hand, she hadn't had a free weekend in as long as she could remember. Having both girls at their dad's meant she could plan something fun in the company of adults. She loved her girls, but often longed for conversations that were above an 8th grade level.

And dare she allow herself to entertain thoughts about dating in earnest? This could only add more confusion to the mix. Up to now, she had strictly confined her dating activities to the summers when the girls were gone.

Kay thought about her divorced friends who had immediately returned to the dating scene with unbridled enthusiasm. She admired their courage to get back in the game, but she had never felt comfortable playing the "single gal" in front of the girls.

If Cory changed her mind, she might finally be able to attend a meeting of the singles group she'd impulsively signed up for   three months prior. Kay had always looked at these groups as being kind of "loser-ey" and swore she'd never sink to such an artificial level to meet men. In this instance, though, her curiosity had been piqued by a newspaper article describing a new social group recruiting and screening for "professional" singles.

Kay had pored over the article with a mix of curiosity and horror wanting to know who these professionally-single people were. It was only after reading past the first few paragraphs she realized her misunderstanding. They weren't looking for professional singles but people who had college degrees and worked at a professional level.

To her surprise, she found herself calling the number mentioned in the article and was the very first person to be interviewed and invited into the group. But that's as far as it had gone. Unfortunately, scheduling conflicts due to the girls' activities had prevented her from attending.

Why, I haven't gone to a single meeting. She chuckled at her silly pun.

Kay wasn't looking for true love. It was embarrassing to admit, but she wasn't completely over her divorce. She just wanted an opportunity to take her social skills out for a spin every now and then. She needed to be sure Kay The Person, hadn't been completely overtaken by Kay The Mom.

Kay loved being a mom, but she thought it was important to guard against it becoming her entire identity. Not because being a mother was something to look down on, but because it just seemed too risky - putting all your eggs in one basket. She knew one day the girls would be grown and gone and she didn't want to be left wondering who the heck she was when there was no longer anyone at home calling her "Mom." And being a funeral director was a job, not an identity.

Before the divorce she had been proud to stay at home with her girls. From time to time she'd encounter some woman who wasn't shy about expressing her scorn for women who'd chosen to raise children rather than earn a paycheck. Kay never took it personally because she knew there was usually something much deeper going on behind the woman's need to ridicule. Especially in the case of one particular woman.

Kay's stomach twisted thinking back to the unpleasant encounter that took place when she and Dave were still married and his affair with Sandy was in full swing.

His company's city league softball team had just finished a game and everyone had gathered at a nearby pizza parlor to celebrate their win.

Kids had always been naturally drawn to Kay and this day wasn't any different. She was sitting in a booth waiting for Dave to bring their pizza when several of the kids who had come to see their parents play spontaneously piled into the seat with her.

Sandy, the company's receptionist at the time and Ellen Cleary, the company's bookkeeper, were sitting in the adjoining booth facing Kay. Sandy took one look at her in the middle of all those kids and snickered. Then, loud enough to make sure everyone heard, she said in a snotty, condescending tone, "Oh Kay…you're such a mother," emphasizing "mother" and obviously leaving off the "fucker" part of the description. Sandy turned to Ellen and the two of them elbowed each other and giggled like a couple of junior high mean girls. Kay had been humiliated…not because she was sitting under a heap of children, but because she knew Sandy was making it clear to everyone who the real woman was in Dave's life.

So down, down, down the rabbit hole of her spiraling thoughts Kay fell, until without knowing it, she had reached the turn-in to the mortuary parking lot. She shuddered with alarm realizing she had no memory of how she'd gotten there.

So, is this how it's gonna be?

Kay carefully brought the car to a stop and slid the gear shift into Park. She lowered her head onto the steering wheel, keenly aware of the tightness that had built up in her neck and shoulder muscles.

Seven years of peace and serenity down the drain?

No. This would never do. She had worked too hard to regain her emotional footing after the divorce. To let herself become that crazy person again was unacceptable. For the sake of her sanity, as well as the safety of other drivers, she would have to be more mindful about staying in the present moment and dealing with matters right in front of her. In this moment a family was counting on her to help them arrange a fitting celebration of their dying-mother's life.

Kay raised her head, turned off the car and took some slow, deep breaths. As soon as the brick on her chest finally dissolved, she got out of the car and headed toward the employee entrance, head held high as if nothing in her world had changed.

3

The Black Dahlia

"Kay, just a reminder your appointment at the McNab's is at 9:30," Ruth announced over the office intercom.

Ruth Linton was the office manager and receptionist at Salinger's Mortuary, positions she had proudly held for over twenty-five years. Her soft, grandmotherly appearance and demeanor were perfect for easing the fear and discomfort that usually came with being in a mortuary for the first time. But as often is the case, looks were deceiving. Ruth was tough-as-nails and Ed Salinger implicitly trusted her with the day to day operation of the business.

"Thank you, Ruth. I was just getting my paperwork together." Kay replied.

She panicked for a split second when she couldn't find the file folder marked "Emily McNab" she had pulled from the file cabinet on Friday afternoon. She was still a little rattled from her upsetting drive and wasn't thinking all that clearly. There it was, right where she'd left it, in her In-box desk tray.

Mrs. McNab had been battling leukemia off and on for the last six years and even though she was currently in remission, she decided it was time to get her affairs in order. During the call to set the appointment she'd said to Kay, "my mother did this for me, and it was a true blessing. I want to do the same for my family." She told Kay that with everything they'd gone through over the years, she didn't want her family burdened with the difficult task of arranging her funeral after she was gone.

Today, Kay was paying a visit to the McNab home at Emily's request. Kay had done hundreds of pre-arrangements, typically for people who were healthy and just, smartly, planning ahead. Providing these services to families who knew death might be lurking right around the corner was another thing all together. It's what made her job so special. It was like being asked to come along on a very important journey and then trusted to handle intimate details of the trip. As emotionally daunting as it was, for everyone concerned, the sense of relief, peace and lightness that filled the room at the conclusion of the meeting was really a wonder to behold. The gratitude expressed by family members taught Kay what it was to feel truly humble.

With a quick double-check of the file to make sure she had all the necessary papers and forms, she grabbed her keys and let Ruth know she was leaving.

* * *

Two and a half hours later Kay was back in the office treating herself to her first cup of coffee of the day. It was her own little private celebration in honor of everything going so smoothly with the McNab's. She was bringing the cup to her mouth, taking in the delicious aroma, relishing the anticipation of its hot, full-bodied richness when the buzz of the intercom made her jump, causing her to scald her lips and dribble coffee down the front of her blouse. "Crap," Kay muttered as she carefully put the steaming cup back down on the desk.

"Yes?" Kay answered, blotting the wet mess from her blouse with the closest thing she could find - a crumpled-up Kleenex hastily pulled out of her wastebasket.

"Kay, Mrs. Burleigh is here and she'd like to see you." Ruth said. "Are you free?"

Kay looked longingly at the cup of coffee getting colder with each passing moment. "Is it the usual?" Kay groaned, knowing Ruth understood what she meant.

"That's correct," Ruth said in that telephone code meant to sound professional but really intended to keep the other person from knowing they're being talked about in front of their backs.

"Aw, geez," Kay replied. "Ok. Give me a sec. I spilled coffee on my blouse and I need to clean it up."

"Ok. I'll ask her to wait." Ruth spoke with her usual air of competence.

Evelyn Burleigh, aka The Black Dahlia, was here for her monthly review of her funeral pre-arrangement file. The reason for the inspection changed from month to month, but it was usually due to some impending crisis of the utmost urgency.

Last month's visit was prompted by a serious medical crisis. Evelyn had to be sure her final wishes were in order because, while enjoying herself at the senior citizens' dance in the arms of Horace Bledsoe, jitterbugging to Glenn Miller's, In The Mood, her "uterus fell out." The gynecologically-challenged woman explained to a stunned Kay the official diagnosis was uterine "relapse" and it could happen again at any time.

The truth was Evelyn was a lonely old woman who just needed someone to talk to now and then. Tony, her 40 year old, unemployed son lived with her but spent the majority of the time in his room watching TV, emerging only when he wanted something to eat.

Kay had christened Evelyn, The Black Dahlia, because the woman reminded her of those "big brassy dames" of the Silver Screen. She always wore a huge, black floppy-brimmed hat and big black sun-glasses that when removed, revealed seriously-smudged black mascara. All that was missing was a smoldering cigarette at the end of a long black cigarette holder to complete the picture.

Evelyn was in her early seventies but carried herself straight and tall with a theatrical elegance which she attempted to insert into her speech. Her sentences included plenty of "Dahlings" and were punctuated with big, dramatic arm and hand gestures. The only problem was she didn't have a good grasp of everyday phrases and expressions and her mangled deliveries were a source of great amusement for Kay.

From her office doorway Kay could see Evelyn, in full black regalia, nervously pacing back and forth in front of Ruth's desk. As she neared the reception area she realized Evelyn was not alone. Slumped in a chair across from Ruth was Tony, looking bored or dim-witted...Kay couldn't decide which. The blue sweat pants he was wearing were badly faded, full of holes and in desperate need of laundering. His red t-shirt, obviously two sizes too small, failed to cover his large, protruding stomach.

Take off the pants, and you've got Winnie the

Pooh.

Kay was already getting in the spirit of the comedy show about to start.

"Evelyn, how good to see you," Kay said, extending her hand to greet the old woman.

"Dahling, I'm so glad you're here," she said, ignoring Kay's hand and enveloping her in a dramatic embrace that almost knocked Kay out of her pumps. "You remember my Tony," Evelyn said, pushing Kay away and proudly nodding toward the moping mass in the chair.

"Of course I do. Hello, Tony," Kay said, trying to be enthusiastic for Evelyn's sake.

Keeping his gaze on the floor, and using every ounce of energy he could muster, Tony snapped his arm up at the elbow in one of those limp, "heil Hitler!" salutes.

Kay returned her attention to Tony's mother, still beaming with pride at her brooding blob. "What can I do for you today, Evelyn?"

"Something has come up and I need to check my pre-arrangement file."

"Of course, Evelyn. No problem. Let's go back to my office." Kay said. She was surprised to see Tony quickly rise from his chair and follow behind.

Looking for sympathy, Kay shot a quick glance back at Ruth, but the ever-professional woman had already turned her attention back to her computer screen. Kay was on her own.

"Please, sit," Kay said as they entered her office, gesturing to the two chairs in front of her desk.

Her workspace was small but seemed larger thanks to two large windows which provided ample light. An attractive array of potted plants and tastefully-hung pictures helped to make the little office pleasant and comfortable - as much for Kay as for visitors.

Tony accepted Kay's invitation and slunk into one of the chairs, maneuvering into the seat with all the grace of a huge jungle python having just swallowed a small antelope. The bored/dimwitted expression never left his face.

Evelyn declined. "No thank you, Dahling," she said, resuming her pacing. "I'm too upset to sit."

Evelyn walked over to the window, peering back and forth in search of some unseen menace.

"What's going on? It sounds serious." Kay was anxious to hear what the story was *this* month.

"Oh, Dahling, it's more than serious," Evelyn said, still searching through the window. "My Tony informs me my in-laws on my dead husband's side are having the verge to murder me." Evelyn pulled a tissue from her sleeve and dabbed at her eyes, pushing the smudges around.

Kay was "having the verge" to laugh, but didn't want to be disrespectful.

Kay looked at Tony. "Is this true?"

Tony, still staring at the floor, shifted his girth uncomfortably in the chair, shrugged and muttered, "I don't know. I guess."

Evelyn finally turned away from the window and approached Kay's desk. "Dahling, they've always hated me, but this has to be the final nail in the coffee.

They're jealous because their mother gave me her diamond pendulum on my wedding day. Now they're demanding it back. They hound me day and night. My God, it's like they have channel vision." She walked back to the window and resumed her search. "But they're going to have to kill me to get it."

Wow, this is one of her better performances.

But despite the entertainment, Kay couldn't help feeling sorry for the woman. "Evelyn, no!" Kay said, hoping to convey genuine concern. "I can understand why you're so upset. Have you gone to the police?"

"The police?" Evelyn said indignantly. "They can't help. You know how they are. They won't do anything until a crime's been permitted."

"What are you going to do?" Kay asked, deciding to indulge Evelyn's drama.

But just as Evelyn opened her mouth to respond, the intercom buzzer interrupted. "I'm sorry to bother you, Kay," Ruth said, "but Mr. McNab is here with a picture for his wife's obituary. He also has some changes to the list of pallbearers."

"Ask him to have a seat, Ruth. I'll be right out," Kay said. She was a little disappointed Mr. McNab had chosen this exact moment to show up.

"Evelyn, you'll have to excuse me. I have something I have to take care of in the front office. It shouldn't take too long."

Kay walked over to the file cabinet, searched the B's and pulled out the one labeled "Burleigh." The folder had been handled so many times, the edges had become frayed and it was beginning to come apart at the crease.

"Here's your file," Kay said, handing it over to Evelyn who was finally sitting. "Look it over and when I come back you can let me know if there are any changes you'd like to make."

Kay made her exit, but before she was able to completely close her office door, she heard Tony complain in a menacing voice that took her by surprise. "Look, Old Woman. You promised if I came with you, you'd take me to Clucky's Chicken Hut. I wanna get outta here and go eat. NOW!"

Behind the closed door Kay could hear the muffled sounds of a bullied mother trying to pacify an over-grown brat. Kay's heart broke for the woman who had to live with this nasty Baby Huey.

Kay took a quick detour through the small hallway separating the display room from the auxiliary chapel. At the end of the hall was a drinking fountain and Kay badly needed the refreshment the cool water had to offer. She had just leaned over to catch the arc of liquid in her slightly parted lips when her boss, Ed Salinger, appeared behind her, causing her to choke on a tiny trickle of water going down the wrong way. He waited patiently for her coughing fit to subside before he spoke. "Sorry about that. Listen. Is there any way you'd be able to work the Campbell viewing this evening? I have to pick up a body at the airport. I can't get a hold of Uncle O, so I have to go myself."

Owen Salinger was Ed's uncle. He'd been helping out at the mortuary since his retirement from the Post Office five years earlier. Whenever there was a death call, Uncle O was usually dispatched to the hospital, nursing home or private residence to pick up the deceased and transport it back to the mortuary. He wasn't officially on the payroll, so he didn't feel obligated to always be available.

"Hmmm," Kay said. "It shouldn't be a problem. I just have to let the girls know."

"Thanks. You know I wouldn't ask unless it was absolutely necessary." Ed, perpetually in a hurry, spoke over his shoulder as he made his exit through the display room.

Ed Salinger was not only one of the best-looking men Kay knew, but also the busiest. In addition to successfully operating a prosperous business, Ed was an active member of the community, sitting on boards and chairing committees in a host of civic organizations. In his spare time he played tennis, coached pee wee baseball, and was a starting forward on an inter-city basketball team. Kay thought it was a good thing Ed was single, because she couldn't imagine any woman who'd be willing to be shoehorned into his long to-do list. Though, from time to time, she'd certainly entertained the idea herself.

Kay thought about Ed's request. This was Monday, which meant Cory had a 7:00 p.m. appointment with her therapist. Here was an occasion when she was going to need Dave's help. She felt her breath coming a little faster. Unlike the stupid excuses she'd contrived in the past to call him when she missed him, now she had a valid reason to make contact. She was curious to see if he was going to make good on their agreement.

Mr. McNab apologized profusely for following Kay back to the mortuary, but he had come at Emily's insistence. Seems she didn't want the slightest detail overlooked.

It didn't take long to get Mr. McNab squared away and Kay headed back to her office determined to speed the bizarre Burleigh duo on their way. Fortunately, they had already emerged from her office and were headed toward the rear exit when Kay met up with them.

"I hate to rush off like this, Dahling, but my poor Tony missed his breakfast and I'm afraid he's feeling a little peckish," Evelyn said in a thin, stressed voice.

*Whadda ya know…she got one righ*t.

Kay was tempted to say, "Don't you mean prickish?" but instead said, "I'm worried about you, Evelyn. Are you going to be ok?" Kay was sincerely concerned - not about Evelyn's impending murder, but about the emotional abuse she was suffering at the hands of her browbeating baked-potato of a son.

Ever the big brassy dame, Evelyn jutted out her chin and defiantly said, "Que sera, sera, Dahling. I have peace of mind knowing Tony won't have to worry about my final wishes. I've taken care of everything."

"So there won't be any changes?" Kay asked, knowing in a year of monthly reviews, Evelyn had yet to alter a single detail of her final disposition.

Much to Kay's surprise Evelyn responded, albeit sheepishly. "Well, actually, I do have one. When I opened the folder it tore in half. Would you mind giving me a new one?"

"I'd be happy to," Kay replied.

She walked them to the door and said her goodbyes. As she made her way back to her office, she passed the hallway window just in time to see something strange streak past. When she stopped to get a better look, she couldn't believe her eyes. It was Tony, running in a full sprint toward Evelyn's car, apparently answering the call of extra-crispy thighs and drumsticks.

Kay chuckled, trying to imagine what Evelyn might say about Tony's uncharacteristic burst of energy: "Dahling, he had to run. The chicken had come home to roast."

4

The Stage is Set

After her whirlwind of a morning, Kay looked forward to settling into her desk chair and catching up on some paperwork. Filling out death certificate forms was just the type of mindless busy work she needed to pass the time before she had to call Dave.

Unfortunately, it wasn't the distraction Kay had hoped for. She began to obsess over her tendency to become flustered and breathless whenever she spoke to Dave on the phone. She couldn't understand why it never happened when they were together, face-to-face. The annoyance always present in his voice made her speed up and talk like Alvin the chipmunk, so as to get out whatever she had to say. He had a way of making her feel she was always taking up his valuable time.

No wonder he acts like he runs the show. I've made him the director.

Kay decided that shit was going to stop today.

If he wants me to cooperate with this crazy child support-slashing scheme, he's going to have to meet me on an equal footing.

Kay pulled Emily McNab's death certificate form from the file folder. Except for the official "Cause of Death" and the doctor's signature, the form was complete. This left two other certificates to fill out and get signed. Normally, she would have asked Leo, their errand-and-whatever-else-needs-doing guy, to deliver the forms to the doctors' offices; she wanted to take care of the task herself so she'd have a break before the long evening ahead.

The Department of Vital Records' new computer program for processing death certificates was still several months away from being user ready, so she had to rely on an old IBM Selectric. But she didn't mind because the machine had a correcting function that erased mistakes with a quick stroke of a key. And it never crashed the way her computer so often did.

She had just inserted a blank certificate into the typewriter when the telephone rang, followed by the buzz of the intercom. "Kay, Line 1 for you," Ruth said.

Kay got up from the small, portable table where the twenty year old machine was stationed, walked over to her desk and jerked up the receiver of the phone. "Is it anything you can take care of? I hate to ask, but I'm running against the clock to get a couple of death certificates out," Kay said. She immediately felt guilty for snapping at the busy receptionist.

"It sounds like a personal call, Kay. I believe the caller said his name is Dave."

At the sound of his name, her insides began to vibrate. Her breath came faster and that familiar fluster swooshed up and around her just like the dust devil swirling past her window at that very moment. Under different circumstances she might have smiled at the coincidence, but instead, she swallowed hard and tried to respond. Nothing came out.

"Kay? Are you there?" Ruth asked.

Kay cleared her throat. "Would you please take his number, Ruth, and tell him I'll call him back?" She knew she was in no condition to have the "equal footing" conversation she had promised herself just a few moments earlier.

"Sure," Ruth answered, a little confused about what was going on at the other end of the intercom.

Even though she was mad at herself for almost falling apart at the sound of his name, Kay had to pat herself on the back for having the presence of mind to delay talking to him until she could get a hold of herself. That old, familiar apprehension was creeping in. Why in the heck he was calling her?

Uh oh. Are those the bomb bay doors I hear opening again?

Her composure began to return when she remembered his promise to call with child support details.

Just then Ruth walked into her office holding the little pink phone message form on which she had written Dave's telephone number. Hand-delivering messages was something Ruth didn't make a practice of doing, but Kay's strange behavior begged a little investigation.

"Are you ok?" Ruth asked, handing Kay the pink piece of paper.

Kay looked up with a fake expression of puzzlement and responded, "Who? Me? I'm fine. Just fine," Kay said, as her eyes hungrily devoured the writing on the paper just handed to her. No message. Just a check-mark next to the "Please Call" box and a return phone number.

Ruth wasn't convinced, but decided not to pry. "Ok. You sounded a little strange on the intercom and I just wanted to make sure everything was alright."

Kay couldn't be sure if Ruth was truly concerned or just nosy. After all, they weren't exactly friends. Ruth was a warm person but didn't go out of her way to encourage personal relationships with the other employees at Salinger's. Kay had always chalked up Ruth's arm's-length distance to an over-developed sense of professionalism. Apart from that, Ruth was kind of a mystery. Nevertheless, Ruth's uncharacteristic show of concern had opened a door and Kay saw a chance to get a new perspective from someone, besides her sister, whom she assumed was wiser and more experienced.

Ruth turned to leave but Kay stopped her. "Uh…Ruth, do you have minute?"

Not totally surprised, the woman turned back to Kay. "Sure, Dear.   What can I do for you?"

"Well, would you have a couple of minutes to talk…about something personal, I mean. I'd like your opinion."

The woman's expression softened and she gave Kay a shy, but grateful smile.

"My goodness. It's been a long time since anyone has wanted my opinion. I'd be honored." Her response was quick and sincere, making Kay glad she had asked. "But do you mind coming up front? I'm expecting a couple of deliveries from the florist and I don't want to leave the office unattended." The dutiful receptionist resumed her walk back to her desk.

"Not a problem," Kay gratefully called after her. "Just let me turn off the typewriter and I'll be right there." The death certificates were going to have to wait.

Accompanied by four generations of the Salinger family, Kay walked up the long, narrow hall that led to the front office. As usual, they were silent as she passed their elegantly-framed photographic portraits.

Kay had always thought the Salinger's were a proud, good-looking lot, but none as striking as Lorraine Salinger. The oldest child of Edward Salinger, Sr. the founder of the mortuary, "Lorri" was not only beautiful, she had the distinction of being the first licensed female funeral director in the state. This impressive, but little-known achievement had captured Kay's imagination. Even though this was the twenty-first century, Kay knew, first hand, the challenges of being a female in a male-dominated profession. She couldn't imagine the hurdles the late Lorri Salinger must have had to overcome launching her career in the 1940's. Ruth had been fortunate enough to work with Lorri back in the day and Kay had always wanted to ask her about their association. But until today, Ruth had never encouraged personal conversations.

Kay was about to take a seat in an extra office chair located behind Ruth's desk, when the receptionist stopped her. "On second thought, why don't we sit on the sofa." Ruth nodded toward the family room just beyond her formal office setting. "We'll be more comfortable and I can still keep an eye on things."

Common to most mortuaries, the family room contained a tasteful but comfortable arrangement of living room furniture. This setting was a holdover from the old days of the funeral "parlor." Long ago, the custom was to have the casketed deceased in the family home where loved ones and friends could come to pay their respects. Over the years, things had moved to the mortuary, but achieving a feeling of "home" was still a mainstay of the services provided.

"So what's going on?" Ruth asked as she settled herself on one of the sumptuous cushions of the sofa. She pulled the hem of her dress down to cover her exposed knees. "Does it have anything to do with that man who called?"

Everyone at Salinger's knew Kay was divorced, but she had never felt the need to fill them in on any of the gory details.

Kay exhaled deeply and laid out her story, clearly and succinctly. She told Ruth about Dave's recent return after a seven year absence and the questionable agreement she had made with him. She explained her difficulties with talking to him on the phone and how she wanted to be calm and composed when she put his part of the agreement to its first test. It wasn't any more complicated than that. In fact, when Kay heard herself speaking the words, she felt a little silly for making such a big deal about it.

Ruth listened intently, a little disappointed there wasn't more to the story. Anyway, it was pretty apparent Kay didn't need an opinion as much as encouragement and inspiration. Little did Kay know Ruth was just the person to give her both.

"Well, it's easy to see why he still rattles you,"

Ruth began. "From what you've told me, your divorce was still fresh when he moved away. It only stands to reason things between the two of you would be suspended in time. Now he's back and you're right back where you left off. But you have to remember he thinks he's dealing with the Kay he knew seven years ago. I mean, why else would he have the balls - excuse the expression - to ask you to agree to such an outrageous proposal?"

Kay could feel herself tearing up, grateful for Ruth's savvy insight into her situation. She also thought it was cute Ruth felt the need to apologize for saying "balls."

"You're right," Kay sniffed. "I hadn't thought about it that way, but it makes perfect sense."

Ruth pulled a couple of tissues from the box sitting on the coffee table, handed them to Kay and continued. "From where I'm sitting it's clear you really do have the upper hand. He knows it, but he's counting on you *not* knowing it. That's why it's so important you make that crystal clear when you talk to him."

Kay nodded in agreement. "The thing is, though, I feel confident sitting here talking to you, but I'm afraid it's gonna evaporate the second I hear his voice." Kay hoped her display of irrational fear wouldn't cause Ruth to lose respect for her.

"Well then, we'll have to make sure that doesn't happen." Ruth's tone was maternal and reassuring.

Kay was definitely intrigued. She was just about to ask how Ruth was going to help rescue her from herself, when two elaborate standing floral sprays with legs walked through the front door, stopped and spoke. "Campbell?" came the question from a deep voice hidden behind the profusion of flowers.

"Main chapel," Ruth said pointing to the room where Herbert Campbell was currently lying in state.

"Send my guy in there, will you? He's got the casket spray," he said over his shoulder as he headed for the chapel.

Ruth stood up. "I'd better go help these gentlemen get situated and then we can continue our little talk. They tend to be a careless with how they set the flowers and it really upsets Ed." She waited for the delivery man's helper and signaled for him to follow her. The two disappeared into the scented cloud left behind by roses and lilies.

Kay smiled to herself. She was proud to work in a business where attention to detail was so important. Flower arrangements were one small part of that attention. Part of Kay's training had been learning the important role flowers played as visible expressions of condolence sent by well-wishers. As such, it mattered how they were displayed. Mortuary staff and flowers, alike, were put through their paces moving from chapel, to church, to graveside - each location requiring an entirely new setup. Before the flowers left the mortuary, it was Kay's job to collect and save every card accompanying each flower arrangement and/or potted plant. They were then presented to the family for proper acknowledgment at a later time - a necessary detail that could be easily overlooked during all the activity surrounding the funeral.

Kay felt stupid sitting all by herself watching the florist's assistant going in and out to retrieve his delivery van's payload of sympathy; she decided to follow Ruth and see if she could lend a hand. Anything to quickly get them back to their conversation.

Kay couldn't get over how Ruth seemed to really get it, and didn't make her feel foolish for making such a big, dramatic deal about everything. Kay was confident the older woman's advice was going to give her the boost she needed to deal with Dave.

Ruth dismissed Kay's offer of help with a wave of her hand; she just stood back and watched the two men rolling their eyes at each other as Ruth corrected and adjusted every one of their unacceptable placements.

The assistant delivery man spotted Kay, walked over and asked, "What's that thing?" pointing to a sheer, netted covering draped over the lid and opening of the casket, making it difficult to get a clear view of Mr. Campbell's body.

"It's a casket veil," Ruth responded before Kay had a chance to tell him she didn't know. She had never seen one before. "It's put there to discourage people from touching the deceased." She continued fussing with the various flower pots and vases.

"Oh," said the man, apparently not requiring any further explanation.

Ruth stood back and took one last assessment of the display. With a sigh of satisfaction, she turned and said, "Thank you, gentlemen." Arms outstretched she herded them toward the door. "I'll be sure to let Mr. Salinger know how helpful you were."

The two men shrugged, murmured "thanks" and quickly made their exit.

Kay was puzzled, but curious about the reason for obscuring Mr. Campbell's appearance with the gauzy cover.   "Ruth, I don't understand. How is the family supposed to see Mr. Campbell through that thing?"

Ruth gave Kay a knowing smile, took her by the elbow.   "Here. Stand in this spot. I'm about to dazzle you with a bit of old-school mortuary show biz magic."

Ruth lightly patted Kay on the back before walking over to a pair of heavy, light-blue velvet drapes hanging on the wall a few feet from the foot of the casket. She pulled back one of the drapes, secured it with a tie-back mounted on the wall and disappeared through the opening to the tiny alcove that housed the mortuary's dual keyboard Wurlitzer organ.

Kay tried to imagine what kind "magic" Ruth could possibly perform.

Maybe she's going to bring Mr. Campbell back to life with the Light My Fire organ riff.

But instead of hearing Ray Manzarek's iconic rock intro wafting out from the little organ room, a bone-rattling "clank" shot through the opening in the drapes, followed by a tentative illumination of a row of lights hidden behind the soffit on the chapel ceiling.

"Are you ok?" Kay called to Ruth.

"I'm fine. Just stand there and watch."

Kay did as she was told and was rewarded with a jaw-dropping display as the overhead lighting was brought up high, then brought down low, then raised again, finally settling on a medium, soft glow. As if by magic, the casket veil seemed to disappear and Mr. Campbell's body came into distinct focus.

After a few more minor adjustments, Ruth walked out to the check the results of her handiwork. "I've still got it!" she boasted with pride.

"Wow, that's impressive. But I still don't understand what it's all about."

"It's an old stage lighting technique used for preparing severely damaged bodies for viewing," Ruth said. "Mr. Campbell was thrown from his truck and his face took the brunt of the impact."

Kay inched up closer to the casket to take a better look. She had never seen a case as serious as Mr. Campbell. Now she could see the heavier-than-normal layer of makeup and restorative wax Mr. Campbell had been repaired with; Ed had applied it so expertly it was almost impossible to detect any evidence of the massive cuts and abrasions Mr. Campbell had sustained in the accident.

"But wouldn't it be easier to have a closed casket?" Kay asked, assuming the obvious alternative. "You have to admit all those cosmetics make him look less than natural."

"We gave the family that option but they still requested an open casket. And, to the extent we're able, we like to honor our families' requests. Thus, the reason for the stagecraft. All it takes is a little direct and dispersed lighting, bounced off a light-pink ceiling with the casket veil acting as a scrim and the family can remember Mr. Campbell intact, rather than road kill." Kay was shocked by Ruth's irreverence.

Ruth walked back to the organ alcove with Kay close behind.

"Here's our little magic maker," Ruth said, pointing to a peculiar round, black-enameled, metal apparatus mounted on the wall above the organ. Kay thought it looked like a car wheel missing its tire. A long metal bar was attached at the center of the "wheel" with a black wooden handle on one end and a small, hammerhead-looking thing on the other.

Maybe that's the jack.

"This is one of the first electric light rheostats ever made." Ruth grabbed the black wooden handle and turned it, causing the lights in the chapel to change.

"Ed's grandfather was an amateur actor and saw one of these used in a production he was appearing in. Being the forward thinker that he was, he instantly saw the benefit of using it to help "stage" our deceased clients."

Ruth went on to explain to Kay how old man Salinger had learned everything he could about lighting techniques and then taught them to everyone who worked at the mortuary.

"I learned from Lorri," Ruth said. Kay could tell the woman was proud of being a part of this morbid showbiz tradition.

Ruth dialed the rheostat back to its ideal setting before turning off all the lights. She freed the drape from the tie-back allowing it to swing back into place, once again, concealing its theatrical secrets.

"C'mon," Ruth beckoned to Kay as she headed for her office. "As I recall, I was just about to give you the solution to your problem with your ex-husband when we got interrupted."

5

With a Little Help from My Friend

"Hello, this is Kay Manning, calling for Dave Noland, if he's available," Kay said, using her best telephone etiquette. She had always hated callers who made you ask, "who's calling?" and made it her personal crusade to model good phone manners - even when she was calling people she'd rather not talk to.

There was a weird, but oddly-familiar, little beat of silence before the receptionist gave Kay a frosty, "Please hold." A breath of a shiver went down Kay's spine.

What the hell was that?

Fortunately, the paranoia threatening to overtake her senses was thwarted by the terrible hold music playing on the phone. Even though she would have preferred a silent wait to the elevator music, Kay found herself providing the words to the corny instrumental rendition.

"Cracklin' Rosie geet on board…"

Thanks to Ruth, there wasn't a trace of nervousness in her body and she was actually looking forward to having a friendly conversation with her ex.

"Crack-e-lin' Rose you're a store-bought woman…"

"Hello, Kay." Dave broke in right as Kay's song began its famous crescendo.

"Hey there, Dave," she said with a startled

laugh. "Please excuse my little song, but your hold music is kinda catchy."

He ignored her merry greeting. "Thanks for getting back to me. There's something I need to run past you."

Normally, Kay would have been thrown by his impersonal response to her attempt at being friendly, but not now. Seems nothing could ruin her spirits.

"Let me guess. You've knocked the socks off your new boss, he's given you a big raise and you don't have to cut my child support after all." She was trying to kid him into the easy camaraderie that had once come to them so naturally.

She punctuated her silly guess with another giggle but Dave was having none of it. His purpose for calling was simply to get her bank information. Seems he wanted to set up a monthly automatic deposit from his bank to hers, so he wouldn't have to write and mail a check, as he'd been doing for the last seven years.

The less personal contact the better, right? Kay wanted to say, but didn't because it was pointless. *Even the thought of us touching the same piece of paper is too much for him.*

But somehow, that didn't matter.

Isn't that what Scarlett O'Hara said after Ashley gave her the ole' heave-ho?

Kay giggled again. She could feel Dave's annoyance ooze through the phone. But Kay didn't care. As it was, she had some business of her own to discuss with Dave and the timing was perfect.

Without question or comment she complied with his request and then quickly segued to her own pressing demand.

"I was going to call you myself this afternoon. I have to work a viewing tonight, so you're going to have to take Cory to therapy." Her confidence was such she didn't bother to ask whether or not it was convenient.

Despite her Ruth-inspired boldness she, nevertheless, expected him to put her off until he had the chance to check with his wife. Apparently, since his marriage to Sandy he'd become a new kind of husband, making sure to consult her on even the tiniest of details.

"I tell her *everything*," he had once declared to Kay, proud to let her know he had turned over a new leaf from his days of lies and deceit.

But much to Kay's surprise, Dave's mood made an about face. "Sure. No problem. What time is her appointment?"

She wasn't expecting this quick eagerness to cooperate and she felt those old "give-the-guy-a-chance" feelings rising to the surface.

I guess Les is right. When it comes to Dave, I am a big pushover.

She was about to lay out the details of his parental assignment when she was interrupted by the loud buzz of his office intercom. "Do you need to get that?" she asked, with polite concern.

"It's ok. This isn't going to take long, is it?"

She launched back into her description of the

therapist's address and a suggestion for the easiest way to get there, when the buzzer went off again - this time twice - daring Dave to ignore it.

He took the hint. "Could you excuse me a second? This may be important."

Back on hold she went. With the strains of the Muzak version of "Love Will Keep Us Together" in her ear, Kay couldn't help but smile at the irony. She and Dave were still together...sort of...and it wasn't because of their love for each other but their love for their daughters.

"...When those girls start hanging around, talking me down..."

The lyrics suddenly brought back her earlier encounter with the receptionist. Was she imagining things, or had the woman been personally annoyed by her call to Dave? As much as she wanted to deny it, the woman's displeased demeanor had struck a familiar chord of discomfort.

Oh, my God, Kay. Will you please stop mind-fucking yourself?

Dave came back on the line and Kay instantly detected an air of agitation. "Listen, Kay. I'm gonna have to go. I'll let you know when the bank transaction has been set up."

"But I haven't finished giving you the directions to the therapist's office."

"I'm sure Cory knows how to get there. Talk to you later."

"Wait, Dave! The appointment is at 7:00 and you have to take Mariah with you."

"Will do. Bye."

"Dave!"

"For christsake, what?"

"You're going to have to take care of the co-pay. I'll reimburse you for your half this weekend.

"Fine. Whatever. I gotta go."

Their roller coaster of a conversation was over. Normally she would have spent time taking apart and analyzing every word…every inflection, every nuance. But she shrugged and decided she couldn't be bothered.

This was new behavior for Kay and she wasn't sure if it was coming from her own growing maturity or the artificial kind Ruth had been so gracious to supply. It had been years since she had smoked pot, and she had forgotten its power to mercifully obscure her undesirable shortcomings.

When Ruth first suggested taking advantage of a little cannabisial assistance, Kay couldn't believe what she was hearing. Seems Ruth's doctor had prescribed medical marijuana for a long list of maladies plaguing Ruth's day-to-day existence. Although the prim and proper woman had initially encountered great difficulty coming to grips with using a substance associated with hippies, drop outs and slackers, today Ruth was proud to be "licensed to carry," and was one of its greatest proponents. She had overcome her great reluctance to even speak about the matter and was now extolling its benefits to anyone who would listen…with the greatest of discretion, of course.

Duh. That's why I'm paranoid.

The receptionist at Dave's office wasn't protecting her personal territory. She was just one of those nasty bitches occupying a position she was completely ill-suited for. It was like casting Joan Crawford in a part made for Shirley Temple. She'd never be able to understand employers who hired these sour personalities when they were charged with making the all-important first impression of their company.

Happy she had solved the reason for her troubling twinges of discomfort, she set about to contact her girls to let them know about the plans for the evening. She wasn't sure if Cory would react with pain or pleasure, but she knew Mariah would be delighted. A quick glance at the clock let her know the girls were home from school.

Mariah answered on the first ring and after the cursory question and answer session about the goings-on at school that day, (Kay: "How was school?" Mariah: "Fine." Kay: "What did you do?" Mariah: "Nothing.") she asked to speak to Cory. While she waited for her elder daughter to come to the phone, Kay imagined a conversation where the tables were turned (Mariah: "How was work?" Kay:"Fine." Mariah: "What did you do?" Kay: "I got stoned.").

"Hi, Mom. Don't forget I have therapy at 7:00," Cory said.

"That's why I'm calling. I'm working late tonight so Dad's going to take you. He'll be picking you and Mariah up around 6:30, so please be ready."

"Wow. How did that happen?" But before Kay could answer, Mariah interjected, "Oh, God. Please tell me Sandy isn't coming."

It had never occurred to her to ask Dave if he'd be bringing his family along. Kay couldn't imagine Sandy wanting to sit around with a rambunctious little boy waiting for Cory while she spilled her guts about her nasty step-mother.

"I really don't think she'll want to bring Little Dave out at that hour. I'm sure Dad is coming alone, but Mariah will have to go with you guys. Please make sure her homework is done before Dad gets there."

"Mom, she's not going to listen to me. Will you tell her so she won't give me any shit?"

"Cory! Do you have to use that language? It's so disrespectful." Kay hated to see Cory taking on the inevitable bad habits that come with growing up.

"Sorry, Mom. It slipped. But, will you please tell her?"

Kay did as her daughter asked and even though Mariah griped, Kay knew spending time with her dad would be the perfect incentive for Mariah to get her schoolwork done. With a few last second maternal instructions for remembering to eat and wearing a sweater, Kay hung up the phone, encouraged this little arrangement with Dave might just work out better than she imagined.

"So, how did everything go? By the look on your face I'm assuming it was a success." Ruth was wearing her coat, apparently getting ready to leave for the day. Kay thought it was amusing the once, standoff-ish woman was now becoming a regular visitor to her office.

"Let's just put it this way. I couldn't have done

it without you." Kay smiled at the woman with a new-found intimacy. "It gave me the leg-up I needed."

"I'm so glad. We women have to stick together. But I am counting on you to be discreet. I don't think Ed would approve."

"Don't worry. Now that I've gotten over the initial hump, I doubt I'll need your help again…except maybe to talk things over every now and then."

Ruth smiled back at her new friend. "Don't forget to lock up after the viewing. The front door can be a little hinkey, so make sure it's secure before you leave. I'll see you tomorrow."

Kay wondered if Ruth was going home to get high.

* * *

The Campbell viewing was in full swing. Kay was back in her office trying to finish the paperwork she had intended to complete before the afternoon had so quickly gotten away from her. She could tell by the rising and falling sound levels of muffled crying and low conversation reaching all the way back to her office, they had a full house.

A viewing was a family affair that didn't require the presence of mortuary staff, other than to refill tissue dispensers, give directions to the restrooms, or on the rare occasion, provide smelling salts to a mourner overcome with grief.

Funeral fainting was more of a dramatic show than a true, grief-induced loss of consciousness. Ed had told her the way you could tell if someone had truly passed out was if their head bounced off the floor when they swooned. In any case, it wasn't staff's place to judge the authenticity of the collapse, but to make sure the fallen were helped up off the floor and back to their seat.

The after-hours business line rang and Kay was on phone duty. She walked over to her desk and reached for the receiver, hoping it wasn't a death call. With Uncle Owen being MIA, Ed would have his hands full transporting two bodies. Nope. Just someone wanting to know what time the Campbell viewing started. "7:00 o'clock," she replied. "Funeral tomorrow at 10:00 at St. Mary's," she added before the caller had a chance to ask the inevitable follow-up question.

She was heading back to her little typewriter station when out of the corner of her eye she spotted a woman, obviously upset, standing in the middle of the family room. Kay recognized the woman as a member of the Campbell family. The moment the fretting woman saw Kay she beckoned her with a rapid-fire crooking of her finger.

Is the restroom really that hard to find?

Reluctantly, she responded to the urgent summons. As she got closer to the distressed woman Kay noticed the sounds from the chapel had become quite boisterous…almost as if there was a party going on.

"Thank God. I didn't think anyone was here," the woman said, frantically grabbing Kay's arm. "You have to come see my brother. He looks like he's starting to smell."

Kay's blood ran cold and she stood paralyzed, not sure she had correctly heard the woman.

Oh, God! Please don't tell me he wasn't thoroughly embalmed.

Kay managed to keep her panic to herself and with all the professional poise she could muster, she led the woman back to the chapel to investigate the potential disaster.

As she rounded the corner from the hallway, Kay almost knocked over a little girl holding the casket veil above her head, twirling around like Salome dancing for the head of John the Baptist. She scanned the room expecting to see other signs of undignified revelry. The intensified noise she had worried about was nothing more than lively conversation between attendees catching up on each other's lives since the last family funeral.

She cautiously approached the casket, discreetly sniffing the air; the only detectable smell was flowers. A small group of mourners stood at the casket blocking her view of the body. Even though she was anxious to see what was happening to Mr. Campbell, she respectfully held back, not wanting to intrude on their final moments with their loved one/friend.

That's funny. These guys aren't gasping in horror or holding their noses.

However, from where she was standing she became aware of several large, ghastly brown smears matting the nap of Mr. Campbell's blue high pile casket. Unlike the sleek, polished finishes of wood or metal, high pile caskets were finished in what can only be described as sculptured carpeting. The high pile was available in blue or pink and because of its affordable price, it tended to be one of their biggest sellers. Kay had always thought the casket should come with a pair of fuzzy dice hanging from the casket lid.

Kay was certain these unsightly stains hadn't been there this afternoon when Ruth was setting the lighting. She couldn't imagine how the casket had become so filthy.

Once the mourners returned to their seats, Kay was able to get a better look. She sighed with relief. Mr. Campbell wasn't decomposing before everyone's eyes. Rather, the family, unable to keep from touching him, had removed the casket veil and in the process of lavishing him with affection for the last time, had made a mess of his cosmetic restoration. With his "face" coming off in their hands, it was easy to see why his sister thought he was starting to "smell." What wasn't easy to see was why, with the tissue dispenser just two feet away, they'd felt the need to clean their hands on the casket. She made a mental note to tell Ed the stains would have to be removed before tomorrow morning's funeral service.

After reassuring the sister that her brother wasn't rotting in full public view, Kay retrieved the casket veil from the dancing girl, re-draped it over the casket and stationed herself nearby, guarding against any more destructive pawing of the body. Fortunately, back under the veil, Mr. Campbell resumed his almost-natural appearance. The transformation, courtesy of theatrical tricks of the trade, made Kay think of the famous Shakespearian quote, "All the world's a stage, and all the men and women merely players: they have their exits and their entrances…"

Mr. Campbell had been given his cue and he was about to make his exit.

6

Cursed by Good Energy

"I'm ho-ome," Kay called out, wiggling and jiggling the key, trying to pull it from the stubborn dead bolt lock.

Silence.

Kay let out a grateful sigh. She was anxious to hear how things had gone with the girls and their dad, but was glad for the opportunity to wind down from her long, crazy day. She poured herself a glass of her favorite Pinot Noir and headed for the welcoming caress of her sofa's poofy cushions.

She was getting home much later than she would have preferred but Ed had returned just as she was locking up. She stayed to give him a hand moving his retrieved deceased from the gurney to the embalming table, debriefing him on the unusual events of the evening. He smiled and shook his head, saying as far as viewings go, Mr. Campbell's was pretty much par for the course - he had seen much worse. Then, before he'd sent her on her way, they cleaned Mr. Campbell's face off the casket. When they were finished, the blue high pile looked like new.

Unfortunately, Kay's welcomed lull didn't last long. She had just put her feet up on the coffee table when she heard the rising volume of the girls' voices as they neared the front door. They didn't bother to use their key, but instead, one of them laid on the doorbell with a heavy finger.

Ding, dong, ding, dong, ding, dong, ding, dong

- followed by insistent knocking. Kay jumped, nearly knocking over her glass of wine.

"Ok, ok, I'm coming," she hollered, hurrying to put a stop to the racket.

She opened the door and Mariah came in with a little skip and exuberant, "Hi, Mom."

Cory blew right past her mother, looking glum as usual.

"There're my gorgeous girls," Kay said. She wanted to find out about the events of their evening but she knew it was better to keep her curiosity in check. Both Mariah and Cory hated being interrogated about their time spent with their dad - something Kay, regrettably, wasn't able to resist when the separation was new and she was at the peak of her craziness. It took her a while but she eventually learned if she stayed quiet long enough, the girls would volunteer all the information she needed to know.

She closed the front door and headed back to the couch and her waiting glass of wine. "Did you guys eat?" Kay asked, hoping her tiring day was over and she wouldn't have to feed anybody.

"Dad took us out for a burger," Mariah said, plopping on the sofa next to Kay.

"He took YOU out, you mean," Cory said with disgust. "I was stuck with Dr. Fulmer. All I got was a cold hamburger and fries. He didn't even buy me anything to drink."

"It wasn't that fun," Mariah said. "He spent the whole time on the phone." Kay thought it was sweet that Mariah was trying to make her sister feel better.

"I guess Sandy just wanted to know everything was going ok," Kay said, trying to make both girls feel better.

"I don't think he was talking to Sandy, Mommy. He was laughing a lot." Even at nine years old, Mariah was already an astute observer.

Kay's ears pricked up, but her exhaustion prevented her from indulging in speculation about who might have been amusing her humorless ex husband.

"How was therapy?" Kay asked, turning her attention to her sulking daughter.

Cory let out a sigh. "It was ok. Except Dr. Fulmer made me mad. He thinks I should try going to dad's this weekend."

"Hmmm. That's interesting," Kay said in her own noncommittal, therapeutic tone.

"I asked him why he was trying to lay a guilt trip on me. I mean, I get enough of that crap from Dad."

Kay tried to explain to a stubborn Cory the therapist wasn't trying to make her feel guilty, but was encouraging her to confront her problems head on. It went right over the immature girl's head. Like most kids her age, Cory was of the opinion all adults, even those with a license to practice psychology, were stupid and didn't have a clue about what was really going on.

"And of course, Dad started in on me as soon as I got in the truck. He didn't even ask me nicely if I would come this weekend. All he did was bitch about how bad Sandy and Little Dave were going to feel if I didn't show up. So much for the adult conversation you wanted me to have with him. "

"I think you're wrong, Cory. He really wants to spend some time with you," Kay said.

"So how come he doesn't say *he'd* feel bad? Why does he put it all on Sandy when we all know she doesn't want us around?"

Kay didn't know how to respond. Dave had always had difficulty with taking responsibility for anything, especially his feelings. But she didn't think it was appropriate to get into that with Cory. The little girl would soon figure it out for herself...if she hadn't already.

Cory helped Kay out of her obvious internal struggle by changing the subject. "Did you get the message I left for you by the phone?"

"I didn't bother to check. I just wanted to sit and not have to think. Who called?" Kay said.

"Some Virginia Something-or-Other. She wants you to call her."

Cory retrieved the piece of paper and handed it to Kay.

Virginia Voorhees. 555-6473

"Did she say what she wanted?" Kay asked, not recognizing the name.

"Nope. Just wants you to call her back."

Kay shrugged, then frisbeed the message on to the coffee table. "I'll call back tomorrow. Probably just wants to sell me something," she muttered.

Cory joined her mother and sister on the sofa. Both girls leaned into Kay in a vertical cuddle that felt especially delicious to the exhausted woman. The three of them sat there without saying a word, content to end a hard day in the sweet familiarity of each other's company.

* * *

"Good morning. Executive Connections. Virginia Voorhees speaking."

It all came rushing back to Kay. This was the woman who had interviewed her for the singles group.

"Good morning, Virginia. This is Kay Manning. You spoke with my daughter yesterday and left a message asking me to call you."

"Yes, Kay. How good to talk to you again. I know it's been a couple of months since your interview but since we haven't seen you, I was checking to see if maybe you hadn't run off and gotten married."

"Oh my goodness, no!" Kay said, a tad too emphatically.

"Well, that's ok," the woman responded, a little too condescendingly. "Anyway, I just wanted to let you know we've had a big boost in membership and there are some very interesting people I think you would enjoy getting to know."

Kay looked behind her - right then left - making sure the girls didn't know she was having this conversation. There was still something unnatural about participating in this proposition that made Kay feel like a loser. But she couldn't admit that to this woman who seemed sincere in her efforts to play matchmaker to the executive lovelorn.

"You know, Virginia, I've had every intention of coming to a meeting but it seems like something always comes up."

Ignoring Kay's lame excuse, Virginia said, "No problem. I completely understand. We're all so busy these days. But just in case you're free on Saturday, you may want to check out our meeting. It's at 7:00 at my house. We're planning a houseboat weekend at Lake Beauchamp while the weather is still warm."

A houseboat weekend?

Seems Kay had missed out on quite a bit if these people were at the point of planning weekend get-aways.

"Wow. That sounds like fun," Kay said. "The group must be pretty friendly to share a houseboat. I mean, I'm assuming the accommodations are coed."

Virginia laughed. "I'm sure some of the guys wouldn't object to a set up like that, but no. The plan is to rent two houseboats, one for the men and the other for the women. A couple of our members have even offered to pull their speed boats so we can water ski."

Her misgivings allayed, Kay was now intrigued. A weekend at the lake, relaxing, water skiing and partying with adults sounded tremendously appealing. "I'd love to hear more."

"I hoped you'd be interested. You have just the kind of energy this group needs.

After all these months, Kay was doubtful the woman remembered anything about her, let alone her energy. In any case, the suck-up wasn't necessary. She was definitely interested. It had been a long time since Kay had had anything like this to look forward to. Unnatural or not, she couldn't pass it up. She was going to attend that meeting whether Cory chose to go to Dave's or not. If she had to, she could leave her twelve-year old home alone for a couple of hours.

Before she hung up Kay took down the directions to Virginia's house and gave her assurances she'd be there.

"Are you really going on a houseboat?"

Kay jumped, not aware Cory had come into the room.

"Don't sneak up on people, Cory. You startled me."

"Sorry, Mom. I didn't want to bother you while you were on the phone. What's the deal with the houseboat?"

"Excuse me, young lady, but that was a private conversation. You know it's rude to eavesdrop."

"Sorry, Mom. I didn't mean to be rude. It's just that you sounded so excited."

Kay wasn't aware she'd telegraphed her enthusiasm and she could feel her cheeks heat up. "Well, it's not a for-sure thing. I don't know if I'm going." Then she underhandedly added, "I'll find out more about it on Saturday when you and Mariah are at your Dad's."

Cory gave Kay a stone-faced look, cracked half a smile and said, "Nice try, Mom."

Kay chuckled. "It was worth a shot. Anyway, I got the feeling last night you might have changed your mind about going," Kay lied, giving her manipulation one more try.

Much to Kay's surprise, Cory confirmed her fictitious suspicion. "The truth is, I was gonna go, but I got an email from Violet this morning. Her family is going camping this weekend and she wants me to come. Can I, Mom?"

Kay laughed again - this time at the uncanny timing of her daughter's last-minute reprieve. "Saved by the bell, huh?"

Now it was Cory's turn to be embarrassed. "No, really Mom," she protested. "I thought about what you said about Dr. Fulmer wanting me to face my problems. I mean, I don't really think it'll change anything, but I guess I owe it to myself to try. I'm only sorry it'll have to wait until the next visit. That's if you say I can go with Violet."

Kay was pretty sure her daughter's sudden show of thoughtful maturity was just that - a show. Teenagers were so obvious when they were trying to get their parents to give them something they wanted. But Kay couldn't fault the girl - especially in light of her own attempt at shifty maneuvering.

"Well, before I say yes, I'll want to call Bonnie for the details. You're probably going to need some camping equipment."

Cory bobbed up and down on the balls of her feet and a wide grin exploded across her face. "Thank you, thank you, than…"

Kay put her hand up, interrupting her daughter's buoyant expression of gratitude. "But there's one condition. You're going to have to call your Dad and let him know you won't be coming this time."

That stopped Cory in her tracks. "Really? You're going to make me call him?"

Kay dropped her chin and stared disapprovingly at Cory from under her brow.

"All right, all right," the girl reluctantly acquiesced. "I hate when you give me that look. I'll call him. But I know he's going to give me a bunch of shit."

"Good. But don't call until I have everything confirmed with Violet's mother."

Cory nodded dejectedly and headed for the stairs.

"Look at it this way, Honey," Kay said, stopping Cory with a gentle touch of the shoulder. "If you're sincere about giving your dad a chance, this call is a good way to start."

Cory looked at her mother, rolled her eyes and said, "Whatever." She disappeared up the stairs in her usual churlish fashion, leaving Kay to quietly return to the excitement of contemplating the possibilities of her upcoming lake-side social prospect.

"Mom?" came the timid call from the top of the landing.

Here it comes.

Kay braced herself for a last ditch plea. But to Kay's pleasant surprise, Cory said, "I really do hope you get to go on that houseboat. You never get to do anything fun."

Kay was so taken aback and touched by Cory's, seemingly, heartfelt sentiment she felt moved to offer to make the call to Dave after all.

Really…what would it hurt?

But just as she opened her mouth to tell Cory she had reconsidered, the realization she was being played again tossed her off her little pink cloud. Kay had to admit she was impressed.

Does my kid know me, or what?

"Thank you, Stinker. That's sweet," Kay called back up the stairs. "Now go call Mariah. You guys have about ten minutes before the bus comes."

The derisive little snort she heard in response let her know her suspicions were right on the money.

Do I know my kid, or what?

7

Disappointment, Thy Name is Sapphire Moon

With a sigh of contentment, Kay nestled a little deeper into her mattress. Sleeping in on a Saturday morning had to be one of life's more-delicious pleasures. The week was over, mercifully taking with it the pressures of raising two growing kids and an exacting boss. She was free!

Kay lifted her head to turn her pillow in search of a cool spot. Once satisfactorily repositioned, she tried to drift off back to sleep. The image of an unhappy Mariah at her dad's tried to sneak in and disturb the peace, but Kay shooed it away. Even if Mariah might not be having the best of times, Kay, nevertheless, knew her little girl was safe. And Cory was off on her camping trip having the time of her 12 year old life, unconcerned about parents, step-parents or siblings. Yes. Kay could lay down the heavy mantle of motherhood without guilt or worry…at least for the next two days, anyway.

Camping! The 7:00 singles meeting!

So successfully had Kay put the event out of her mind lest her anticipation cause the week to go by any slower than it already had, the out-of-left-field-reminder hit her with a jolt. If there was any hope of going back to sleep, it was gone. Kay rolled over on her back, drew up her knees and folded her hands across her stomach. She lay there, staring at the ceiling, faced with making some very critical decisions.

What was she going to wear?

How should she do her hair?

What kind of nosh should she bring? (a follow-up email from Virginia informed Kay the refreshments were provided pot-luck style)

How would she handle it if some guy hit on her?

Stop. Remember, it's just about the houseboat weekend.

There was no use spending anymore time in bed. Robed and slippered she padded to the bathroom, humming as she happily anticipated the mind and body cleansing benefits of a hot shower.

* * *

It took three trips around the same block to convince a stubborn Kay she should pull over and re-check Virginia's directions. She immediately realized her mistake. She had made a right turn one street too soon. When she finally pulled up in front of the house she still wasn't sure she was in the right place. It looked deserted. Where were all the cars? She checked the house number again. It was correct. Could she have gotten the date wrong? Why didn't she think to write Virginia's number on the directions?

She sat there for a few moments, her uncertainty and disappointment urging her to head on home. But she had come too far to turn back now. Kay was going to make the best of it.

She approached the front door with all the

confidence of someone who knew they were "lookin' hot." She was the picture of casual sophistication in her skinny jeans, bulky maroon pullover accented with a gray, cable knit scarf and finished off with tan, suede trooper boots. Kay looked like a "professional" single who knew how to relax and have fun.

Suddenly a picture of Sandy, in her old-lady denim jumper and sensible shoes, with a well-dressed, handsome Dave at her side, popped into her head. She would never be able to understand what Dave found attractive about his new "old lady."

I guess there's just no accounting for taste.

Kay rang the doorbell and stood there, shifting her weight from foot to foot. The anticipation of discovering what awaited her on the other side was too much for her to keep still. She was looking down, carefully transferring the bamboo, insulated food tote from one hand to the other when the door finally opened. She looked up, expecting to see Virginia, but instead was greeted by one of the most unattractive men she had ever seen.

The instant he saw Kay he opened his eyes wide to take her all in, causing his fore - make that five - head to slide from front to back. A thin little tiara of curly hair arched over his head from ear to ear in a goofy kind of halo.

His obvious delight at seeing her was as instant as her second disappointment of the evening, which she hoped wasn't as evident. "Well, h e l l o," he sang, with a creepy excitement. "Here. Let me help you with that." He thrust his arm forward to grab for the tote.

"Oh thanks," she responded with all the grace she could muster. "It was starting to get a little heavy."

Kay avoided making eye contact with him during the hand-off, lest she be devoured by another hungry leer. Once the tote was securely in his hand, he took a step back to allow Kay to enter the house.

"Everyone's in the kitchen," he said, gesturing with his chin upward to the right. Kay took off in that direction, with her eager helper close behind. "My name is Delbert Schumacher, by the way."

Of course it is.

"Nice to meet you, Delbert," she said. "I'm Kay Manning."

The kitchen was abuzz with a small mix of men and women busy putting out their snacks. Disappointment #3 was realizing there were more women than men. And all the men in attendance seem to fit into a general "nerdy" category. Kay made an effort to push disappointment #4 out of her mind.

Just then, Virginia who was standing at the sink trying to break up a bag of ice with a metal meat tenderizer, spotted Kay, smiled and shouted, "Kay! I'm so glad you could make it."

With Virginia's friendly greeting, Kay finally felt comfortable enough to enter the kitchen the rest of the way.

"Would you like me to put your bag on the table?" Delbert asked, reminding Kay he was still behind her.

"Oh. I'm sorry. I forgot you were there," she said. She relieved Delbert of his burden.

"Yeah. That happens a lot," Delbert responded with a tone of fatalistic resignation. Kay felt a sudden pang of guilt, sorry her innocent comment may have been taken the wrong way. But looking at Delbert it was easy to see why he didn't stay on many women's radar.

Rather than make things worse by trying to explain herself, Kay changed the subject. "Do you like chile con queso?" she asked as she removed the small crock pot from the bottom of her insulated tote.

To no one's surprise, Delbert answered, "Well, not exactly. I'm lactose intolerant. The last time I tried to eat some of that stuff you couldn't get near me for the horrible gas."

Is there a school somewhere that offers a degree in nerdery?

But because she felt obligated to reciprocate his kindness she offered him a little empathy for his delicate digestive disorder. "Really? That's too bad. I have a cousin who suffers from the same thing," she lied.

Luckily, Virginia showed up and saved Kay from the inelegant conversation. "Oh, your queso looks great. Do you use the Tio Taco chiles?"

"Is there any other kind?" Kay said with a laugh.

Floundering there with nothing more to say, Delbert shoved his hands in his pockets and slunk away from the table. He was quickly replaced by a very tall, slender man who walked up to Virginia. "Sorry to interrupt, Virginia, but we've got all the chairs set up."

72

"Thanks, Lance," Virginia said. She turned and addressed the small group in the kitchen. "Hey, listen everyone. We're about to get started. If you've got your dish on the table you can start making your way to the living room." She gently waved the remaining people away from the refreshments and toward the kitchen door. Then she turned back to Kay. "C'mon Kay. I'm looking forward to introducing you to the group."

Virginia's living room had a large, sunken, horseshoe-shaped conversation pit carved out of one end of the room, protected by a low decorative wrought iron fence around the outer edge. Kay walked down the three steps and took her seat among the folding chairs placed along the wall of the pit. The placement of the chairs made for easy reconnaissance of all in attendance.

Kay counted six men and nine women - ten if you included Virginia - not exactly the teeming throng she had pictured during her phone conversation with Virginia. Kay's guessed ages ranged from the low 40s to the mid 60s. And from the look of things, no one, it seems, had felt overly compelled to fix themselves up. They all looked clean and groomed, but their clothes screamed, "I couldn't be bothered." But then Kay realized she felt overdressed because she was the new kid. Everyone here had already made their debut and could now relax.

Virginia stood up in front of the group and got the meeting going. After a few announcements (the meeting was moving to the *second* Saturday of the month; membership has now topped 38), and reminders (please don't block the neighbors' driveways; don't forget the donation basket on your way out), Virginia smiled and said, "It gives me great pleasure to welcome Kay Manning to our group. Kay was the first person to answer my ad and the first person I interviewed and invited to join." Virginia looked at Kay and winked. "Unfortunately, the body shop where she works keeps her so busy this is the first opportunity she's had to come and introduce herself to everyone. Kay?" Virginia sat down, turning the floor over to Kay.

Kay stood up to a smattering of polite applause. Everyone was staring up at her, waiting to see evidence of Virginia's endorsement as the group's wonderful maiden candidate.

"Hi everyone. It's a pleasure to be a part of this group and I'm looking forward to getting to know each of you personally. Thank you." And with that she sat down.

"Aren't you going to tell us a little about yourself?" a pudgy man with a bad case of rosacea and a wide gap between his front teeth interjected.

"Oh," Kay said from her seat. She stood again and said, "Right." She hadn't been prepared to speak. "Well, let's see. Like Virginia said, my name is Kay Manning. I was born and raised here - graduated from local schools. I'm a working mom, raising two girls, Cory, twelve and Mariah nine."

She was about to clear up any misconception Virginia may have created with her little body shop joke, when the man who parted his teeth in the middle beat her to the punch. "Do you work on foreign cars?" he asked innocently.

Kay looked over at Virginia who was obviously

delighted by the question. "Well..." she began tentatively, "We...I'm sorry. What's your name?"

"Jim. Jim Blake," the man answered. Kay thought he might be blushing but she couldn't tell because of his rosacea.

"Well, Jim, I do work in a body shop, but it's not the automotive kind. It's the dead kind." She was trying to keep things light.

He looked at her as if she was speaking Chinese. Some of the others in the group were starting to get it and a little giggle went around the half-circle.

"I'm an apprentice funeral director, Jim. I work in a mortuary. But, I'd be happy to refer you to the guy who works on my Honda."

Kay could have sworn that, in a split second, Jim's face displayed three of the Five Stages of Grief. But it wasn't anything she hadn't encountered a hundred times before. When someone learned about her profession, they reacted either with horror, curiosity or admiration. It usually depended on the extent of their personal experience with death and dying. Making fun of her job was an easy way to move past the inevitable awkwardness. But she was used to it. It came with the territory.

Kay didn't have anything more to say so she sat down. Her only purpose for being here was to find out about the houseboat weekend.

Let's get on with it.

Virginia launched into the group's scheduled presentation. Tonight's was on the importance of making positive first impressions. Kay wondered how

75

professional these people could be if they had to be lectured about stuff they should have learned in high school.

Virginia's remedial tutorial finally came to an end and she turned the meeting over to Carol Ann, the head of the planning committee for the houseboat weekend.

The attractive forty-something, buxom blond, with big blue eyes and chicklet-white teeth walked authoritatively to the front of the group, clipboard in hand. She stood there for a moment, nervously flipping the top page back and forth as if she was looking for something that had previously been there but was now gone.

"Ok," the woman began, "We've run into some problems with the houseboat rental."

Low murmuring rumbled through the group.

"First of all, I found out it's not going to make sense to rent two boats. The smallest boat they have sleeps twelve and it costs around $1000 for the weekend."

She paused for reactions, but the group was silent. So she went on. "But then I was told to add another 50% to cover gasoline and food. With twelve people that would come to around $125 a piece."

That's a deal! Kay enthusiastically nodded.

"Unfortunately, as of today, only four people have confirmed," she said. There was a disapproving edge in her voice. "We have to send a deposit by the end of next week so unless we can get at least six more people to sign up, ASAP, I don't know if it's going to be worth it."

Kay did a quick calculation in her head. If she signed up, and nobody else did, it was going to be a $300 weekend. And while she didn't mind spending the money, it was a little steep for being locked up in close quarters with four people she didn't know...or worse...the gassy Delbert Shumacher.

In an effort to entice more sign-ups, Carol Ann took a brochure from her clipboard and asked Virginia to pass it around. But with the speed at which the pamphlet was traveling around the semi circle, one could assume interest was minimal.

It finally reached Kay. She took one look at the cover picture of the long, sleek, Sapphire Moon docked at the marina just waiting to welcome the next group of weekend revelers, and she was overcome with the urge to jump up and scream, "What's wrong with you people?" Instead, she just looked longingly at the pictures in the inner folds which showcased the luxurious style and comfort of the boat's interior. She let out a sigh, imagining being lulled to sleep by the sound of gentle waves as they lapped up against the side of the boat while she relaxed in one of the six private staterooms. Was that a gas barbecue grill she spotted on the topside deck, next to a long line of lounge chairs?

Virginia spoke up from her chair. "As some of you may know, one of the playoff games is being televised tonight. I'm assuming that's the reason for our small turnout this evening. Carol Ann, do you think it would be worth it to contact every member with one last reminder and see if we can possibly get six more people to sign up?"

"It might be," Carol Ann answered, "but I'm

very busy this week and I don't think I'll have time to do it" It was obvious Carol Ann was tiring of her role as planning committee chair.

"How about your committee? Is there somebody who might be willing to help out?" Virginia asked, not ready to let this go.

"Well, neither Phyllis or Alvin are here, and they weren't all that helpful. Frankly, I wouldn't be comfortable asking them to do this."

If there was any hope of keeping the weekend on the Sapphire Moon afloat, Kay was watching it quickly sail into the sunset. It seems no one's heart was in it and Kay was totally baffled as to why.

"I have to tell you Virginia, I think most people signed up for this group to meet someone they could go out with, one on one," Carol Ann said. "I mean, who wants to go on a date with a group…especially a date that lasts three days?"

"I understand, Carol Ann. But if you recall, there was a lot of support for changing things up from these "humdrum" monthly meetings and everyone seemed really excited about doing the houseboat thing."   She turned to the group and said, "Maybe we should put this up for a vote."

Long, lanky Lance spoke up. "That doesn't seem fair with so many members absent. Maybe we should postpone a vote until next time."

"How's that supposed to work?" Carol Ann sneered. "Boating season will be over before our next meeting. We'd be voting on a weekend for next summer."

"Well, I'm going to make an executive

decision," Virginia declared. "We need to finish what we started. Carol Ann, I'd like you to send one last email to everyone on the membership list."

"That's a lot of emails, Virginia. I told you I don't have time," Carol Ann said.

"No, that's one email, mass-mailed to everyone on the membership list. If you stay for a few minutes after the meeting I'll show you how to do it. Give them the information you presented here tonight, along with a deadline to respond. We can even scan the brochure and attach it to the message. Give them the link to my email address, and I will manage the responses."

Kay was hoping Virginia's "take-charge" attitude might just turn things around.

Carol Ann was not finished throwing up roadblocks. "But how are we going to collect the money? Does this group have a bank account? How will you pay the deposit?"

By the way Virginia was standing there chewing her bottom lip, Kay thought her next executive decision would be to fire Carol Ann and her committee. But she just shook her head, sighed. "It's my fault for not checking in with your committee, Carol Ann. I just assumed you guys were handling all these details."

Carol Ann opened her mouth to make an excuse, but Virginia cut her off by addressing the group. "Well, it's clear the time constraints involved with tying up all these loose ends mean the houseboat weekend is probably a no-go." Then she glared at Carol Ann and said, "But we're still going to send that email and let everyone know what's going on. Maybe we can give it another try in the spring."

If there was anything else on the agenda it was clear Virginia didn't have the wherewithal to bring it up. She was done. The meeting adjourned to the kitchen and Kay asked for directions to the bathroom. She needed to splash a little cold water on her face.

"Well Kay, that's what you get for not listening to your gut," she said aloud to herself in the mirror. She had wasted a gorgeous outfit, not to mention an entire Saturday evening. Kay knew she wouldn't be making this mistake again.

Oh well, you probably dodged a bullet.

She pictured Delbert Schumacher standing on the topside deck of the boat, clad in Bermuda shorts, Hawaiian shirt, black socks and sandals, big straw beach hat with the frayed edges, offering her a pina colada with that hungry wolf leer while he ripped a big, stinky, lactose-intolerant fart.

As much as she wanted to, Kay knew she couldn't hide in bathroom all night. With a deep breath, she rejoined the group in the kitchen standing at the refreshment table chatting while they plunged chips into dip, speared cocktail franks with toothpicks, and built slider-sized sandwiches from an array of cold cuts and cheese. Nothing appealed to her, including the conversation. Luckily, she spotted a makeshift bar set up on one end of the table and made a bee line for the bottle of red wine so graciously provided by someone who clearly understood the need for liquor at this queer gathering.

It was a cheap Merlot, but Kay didn't mind. It

was just what the love doctor ordered. She stood off to the side, sipping her wine, trying to be inconspicuous. Her plan was to finish the drink and then beg her leave.

Oh, shit! The crock pot.

Normally, she would have taken the time to empty what was left into a bowl and wash the pot before transporting it back home. But not tonight. She didn't want any unnecessary delays. The pot lid was going on and it would go, as is, into the bamboo tote.

She took a step toward the table when she heard a man's voice say, "You're not coming back, are you?" She turned to see Delbert, whose amorous leer had been replaced by a look of stony disdain. Even the tone of his voice had gone from welcoming to near intimidating.

"I'm sorry?" Kay asked, feigning ignorance.

"I've seen your type before. You come here with your pretty face, tight pants, and tasty cheese dip, looking for the guys with the six packs and the fast cars. And when you don't find them, you're outta here. You bitches never give nice guys like me a chance. I may not look like Tom Selleck, but at least I know how to treat a woman."

But before Kay could say anything in her defense, Delbert walked away in a huff with an audible "toot" escaping from his backside.

Well, if that's how you treat a woman, you don't deserve a chance.

With her purse and tote in hand, Kay hurried for the front door, not bothering to say goodbye to anyone. She doubted if anyone even noticed. As she turned the corner to the entry, she almost bumped into Virginia who was standing there counting the money in the donation basket. She had a defeated look on her face but managed to smile when she saw Kay.

"I'm so glad you were able to come. I'm afraid we didn't make a very good first impression on you. But I hope you'll give us another chance. Like I told you on the phone, we need people like you." It was sad to see the woman so disheartened.

"It was fine," Kay said trying to bolster the spirits of the crestfallen woman. "Don't let the houseboat thing get you down. You know how hard it is to get people to commit to anything. I mean, just look how long it took me to get here." Kay smiled really big trying to make Virginia feel better.

"Yes, and now I'm afraid you won't be coming back," Virginia said as if reading Kay's mind.

Kay kept the big smile on her face, frantically searching her mind for something to say that wouldn't sound like a lie. "Well, I'm anxious to hear what people's reaction will be to the email you're going to send out."

"Oh my god!" Virginia said slapping her hand to her cheek. "The email! I've got to show Carol Ann how to do the mass mailing. I hope she's still here. Well, bye Kay. Be careful going home." She rushed away, leaving Kay standing alone in the entry.

Kay looked down at the sorry little stack of money laying at the bottom of the donation basket. She dug her wallet out of her purse, pulled out a five and with a sigh tossed it in.

My dues for dis-membership.

8

September Skies

What is it about the blue of September skies that makes it so special from all the rest?

Kay sat gazing out the window of her bedroom, mesmerized by the beauty overhead. She was sure there was a scientific explanation having to do with the angle of the sun this time of year, or some other equally-as-boring reason for its uniqueness. But Kay preferred to imagine it like a divine (either small or big "d") overture playing a sentimental recap of summer which gracefully segued to a seductive preview of the coming autumn.

But as captivating as this little parenthetical season was, there was an ever-present, low grade sadness preventing Kay from fully relishing this special time of year.

It must be "cell memory."

This was the explanation she gave herself for these feelings sneaking up on her every September. Once reminded by her cells, her full memory took over and she could recall in detail, the pain and anguish that were hers in those last weeks of September, when Dave slowly but deliberately made his exit from their family. It also didn't help that she was still feeling the sting of the previous night's social let-down.

Kay looked at the clock on the nightstand next to her bed. It was almost 1:00 p.m. Dave was nearly an hour late bringing Mariah home. Not that she was one of those ex-wives who insisted on strict adherence to agreed-upon pick up and return times. Far from it. Mariah was Dave's child too and if he was a little late it was no big deal. She was with her dad. Kay was just anxious to see how the visit went - especially since Mariah had gone without her sister.

As soon as she saw Dave's truck pull up to the curb in front of her house, Kay ran downstairs to welcome Mariah and say hello to Dave. She wanted the girls to see she was making an effort to keep things civil. But truth be told, she wanted to talk to Dave - friendly-like, in the spirit of new beginnings.

It only took her a couple of seconds to reach the front door, but as soon as Kay opened it she saw a cloud of dust left in the wake of Dave's truck as it zoomed away from its brief parking spot. Mariah stood on the sidewalk where her dad had unceremoniously dumped her, looking as crumpled as the little overnight bag laying next to her feet. Kay felt her heart drop to the floor.

"Wow, I hope your dad at least slowed the truck down before you got out," Kay said, trying to make a little joke. "What's the hurry?"

"Oh, you know," Mariah said with a sigh as she bent down to pick up her bag. "He had to get back home right away so Sandy wouldn't be mad at him."

Kay wondered if Dave actually said this to Mariah, or if she had concluded this on her own.

"Here, let me help you with that," Kay said taking the bag from the little girl's hand. "I'm so glad you're home. I missed you."

"I really missed you too, Mom." Kay could hear pain in Mariah's voice. "I wanted to call you last night, but Dad wouldn't let me."

Kay felt a burning heat slowly inch up her face. According to the terms of the visitation agreement, phone calls to either parent, at any time and for any reason were supposed to be permitted. Kay did her best to remain calm. "Oh, I know how it feels to be homesick. I remember one time…"

"Mom," Mariah said, cutting Kay off. "I wasn't homesick. I was mad and I needed to talk to you."

Kay's insides began to churn. This was the first visit of their new agreement.

How could things go off track so soon?

She gently guided her little girl back into the house.

"Sandy wanted me to show her my homework," Mariah said.

Oh no she di-ent!

School was another area where Mariah had issues. She was a very bright little girl, and well-liked by her teachers. Her participation in class was excellent and she got along well with her classmates. But when it came to doing and turning in homework, Mariah seemed to falter.

Last school term, after more than one parent-teacher meeting where Kay was shown a grade-book with numerous zeros next to Mariah's name, she'd become diligent about checking Mariah's work to make sure it was finished and carefully placed in her backpack for the next day. Unfortunately, for some reason Kay couldn't understand, Mariah wouldn't turn in her work. Kay would find the papers in the backpack right where Mariah had put them the evening before. Asking the little girl for an explanation would just elicit a vacant stare and befuddled, "I don't know."

In the interest of full disclosure, Kay had made sure to keep Dave apprised of Mariah's progress in school, or lack thereof. Apparently he had full-disclosure issues of his own.

The girls were only a few weeks into the new semester and Kay had already alerted Mariah's new teacher to the possibility of a repeat of last term's problems. So far, things seemed to be going ok. Not only was Sandy's meddling unnecessary, it was terribly inappropriate. But, of course, that had never stopped Sandy before.

"So, did you show her?" Kay asked, hoping Mariah couldn't detect the fury building up inside her.

"I didn't take my backpack with me, Mom. I was going to do my homework when I got back from dad's today," she explained. Mariah's voice trembled as if she was about to cry.

"Did you explain that to Sandy?"

"Yes. But she just got mad and started saying a bunch of stuff about how it wasn't right that I was making Dad worry and that I was old enough to do my homework without people having to check up on me like a little baby."

So why is the bitch checking up on her?

Mariah went on."Then she said something

87

else that really made me mad, Mommy." Mariah stopped, obviously apprehensive about continuing.

"What was it, Honey?" Kay wasn't sure she wanted to hear the answer.

"Well..." Mariah hesitated. "She said, "Your mother may let you get away with murder at home, but that's not going to happen here. The next time you come you'd better have your homework with you."

Kay felt pain in her hands from the tight fists she had made without knowing.

"Was your dad there? What did he say?" Kay asked, hoping Dave had stepped in.

"Yeah, he was there. But, as usual, he just sat in his chair watching TV."

"Was that when you wanted to call me?

"Yeah, and that's the only time Dad said anything. He told me it wasn't a good idea."

*So the jerk **was** listening.*

"Then what happened?" Kay said, immediately wishing she had waited for Mariah to continue on her own.

"Well, I didn't want Sandy to see me cry, so I just went to the bedroom."

Kay wrapped her arms around her little girl, kissed her on the forehead and said, "Don't worry, Baby. Everything is going to be ok."

Mariah sank into her mother's reassuring embrace, allowing Kay to hold her longer than she normally would have...being nine and all.

"Here. Take your bag and go put your stuff away. I'll fix you something to eat and then you can go back up and start on your homework."

"Ok. I'm really hungry." She headed up the stairs, but stopped and turned back to Kay. "Do I have to show her my homework, Mom?"

"Well, I think it might be nice if you showed it to your dad. But if you'd rather leave it here and work on it when you get home, I think that's fine. I'll talk to Dad and we'll get everything squared away."

The look of terror that flashed across Mariah's face was instant. "Oh, no. Please, Mom. Don't call him. You're going to get me in trouble with Sandy," Mariah cried.

"Don't worry, Honey. You're not going to get in trouble. I promise," Kay said trying to soothe her daughter, not exactly sure if she could keep the promise.

Mariah stood on the stair step, not moving. She searched her mother's eyes for a moment before dropping her gaze to the floor. Kay knew there was something else, but she stopped herself from asking.

Finally, Mariah spoke in a small voice Kay could barely hear. "Mommy…when Sandy got mad at me I messed my pants."

The room undulated like a reflection in a fun house mirror, making Kay dizzy.

"Did you tell Dad?" Kay asked, regaining her equilibrium.

"Mom! I can't tell him. It's too embarrassing. Anyway, he'd tell Sandy and I'd just get yelled at again."

"Ok…ok. But I'm still going to have to talk to him. This business of not allowing you to call me is unacceptable. Like Aunt Les always says, "silence equals permission." Anyway, Kiddo, if we don't stick up for ourselves, who will?" Kay gave Mariah a reassuring smile. "Finish what I told you to do and then come down to eat."

Mariah gave her mother a look mixed with relief and gratitude, turned around and started back up the stairs.

Kay headed into the kitchen and yanked open the refrigerator door so hard the salad dressing bottles loudly clinked as they bounced off each other. She stood there staring at the contents of her fridge, not really seeing anything. White hot rage was building inside her. She didn't know if she was angrier at Sandy for bullying Mariah, or Dave, for granting Sandy permission with his silence. Her heart broke imagining the helplessness Mariah must feel when the man who is supposed to protect her hands her over to her tormentor.

"Mom, can I have a grilled cheese sandwich?" Mariah yelled from upstairs, bringing Kay back to the task at hand. She opened the cheese drawer and pulled out the pack of American cheese slices. Her hands were trembling.

"How 'bout some soup to go with it?" Kay called back. She hoped Mariah couldn't tell how upset she was.

"Do we have tomato?"

Kay opened her pantry door, did a quick

check and found what she needed.

"There's one can left and it's all yours," Kay loudly reported.

"What about Cory? Won't she want some?"

"I don't expect her until after 7:00. Like I said, it's all yours."

"Super!" Mariah said.

Kay was grateful she could do something to make her child happy...and it was such a little thing. She could already picture the appreciative look on Mariah's face when she placed the simple meal in front of her at the table. Just the thought of that beautiful little smile gave Kay such a feeling of warm satisfaction; she could feel her wrath subside.

What kind of sick satisfaction do you get from terrorizing a child?

Kay took turns between tending the sandwich in the skillet and the small saucepan heating the soup, making sure neither one burned. In between stirs and spatula flips, Kay stole glances at the clock. She wanted to make sure Dave had plenty of time to get home before she called. Calling now and airing her grievances to Sandy would only elevate the importance of Sandy's role in the situation. As far as Kay was concerned, Sandy had no role...other than Dave's wife. Dave was the parent and he needed to start acting like it. If he and Kay couldn't be on the same page when it came to the kids, then maybe the visitation agreement would have to be revised.

There was another reason Kay didn't want to talk to Sandy - one she didn't want to admit. She was afraid of the woman, too. Sandy seemed to possess some strange confidence Kay didn't understand. What else could explain Sandy so brazenly helping her herself to a married man? The woman's shameless proprietary attitude toward someone who, clearly, didn't belong to her, was so steadfast and sure she didn't even care it had cost them both their jobs. It was as if Sandy knew something she didn't.

Mariah's meal was ready. Kay placed it on the table, added a glass of milk and called her down to eat. The hungry little girl wasted no time getting her butt in the dining room chair. She took one look at the plain lunch and grinned as if she was looking at a gourmet feast.

"Thanks, Mom," Mariah said, smiling up at her mother. "Is there enough cheese if I want another sandwich?"

"Eat that first and then we'll see," Kay said, even though she knew it was likely she'd have to make another. But it would have to wait until she made her important phone call.

"Slow down, Mariah. That sandwich isn't going anywhere. I'll be back in a minute."

Mariah was so focused on enjoying her grilled cheese, she voiced no objection to what Kay was obviously on her way to do. Kay knew, deep down, Mariah was grateful her mother was coming to her rescue - even if it was a day late.

Kay closed the door to her bedroom just in case she might have to raise her voice.

Maybe I should take the phone in the closet.

Kay wanted to be sure Mariah wouldn't be subjected to any further stress. But she nixed the idea realizing it would be setting the stage for a heated confrontation. And while telling Dave and Sandy off would have given her a boat-load of satisfaction, she reminded herself this wasn't about her but about Mariah. The best way to handle the situation was to stay firm, cool and detached.

With each ring of the line, Kay's heart pounded in a rhythmic response. The hand holding the phone was cold and clammy with sweat. She was just about to lose her nerve and hang up when she heard Sandy's slow, thick-throated "hullo." In an instant Kay could feel her fear evaporate as the reason for Sandy's menacing behavior suddenly became crystal clear.

"Hello, Sandy. This is Kay. May I please speak to Dave, if he's available?" Kay said, trying to be as polite as possible.

"Jusssst a minute," Sandy hissed through clenched teeth.

Even though Sandy had covered up the receiver with her hand, she couldn't cover up the loathing in her muffled voice as she grudgingly summoned her husband to the phone.

"Hello?" Dave said. He tried to sound as if he had no clue who was on the other end of the line.

"Dave, this is Kay."

"Oh, hi," he responded in fake surprise.

"I wanted to talk to you earlier but you drove away so fast I didn't get the chance," she began. "Anyway, I wish you would at least wait until you know Mariah is safely in the door."

Kay could hear the wheels in Dave's head whirling as he tried to come up with a plausible excuse for his quick get-away.

"Oh. Uh, well, I knew you were home so I didn't think there'd be a problem. But I'll be sure to wait next time. What did you want to talk to me about?"

"Nothing specific. I just wanted to know how the weekend went and if there was anything I needed to be aware of, or if you had any questions for me. Now that you're back I think it's important for the two of us to communicate regularly about the kids."

Kay knew he hated being reminded there was still "the two of us," even if it was only as parents of Cory and Mariah.

"The weekend was fine and there's nothing I can think of that you need to be aware of," Dave said. His voice was bone-chillingly cold.

"That's good," Kay said, trying not to let his frosty attitude throw her off her intended path. "Well, there's something *I* need to ask *you.*"

"What is it?" Dave snapped.

"Was there any particular reason why Mariah wasn't allowed to call me last night? The kids are supposed to be allowed to call either parent, anytime, for any reason."

Kay made sure her tone was non-threatening and business-like. Her straightforward manner threw Dave off more than if she had screamed at him in anger.

"I didn't say she couldn't call you," he said. His

94

cold tone had become defensive. "I just told her I thought it wasn't a good idea. I didn't want her to upset you."

"Oh? And why would I have been upset?" Kay asked innocently, luring her prey into her trap.

I'm going to make you tell me, yourself, asshole.

After a brief, uncomfortable pause Dave said, "Well, I think she may have misunderstood Sandy's offer to help her with her homework."

Kay was insulted by this weaselly explanation but instead of challenging him, continued to tightened the noose. "I don't understand. What was the offer?"

Dave cleared his throat.

"Sandy just asked Mariah to show her where she was with her work so she could see if she could help."

Just then Sandy, who had been secretly listening on the extension, broke into the conversation. "That's ok Dave. I don't need you to defend me. Kay, I asked Mariah to show me her homework because I think she needs to learn to be more accountable. Lord knows if you were stricter with her she wouldn't be having these problems in school."

Kay smiled to herself. *There it is.* Her suspicions had been validated.

"Excuse me, Sandy, this is a conversation between me and Mariah's dad. Please have the courtesy to give us privacy." Kay knew her request would be ignored.

"No, I won't excuse you. Dave is my husband and his business is my business."

"I'm afraid in this case you're wrong, Sandy. It's not your place to get involved in matters concerning the girls. I will not discuss Mariah with you except to say if you continue to harass her I'll have to go to back to court to have the original order reinstated. That includes child support."

"Aw, c'mon, Kay," Dave cut in. "I don't think that's necessary. It wasn't as bad as I'm sure Mariah made it out to be. You have to admit she's pretty sensitive when it comes to talking about her school work."

Putting the blame on Mariah was a cheap shot and Kay wasn't about to let Dave get away with it.

"Yes, Dave, I agree. But you and I both know this went far beyond just school work. She was belittled and made to feel guilty about worrying you. Have you actually told her you're worried?"

"Well, no…not exactly," Dave said.

Sandy butted in again. "He won't admit it, but I know my husband. It bothers him that Mariah might be failing, and he doesn't need the aggravation."

I'm sorry. I had no idea he was so delicate.

As tempting as it was, Kay resisted the urge to mock Dave out loud.

Dave stayed quiet, perfectly comfortable having his wife speak for him. But Kay refused to make Sandy a bona fide participant in the conversation.

"Dave, Mariah is the one who doesn't need

96

the aggravation. Your wife made her feel so bad she messed her pants. Did you bother to worry about that?"

Kay heard Sandy suppress a scornful snort.

"I - I didn't know. Mariah didn't say anything." Dave was clearly taken aback.

"Would you really expect her to? It's humiliating."

"If you ask me, she does it to get attention," Sandy said.

"Nobody asked you," Kay replied, no longer able to ignore the meddling third party. "Dave, would you please tell your wife she can relax. She's got the job. It isn't necessary for her to keep pointing out our short-comings just so you can feel better about leaving us."

With that, Sandy slammed down the extension. But Kay wasn't finished with Dave.

"Look, Dave. I can't allow the girls to be bullied just because Sandy is insecure and you're too passive to do anything about it. I've tried to stick up for you when the girls have complained. Not for your sake, but because they need to believe their father loves them and hasn't pushed them aside for his new family. But there isn't much I can do when your actions prove otherwise, except ask the court to intervene."

"Kay, you have to know I really feel bad about Mariah's accident. Has the doctor said anything else about her problem?" True to form, he was trying to deflect the conversation so he wouldn't have to deal with Kay's justified threat. Kay refused to take the bait.

"I mean what I say, Dave. Mariah isn't in a position to stand up for herself like Cory did. Besides, she really loves you and still wants to see you. Please don't let Sandy make it difficult for her."

She stayed quiet, waiting to see what Dave was going to do now that the ball was in his court.

After a few tense seconds he finally spoke."Why don't I come by sometime this week and take her out for an ice cream?"

Kay knew this was as close to an apology as Mariah was going to get.

"I'm sure she'd really like that. I'll tell her to expect your call. Oh, and just so you know, Mariah is doing just fine in school this semester. So you can call off your dog." Kay couldn't resist getting in a least one below-the-belt dig.

"That was uncalled for," Dave said.

"I'm glad you get it. I was beginning to wonder," Kay said. "G'bye, Dave," She hung up before he had a chance to respond.

Kay walked slowly downstairs, proud she had stood up to both Dave and Sandy. Now only time would tell if her words had gotten through to them. But if history was any indication, she wasn't holding out a lot of hope. She'd have to put her lawyer's number on speed dial.

"How'd, it go, Mom? Is Dad mad at me for telling you what happened?" Mariah asked.

"Not at all. In fact, he's going to come by this week to take you for ice cream. I think he wants to make things up to you."

"Really, Mom?" the little girl said. There was no mistaking the pure delight in her eyes. "When?"

"Sometime this week. He'll give you call."

Kay didn't want to talk about it anymore. Now it was her turn to deflect the conversation. "Are you going to want that other sandwich?"

"Yes, please."

As Kay walked over to the stove to get things ready for Mariah's second grilled cheese her attention was drawn to the kitchen window by a dramatic change of color in the late afternoon sky that mirrored her changed mood. She let out a bittersweet sigh. Her heart ached for this September and all the sad Septembers past.

9

Always Use Protection

Kay carefully backed the gold-colored hearse out of the garage and parked it under the canopy of the mortuary car port. It's sparkling condition, inside and out, was evidence Leo had given it his usual all-out cleaning effort.

Kay knew it was crazy, but driving the hearse for a funeral filled her with excitement. She got to be the lead car directly behind a police escort. Traffic was stopped in every direction to let the slow, sad parade of cars with their headlights on, pass in procession. To underscore the near-thrilling experience, Kay always played her Bee Gee's Saturday Night Fever CD, with the volume turned up to near ear-splitting levels during "Staying Alive."

Everybody's got their little eccentricities.

Once at the church, she would resume her dignified, funeral director persona. This morning she would be directing Emily McNab's funeral, with Ed making a mandatory appearance at the church to satisfy the legal conditions of her apprentice license. Emily had lived a mere six weeks after the day Kay had put her final wishes to paper. With a mixture of sadness and pride, Kay was ready to see Emily's wishes through.

On her trip back to the garage to retrieve the limousine she met up with Ed who had just arrived to begin his day. Kay was struck by how impeccable he looked in his charcoal gray suit, crisp white shirt and burgundy tie. She was about to compliment his appearance when she noticed the un-rinsed remains of shaving cream clinging to the outer rim of his right ear.

"Hey, Kay," he said in a hearty greeting. "Are we ready for this busy morning?"

"Well, I am, but I don't know about you." She reached up and gently brushed the dried foam from her boss's ear. She had never been so familiar with him and by the embarrassed expression on his face, she wondered if she had crossed some kind of unspoken line.

"Thanks," he said with a nervous laugh. "I gotta start shaving *before* I get in the shower."

Instantly, the image of a naked Ed, traces of shaving cream streaked on his handsome face, stepping into the shower, flashed in Kay's head. She felt a surge of warmth in the lower reaches of her anatomy and thought it would be wise to change the subject.

"Leo sure did a great job on the cars," she said a little too enthusiastically. She hurried for the safety of the furthest reaches of the garage where she expected to find the exceptionally clean limousine.

"Come by my office when you're done parking the car," Ed called after her. "We need to double-check a couple of last minute things."

Kay didn't respond but it didn't matter because he was already on his way to his office. She took her place in the driver's seat and let out a raggedy sigh before inserting the key. She started the ignition, put the car in reverse and, because she didn't trust her skills using the rear view mirror, she extended her arm across the back of the seat and turned her head around to guide herself out of the long garage.

"Oh crap!" she said. A mass of crumpled tissues, discarded paper cups, food crumbs and other bits of trash was strewn across the expanse of the stretched rear of the car. She had spoken too soon.

"Damn you, Leo," she muttered under her breath. He had to be located as quickly as possible. Uncle O would be here soon to get the limo for a 9:45 pick up at the McNab's home.

Kay thanked God she was rear view mirror-challenged. Had she not turned around, the stellar reputation of the mortuary could have easily taken a hit. But saving face for Salinger's was the least of it. It pained Kay to remember the look on Emily McNab's face during the prearrangement, when she insisted her husband and family ride to her funeral in the grandeur of a limousine. It was obvious Mr. McNab didn't approve of the unnecessary extravagance (or cost) but couldn't bring himself to deny the dying wishes of his wife. And now, instead of riding in the posh splendor Emily McNab had envisioned, Kay might have to cancel the limousine due to luxury-spoiling filth.

She quickly parked the limo behind the hearse and set out to look for Leo. There was still time for a quick trash removal and vacuuming.

Ed spotted Kay as she sped by the door of his office. "Kay," he called out, "did you forget me?"

"Oh, yeah, sorry," she said, putting on the brakes and making a tight u-turn back to Ed's office. "Have you seen Leo?"

"Yeah. I sent him to the cemetery with the lowering device. Why?"

"Do you know when he'll be back?"

"He just left. He probably won't be back for an hour. Why?"

"Well...it's just that the limo is a mess and Uncle O will be here any minute to go pick up the family."

Kay hated being a snitch, but Leo had put her in an untenable situation.

Ed's bright mood of a few moments earlier quickly turned. "God damn it, Kay! Didn't you just tell me he had done a great job?" Ed was a stickler for perfection, and little hiccups like these usually drove him over the edge.

"I know, I know. It's just, well, the hearse looked great I just assumed the limo would be in the same condition."

Her explanation sounded lame and whiny and she was ashamed she couldn't come up with something better.

Ed pulled back the starched white cuff of his sleeve and looked at his watch. "He'll never make it back in time. Sorry, but you're gonna have to take care of it yourself. I'll talk to him when he gets back. Now, let's go over this morning's timetable."

They synchronized the details of her service, so Ed would know when to make his official appearance at the Episcopal church. When they were done, he pushed his chair back and placed the palms of his hands on the tops of his thighs. "So, I guess I'll see you sometime around 10:15. You better get going on that limo." Then he rotated his chair toward the file cabinet against the wall and busied himself looking for something. Kay had been dismissed.

Leo. You little shit. I hope Ed reams you a new one.

Kay had about 30 minutes before the McNab's were expecting Uncle O. It would be cutting it close, but she figured she had enough time to do an adequate cleaning. On her way to the store room to get the car vac and couple of plastic bags for the trash, she made a quick pit stop at the ladies room to remove her pantyhose. Kay hated the way her bare feet felt inside her expensive pumps but she couldn't risk getting a run in her stockings. And now she was going to be cleaning and vacuuming on her knees in her best Talbot's suit. All because Leo didn't do his job.

Better not forget the rubber gloves.

Thinking of all those dried, snotty tissues was making her madder by the second.

Fifteen minutes, a myriad of cups, Kleenexes and freshly-vacuumed floor mats and seat cushions later, Kay had the interior of the car looking ship-shape. Inching backward out of the car on her knees, she caught a glimpse of one last bit of trash she'd missed hiding under the driver's seat. Lowering her chest to the floor, she stretched her arm under the seat as far as it would go. She grabbed the item and pulled it out and raised herself up from her crouched position. She took one look at the used condom swinging from her fingers, screamed and flung it across the top of the front seat, where it stuck to the air conditioner vents on the dash. She knelt there staring at the thin latex mess, a million scenarios racing through her mind.

Maybe Ed is some sort of kinky mortician who got his jollies from screwing women in the back of a funeral car.

Then she imagined Leo taking advantage of the comfort of the expansive interior and privacy of the garage to entertain female friends. But she quickly put that thought out of her mind. Leo wasn't exactly what you'd call a "ladies man."

Maybe it was a client channeling their grief into lust, stealing away from a boring after-funeral reception, to feast on catered food and other grief-consoling treats.

Regardless, she didn't have the time (or desire) to figure out the repulsive mystery. She was just glad she had discovered it before one of her unsuspecting passengers inadvertently unearthed it. She left the offending prophylactic on the dash until she re-parked the limo behind the hearse. With a new set of latex gloves, she carefully peeled it away and discarded it deeply in the bowels of her trash bags. Unfortunately, there wasn't time to wipe down the vents. Uncle O was at the driver's side door, big smile on his face, proudly ready to assume his chauffeuring duties.

* * *

Kay was in the break-room getting her Slim

Selections Butternut Squash Ravioli lunch ready for the microwave. This morning's limousine mishap had been a close call. She was pleased she'd been able to pull everything off relatively smoothly. Even Ed's appearance at the church had been a small triumph for her. Upon offering his condolences to Mr. McNab, the grieving widower thanked Ed for his services and congratulated him for having such a competent, compassionate staff. Ed had walked to the back of the church where Kay was standing, patted her on the shoulder and said, "good job!" before he hurried back to the mortuary. It was quite a generous gesture from a boss who had a reputation for being stingy with compliments.

The whirring of the microwave masked Ed's entrance into the break-room. Kay was staring at the little glass window in the door with a curious smile on her face as she watching her raviolis spinning round and round.

"That food must be pretty entertaining," Ed said with a laugh, startling Kay out of her reverie. "Mine's boring. It only gets hot."

"Oh hi. I didn't hear you come in."

The microwave beeped, and she pulled her steaming convenience meal out of the little white oven. She grabbed a plastic spoon and a napkin from the counter top and headed over to the table in the middle of the small room.

"I was just thinking about something that happened during my funeral service," she said.

She pulled out a chair and set her place at the table.

Ed opened the refrigerator and pulled out a can of soda. Kay guessed he was probably off to some important engagement and wouldn't make time to eat. With a quick pop of the tab and familiar burp of trapped CO_2, Ed's liquid lunch was ready for consumption. He took a big gulp, uncouthly wiped his mouth with the back of his hand, looked over at Kay and said, "Well?"

"Huh?" Kay answered, not sure what he was asking.

"Are you going to share?" referring to her previous comment.

"Oh," she said with a laugh.

Kay explained to Ed how at the moment she was closing Emily McNab's casket for the last time, the solemn moment had been pierced by a small, but insistent voice from the back of the church. An inquisitive little girl wanted to know, "Mommy, who's that lady in the suitcase?" With the exception of the child's mortified mother, the congregation had enjoyed a good laugh.

"It was so touching, Ed. Mr. McNab went out of his way after the service to talk to the little girl and assure her mother no harm was done. He said he was sure Emily was up in heaven laughing with everyone else. You know, it made me think of that saying...let's see...how does it go? ...*ask not what your country...*, no - wait - that's not it."

"Do you mean, *"grant that I may not so much seek to be consoled, as to console?"* Ed offered.

"That's it!" Kay cried.

"Yeah," Ed said, "It's from the prayer of St

Francis, delivered in Assisi at his first inaugural address."

She had just taken a spoonful of raviolis when the realization of her mistake, combined with Ed's dead-pan delivery, triggered a deep belly laugh that sent her little pasta pillows flying out of her mouth in a very un-lady-like fashion.

The scene disintegrated from there. At the sight of Kay's spit take, Ed could no longer play it straight. He and Kay were both roaring with laughter. Every time they quieted down, they'd look at each other and be off again. They had almost managed to regain their composure when Leo walked in to fetch his brown bag lunch from the fridge.

"What's so funny?" he asked, smiling at the merry carrying-on. In light of the situation with the dirty limousine, Leo's appearance dampered the mood more effectively. With one last smothered chuckle, Ed said, "Oh, nothing." Then, as was his custom, he hurried out of the room, shooting his final comments over his shoulder. "Hey, Leo. When you're done eating, come see me in my office."

"Will do, Ed," Leo blithely called after him, completely unaware of the tongue lashing that was in store for him.

Kay returned her attention to her lunch, which was beginning to get cold. Reheating the meal would have surely turned the pasta to rubber, so she stirred the contents of the little plastic tray, hoping to transfer some of the remaining heat to the colder portions sitting on the top.

Leo planted himself in a chair across the table

from her and proceeded to remove a wax paper-wrapped sandwich from his lunch bag. Without looking, Kay could tell by the smell it was egg salad. He unwrapped his aromatic prize, and dug in with all the gusto of a starved animal. Then he opened his mouth to speak, displaying the egg salad in all its mayonnaise-bathed glory. "I wonder what Ed wants?"

Aptly grossed out by Leo's lack of good chewing etiquette, Kay, nevertheless, made the effort to not visibly cringe. As mad as she was at him, she still felt sorry for the poor sap. He was the guy at the bottom of the totem pole, in charge of all the lowly tasks around the mortuary. Though he had dropped the ball this morning, he could usually be counted on to get things done. She was beginning to feel guilty for ratting him out. Nevertheless, she matter-of-factly told him, "I think he's going to ask you why you didn't have the limousine ready for me this morning."

He scrunched his eyebrows together, completely clueless about what Kay was saying.

"Huh?"

"Yeah. When I pulled it out of the garage this morning, the inside was completely trashed." Then she confessed, "I only told Ed because he wanted to know why I was looking for you."

He sat there for a few moments, chewing, with the puzzled look still on his face. He finally swallowed and said, "I'm pretty sure the limo wasn't initialed on the white board," referring to the large, dry writer hung in the back hallway. It contained a detailed checklist used for keeping track of all the details of each funeral service.

"No, Leo," Kay corrected, "I know I initialed it because it was a special request on a pre-arrangement."

Leo shook his head and countered, "I don't mean to go against you Kay, but if it had been initialed I would have cleaned it."

"Well, this is easy enough to settle. Let's just go check. I haven't erased this morning's service yet."

The two got up from the table, leaving the remains of their lunch uneaten and went around the corner from the break room to the hallway.

"Ok. Here it is," Kay said running her index finger along the grid line containing the service details of Emily McNab's funeral.

Authorization to Embalm: KM

Embalming Report: KM

Hearse: KM

Limousine:

Escort: KM

Memorial Cards: KM

Register Book: KM

Announcement Board: KM

Obit: KM

Flowers: KM

Honorarium Checks: KM

Cemetery: KM

Headstone Order:

Insurance Claim: KM

There it was as plain as day. A blank space next to "Limousine." Kay stood there staring at the empty spot, as if she could will her initials to magically appear. Leo remained, mercifully, quiet. He wasn't the type of jerk who'd enjoy laying an "I told you so" on her. But the fact remained, he was right and she was wrong. Kay knew she'd have to go to Ed, admit her mistake, take Leo off the hook, and take her medicine like a grownup.

"Oh my god, Leo. I'm so sorry. I don't know how I missed it," she said with sincere remorse. Then she quickly added, "Don't worry. I'll explain everything to Ed. Let's go finish our lunch."

Together they walked back to the break room, one person in triumph and other in defeat. Kay took one look at the drying, curled edges of her cold raviolis, and knew lunch was over. Leo, on the other hand, dove right back in where he'd left off. Not giving a thought to his disgusting mouthful of egg salad said, "I bet Ed was pissed when you had to cancel the limo."

"Oh, we used it all right," Kay said as she cleaned up her eating space. "Thankfully, there was enough time for me to give it a quick going over. Of course, it wasn't as perfect as you usually make things," she said with a conciliatory smile. Then she leaned in, lowered her voice and said, "You'll never believe what I found hiding under the driver's seat."

Leo took another big bite off his sandwich and answered with an eager, but gross, wide-mouthed, "Whaaat?"

111

"A used condom!"

Kay shared this with him fully aware of her ulterior motives. Not only was she trying to make things up to Leo by taking him into her confidence, she was also fishing for some kind of tell-tale reaction.

"Oh," he said, with a blase´ shrug. "Is that all?" He was clearly disappointed by Kay's shocking revelation.

"Is that all?" Kay said. "You make it sound like finding used condoms in the limousine happens everyday."

"Hmmm," Leo answered, still chewing, but now with his mouth closed.

He knows something.

She waited for him to swallow, hoping he was going to speak and clear up the mystery. But he just shoved the last bit of his sandwich into his mouth and went on chewing without saying a word.

Kay watched him for a few more moments and when she couldn't take his silence any longer she blurted out, "Ah, c'mon Leo. Don't leave me here twisting in the wind. What's going on that you're not telling me?"

He smiled that smile that only someone with a juicy secret can. He balled up the used wax paper, shoved it back into the brown paper bag, and rolled the whole thing up. "I gotta get going," he said as he pushed his chair back from the table. "If I don't start on the chapels, Ruth is going to be on my ass." He walked to the trash can, tossed in his wadded-up bag, turned to Kay and said, "You're gonna go talk to Ed now, right?"

"Yes. Of course," she said, quickly rising from her chair. "And I'll try to make sure that doesn't happen again, ok?"

He nodded at her graciously and then quickly exited the break-room before Kay could ask any more questions.

So it looked like Kay was going to get to eat lunch after all - a heaping, helping of crow. But she wasn't really concerned about that now. All she could think about was the secret lurking behind Leo's inscrutable smile.

10

The More Things Change

For the next few months, Kay, the girls and Dave settled into their new routine with only the occasional hiccup here and there. Of course, the holidays presented their usual challenges. The girls had their standard complaints about feeling unwelcome at Sandy's brother's Thanksgiving table, and having to sit by and watch on Christmas morning as Little Dave tore into an avalanche of presents where one or two "crappy" gifts might tumble down for them. For the most part, Dave was holding up his end of the bargain, filling in at the last minute when Kay couldn't get away from work. She was proud that she could call him now without the aid of controlled substances. Even the frosty receptionist at Dave's office had thawed and the bad hold music had gone back to being bad and no longer inspired silly singing.

The weekend visits had been, relatively, trouble-free, and Cory even joined her sister on occasion. Kay was always there to see the girls off on Friday evening and again to greet them when they came home on Sunday. Each time she'd secretly hope to engage Dave in a friendly chat. But it never happened. She wanted to know how he was doing at his new job and she longed to tell him all the funny stuff that happened at work. (The mystery of the Limousine Lothario, which remained unsolved, would have been just the thing the two of them would have had a good laugh about.) But those days were gone. He was always polite, but he showed no interest in how she was doing or anything going on with her life. Eventually, his unwavering indifference got to be too painful so she excused herself from any further departure/arrival appearances at the door, and just watched, wistfully, through her bedroom drapes as his truck came and went.

Then, almost imperceptibly, things began to change. Looking back, Kay realized it had all started with an innocent little desk lamp.

In an effort to keep Mariah motivated with her school work, Kay bought her a college dorm-like desk. It was clear from Mariah's delight, Kay's idea had been inspired. Now the little girl would have a grownup work space all her own where she could keep everything organized and conveniently within reach.

But the corner of the room where the desk had been placed was too dark for reading and writing. It needed a desk lamp - one of those items that fell into the category of "extra curriculars" to which Dave had so happily agreed to supply. And indeed, he complied with his usual, enthusiastic, "no problem." He would take care of it during Mariah's upcoming weekend visit.

Mariah came home with the lamp, alright. But it seems getting this simple $10 item involved the kind of secrecy and subterfuge worthy of a John le Carre spy novel.

First, a crafty ruse had to be devised to justify a shopping errand in town. According to Mariah, Dave told Sandy he was taking Mariah with him to the local home building center to purchase supplies for a tree house he promised to build for Little Dave. Once there, Dave bought the desk lamp and hid it in his truck under the lumber, nails and wood sealant; Mariah was sworn to secrecy. If Sandy found out, "there'd be hell to pay."

To celebrate the completion of their secret mission, (or to assuage Dave's guilt) he took Mariah to the local Cream Queen for a double dip soft serve. Naturally, any evidence of their ice cream junket had to be consumed and cleaned up before they got home and no mention of it made, lest Sandy's wrath be incurred.

Mariah was confused. What kid wouldn't be? Her dad was making her feel special and ashamed at the same time, all the while forcing her to keep a secret. Kay thought she needed to confront Dave about his borderline child abusive behavior, but brushed off the thought, telling herself it would be a wasted effort. The main thing was she had asked for Dave's help and he had complied. Mariah had her desk lamp and it would all be worth it when the little girl could proudly show up Sandy in front of her dad with her good grades.

You gotta focus on what's important. We're working together the best we can for the sake of the kids.

But deep in her heart Kay knew she was selling out.

As time wore on, twinges of pain from the impact of her reduced child support were becoming harder to ignore. Dave's reliability for taking up the slack for those pesky "extra curriculars" was slowly, but surely diminishing.

Something as simple as asking for help with school lunches was met with an apologetic excuse about payday and bad timing. Then there was Cory's field trip to the nuclear waste storage facility. When he feigned being unable to pony up half the $25 student participation fee, Kay told him he could still participate as a parent chaperon. Kay had caught him off guard with that one, so he reluctantly agreed to go along.

Not long after that, Cory's trumpet was in need of a valve repair, which meant forking out $125 so she wouldn't miss the district middle school band competition (she was first chair). Even with Kay's offer to split the bill with Dave, he found an excuse for saying no. And each time Dave let her down, Kay would find an excuse for excusing his excuse.

His income's been cut too - or - *the move was expensive and he's trying to catch up.* And the ever-popular, *money's tight for everyone these days.*

She told herself she would cut back on the money requests to give him some breathing space. That way he'd be able to come through if something really big came up. As long as he continued to be available to drive the kids when needed, she told herself she could make do.

But that's just the thing. He was becoming less available.

He couldn't take Cory to therapy because he had to meet clients for a meeting over drinks after work.

He couldn't get a sick Mariah from school because Sandy wasn't going to be home to watch her.

He couldn't pick up Cory's (paid-for) repaired trumpet, because he was going out of town on business *that very* afternoon.

And he certainly couldn't ask his wife to fill in for him. "It isn't her responsibility," he would defensively insist to Kay, when she suggested Sandy help out.

Kay was frustrated and angry, but still unwilling to pay attention to the nagging thought Dave might have played her for a chump. If she did that, she'd have to admit nothing had changed and Dave still had the power to manipulate her; which meant her hard-won triumph over the divorce was a joke.

No. Their agreement just needed to be tweaked to take into account changing circumstances. Kay was sure they could get things back on track. She decided the best course of action would be to set up another face-to-face meeting. There they could review the agreement to see where changes could be made to accommodate everyone's needs and preferences.

Taking charge of the situation gave Kay a much-needed sense of empowerment and hope. She'd give him a call the next evening to make a date to get together at a mutually-convenient place and time.

But Denial is a jealous task master. If it's going to run interference between you and Reality just so you can have the convenience and peace of feeling "everything's OK,"   it's going to continually test your worthiness to receive its services.

By the next evening, Kay's earnest resolve

had been sapped by the stresses of a long, hard day at work. Cory, graciously driven to therapy by Violet's mom, Bonnie, had just called asking to be picked up. The thought of putting her shoes back on and getting back in the car was so abhorrent to an exhausted Kay, she picked up the phone and put in a call to her designated wingman, Dave.

Dave made no effort to disguise his irritation. Her request to retrieve Cory from therapy was met with a flat, "I just sat down to dinner."

She pictured him, taking his place at the table like a king, presented with a hot meal he didn't have to prepare. Whereas she had just driven 30 miles after a taxing day at work to be greeted by a cold, dark kitchen and an empty table. The inequity of their situations fueled a determination to get *something* out of the smug, spoiled sonofabitch.

"Then how 'bout splitting the co-pay with me?" She wondered if he could detect the edge of challenge in her voice. The co-pay was only $15 which meant she was asking for a measly $7.

He didn't even pretend to think about it. His reply was immediate, terse and stone-cold. "I don't have it."

The words slapped her with the realization the window of opportunity to save the agreement was rapidly closing. Hell, it may have already slammed shut.

Kay's emotions were too overwhelming to allow her to stay on the phone and argue for the piddly amount of money. She could only bring herself to quietly say, "Ok. Bye." She stood there, knees locked together, trying to quash the shakes threatening to overtake her tired body. Swallowing the painful lump in her throat trying to push stinging tears from her eyes, she gathered her purse and her youngest daughter and headed for Dr. Fulmer's office.

Enter Denial to the rescue. Kay calmed herself with the rationalization that her unpleasant encounter with Dave was simply the result of two people tired after a hard day's work.

I mean, can you really blame someone for not wanting to get up from their dinner to run an errand?

The issue of the $7 was a little more difficult to justify, so she simply banished it from her thoughts, as best she could. She couldn't allow anything to dampen her hope they could still fix the agreement.

I'm sure he wants what's best for him and the girls.

This was his weekend with Mariah. She would approach him when he came to pick her up on Friday.

But Friday came and she wasn't able to get home in time to carry out her plan. Dave and Mariah were long gone.

"Dad practically begged me to come with them," Cory bragged to her mother. "But I just said, "Maybe next time.""

Kay envied her daughter's power to say no to Dave. She regretted not making him beg her to take his stupid child support deal.

Then I wouldn't be in this position.

Shoulda, woulda, coulda…No, Kay! Don't go there.

There was still a chance to assert herself and get what she wanted. She promised herself when Sunday afternoon came she would be there and she'd make him bend to her will.

For the next two days she stewed and fretted, rehearsing various scenarios so she'd be prepared for anything he threw at her. In her shakier moments, she was tempted to call Ruth to ask for reinforcement; she remembered the hard-working woman was taking a few days off to host visiting relatives. No. She'd just have to dive in the deep end of this pool without an inner tube.

* * *

The doorbell rang and Kay opened the door to a smiling Mariah and a scowling Dave. "Hi, Mom. Bye, Dad," Mariah said. She hurried past Kay to get into the house (or away from Dave?).

"Hey, Baby," Kay called after her, happy her little girl was home. By the time she turned back to Dave he was halfway down the driveway. Kay ran after him.

"Dave, wait."

With a disgusted sigh, Dave stopped and turned around to face his ex-wife. The deadness in his eyes stalled Kay in her tracks and she could feel herself shrink like a wool sweater in a hot dryer.

"Look, Kay. I already told you I don't have your co-pay."

In that moment, all her rehearsals abandoned her.

"No...no. Uh, I just wanted to talk...uh, to see

if we could…I mean, I think we need to talk."

She knew she sounded like a blithering idiot.

"I really don't have time right now. Sandy is waiting for me."

"I didn't mean right now. I was hoping we could set up a time to get together," Kay said. She was trying to ignore the sting of his intolerant demeanor.

He stood there staring at her without any response. After a couple of uncomfortable moments he turned up his palm, raised his eyebrows and said, "Well?" throwing Kay even more off kilter.

"Well, I just thought it might be time to revisit our agreement to see if we can make it more workable for the two of us," she breathlessly got out.

Dave was slowly going from cold to angry. "What the hell are you talking about?"

"C'mon Dave. Please don't play stupid. You know I'm talking about the agreement we made when you cut my child support."

Dave's dead eyes suddenly sparked to life with angry fire. "Listen, I never forced you to take that cut. As I recall, you were more than willing to accept it." Then he let out a snide little snort and said, "Sandy said sooner or later you were going to throw that in my face"

Invoking the name of Sandy was a surefire sign she had hit a nerve.

"I'm not trying to throw anything in your face. I'm trying to work with you so things will be easier for everyone, all the way around. That includes Sandy."

122

His look of contempt was burning a hole through Kay's brain.

"Easier? That's a laugh! I should have known you were going to try to take advantage of me now that I'm back. When are you going to get it through that thick skull of yours I'm no longer your dutiful husband and you can't just pick up the phone anytime you have some stupid errand you're too lazy to do yourself?"

Kay stood there dumbstruck, sliced to pieces. None of this had gone the way she's imagined. The look on her face must have been pretty alarming because Dave suddenly softened and in a much quieter tone said, "That didn't come out right." He let out a big sigh and continued, "It's just that I'm under a lot of pressure at work and they're not paying me what I'm used to."

His explanation was missing an apology, but Kay knew that was as close as he would ever get. Nevertheless, the issue of meeting to discuss their failing agreement was still unresolved, and under the circumstances, Kay thought, badly needed.

"Look, Dave. If you're under that much pressure from work, wouldn't it help to see where we can make some mutually-helpful changes?"

"I don't know. I guess. I gotta go. I'll try to call you this week and we can talk about it."

Squirming to get away from Kay, Dave made a quick escape to the safety of his truck. Neither of them said goodbye.

Kay turned and with great difficulty, willed her wooden legs to move toward the front door.

Thankfully, it was closed. She hoped the girls hadn't heard any of the nasty exchange. Long before they were born, she and Dave had promised each other they wouldn't put their kids through the gut-twisting discomfort they had both experienced as kids during parental battles. It was hard enough for the girls to navigate through difficulties of having divorced parents without having to witness them being at each other's throats.

As soon as she saw Kay walk in the room, Mariah ran up and grabbed her in a big bear hug. "I'm so glad to be home." The little girl's delight radiated into Kay.

The two waddled awkwardly over to the couch, Mariah refusing to break her hold on her mother. Kay could feel herself return to normal at the sound of Mariah's cheerful chatter.

Sitting on the couch, holding hands, Mariah regaled her mother with details of her busy weekend:

A trip to the park to play catch ("Little Dave always misses and it takes forever for him to go get the ball."), Dave's mom's house ("Grandma said I look more like her every time she sees me."), a Chinese buffet ("I hate those fortune cookies. I think they make 'em with rotten rice.") and the mall ("You should see the big screen TV Dad bought. And he paid for it with a bunch of twenty dollar bills.")

Cory, who had been quietly sitting at the table, doing homework, snapped her head up when she heard the last of Mariah's pronouncements and mockingly said, "Oh, I'm so sure. Where do you come up with this crap?"

"Stay out of this, please," Kay said to Cory. Then to Mariah, "Tell me again…about the mall."

Mariah looked at Cory, then back at Kay. With the cheeriness gone from her voice, Mariah reluctantly repeated,

"Dad bought a big screen TV."

Kay let that sink in for a moment. "And you say he paid for it with $20 bills?" Kay asked.

With eyes wide and chin quivering, Mariah slowly nodded her head.

Kay's head was swimming and she felt the urge to scream. But not wanting to create a scary scene, she simply got up from the couch and calmly headed for the stairs.

"She's stupid, Mom," Cory said in a desperate attempt to soften the blow. "She doesn't know what she's talking about."

"It's ok, Honey," Kay said, patting Cory on the shoulder as she passed. "I just need to get something from my bedroom."

As she climbed the stairs she could hear Cory scolding her little sister in hushed tones. "Way to go, Stupid. Why did you have to tell her that?"

"I'm sorry. I didn't know. I was just telling her what we did this weekend."

As Kay closed the door to her bedroom, she could hear Mariah softy crying. She knew she should have walked back down to reassure and comfort her, but in her borderline-hysterical condition, it was well-beyond her capabilities. She walked around the foot of the bed and stood staring out the floor-to-ceiling window that looked out over her driveway. She could see everything and nothing. Continuous cyclones of thoughts stormed through her head, and yet her mind was a blank. The pain in her body was unbearable, but she was numb.

She sat down hard on the bed, pulling her arms in tightly to her sides until she could feel her elbows squeezing her ribs. Her breath was coming fast and hard, causing the tip of her nose to tingle.

Why can't I cry? I need to cry. Kay stayed in her contracted position, waiting for the tears which refused to come.

The phone rang and Kay jumped.

Oh, God. That can't be Dave already.

The phone was two feet away resting on the night stand; she knew she was in no condition to answer it. It stopped ringing. Cory's muffled voice wafted up the stairwell, followed by quick footsteps. She gently tapped on the door and softly called out to Kay. "Mom, it's Aunt Les. Do you want me to tell her you can't talk right now?"

Leslie's timing was a godsend. "That's ok, Baby. I'll take it." Kay dove for the receiver. "Hey, Les. How's it going?" the distraught woman said, trying to sound breezy.

"You can knock off the act. Cory's already told me something bad went down with that sonofabitch father of hers. Are you ok?"

Even though Leslie sounded harsh, Kay could feel the love and support behind her words. Hearing her sister's voice was all it took to release the backlog of humiliation, frustration, anger, confusion and hurt

126

heaped on her by Dave's latest betrayal.   It felt good to let go.

Leslie stayed silent through the two or three minutes of Kay's hard sobbing. Then the crying slowed and quieted, giving Leslie a comfortable opening to start the conversation. "So, what did Asshole do this time?"

Kay knew she was asking for an "I told you so," but launched, anyway, into the account of how Dave, once again, got her to trust him, then dropped her on her head. By the time her story reached the $7 co-pay and the big screen TV-climax, she was crying hard again, this time mourning how she had betrayed herself and the girls.

"How could I be so stupid? I should have laughed in his face when he offered me that ridiculous proposal," Kay choked out through sobs.

"Yup. It was pretty stupid," Leslie agreed. "But don't beat yourself up. You were just giving him the benefit of the doubt - which, of course, he didn't deserve. But, hey. That's who you are. You're a nice person. And he's who he is - an asshole."

Kay was glad her sister had chosen to sum up the situation so succinctly and not to delve any deeper into Kay's possible unresolved feelings for Dave - an uncomfortable reality Leslie attempted to get Kay to admit to from time to time.

"I don't know what to do, Les. I feel so helpless," Kay lamented to her sister.

"Are you kidding me?" Leslie shouted at Kay. "Weren't you the one who told me how you threatened Sandy to take Dave back to court if she didn't ease up on Mariah? Seems to me, given the circumstances, it's time to make good on that threat."

Of course. Kay had forgotten she could still play the legal card. Thinking about that time when she had shown some backbone made her feel better. She wasn't helpless. Yes. A call to her lawyer was definitely in order. Suddenly, the bleak, hollow feeling that had invaded Kay's core was beginning to evaporate and she felt the glimmer of renewed hope.

"You're absolutely right," Kay said, slowly letting herself relax into a lounging position across the bed. "That's just what I'm going to do. Dave's used up his last chance to keep this charade going. I'm officially putting a stop to his game."

"Yeah, you are," Leslie encouraged. "Hey, listen. Remember my friend, Rebecca? The one I told you about who's just gone through a nasty divorce?"

"I remember," Kay said.

"Well, she had a lawyer who was a real barracuda. I could ask Rebecca for her number," Leslie offered.

"Her? The lawyer's female?" Kay asked. She was intrigued with the idea of having a woman represent her.

"Yeah. Her name is Judith Something-or-Other. All I know is Rebecca was very happy with the job this gal did for her."

"It sounds good. How soon do you think you can get the number?" Kay was already anxious to talk to Judith Something-or-Other. "I'll call her as soon as we hang up." Then Leslie's mood turned serious. "Please tell me you're not going to chicken out after you've had a chance to sleep on it."

Kay knew exactly where her sister was coming from and didn't let the comment bother her.

"There's no going back, Les. I've reached my booger moment."

This was a reference to a private code the sisters shared to describe turning-point situations.

The "booger moment," as it had come to be known, was the result of an, otherwise, great relationship ruined when Leslie accidentally caught her sweet, gorgeous boyfriend eating a freshly-harvested booger. For Leslie, there was no going back…or forward, for that matter.

Well, Kay was going to go forward so she *could* go back - back to the order and structure of the original court order, when life was stable, secure and peaceful.

The sisters ended their call with Leslie promising to call back as soon as she had the information Kay needed.

Kay let out a deep, cleansing sigh before getting up and going to the bathroom to splash some cold water on her face. She wanted to rid herself of any remaining traces of her leftover breakdown. She was glad she could return to the girls with a sincere smile on her face and lightness of spirit. Then, for the briefest of moments, she wondered if her old friend, Denial, might be responsible for her lifted mood.

No. She needn't have worried. Things really had changed. And she knew this because, as gut-wrenching as it was, she had finally let go of the need to rely on Denial's false security. Reality was her new ally, and she'd allow it to guide her through whatever was to come. She headed downstairs with a spring in her step. "Hey girls!" she called. "Whadda you want for dinner?

11

Manning vs. Noland

I never imagined I'd be back here again.

Kay waited for the elevator to take her to the fourth floor hearing room marveling at how much things had changed in seven years. The near strip-search and x-ray scan they subjected visitors to in the lobby was clear evidence of the intense emotion and combustible energy coursing through these "halls of family justice." It was a strange system that asked perfect strangers to make life-changing decisions about other perfect strangers.

Where's King Solomon when you need him? Now there's a guy who knew how to settle a custody dispute.

Kay was both dreading and looking forward to seeing Dave. She chided herself as she wrestled with her conflicting emotions. Bringing this legal action against him meant she was going to alienate him even more than he already was. But what choice did she have? He had reneged on his part of the bargain. All she was asking for was a return to the trouble-free days when the original court order was in place.

I don't see how he can think I'm being unreasonable. After all, a deal is a deal.

What was truly unreasonable was the fact that this guy had, once again, made a major fool out of her and here she was, secretly hoping he'd notice how attractive she looked in her best suit - the one she wore when she worked funerals alongside Ed. It was a gorgeous taupe-colored, wool gabardine design with a slim skirt and short, belted jacket that accentuated her small waist. Combined with her best black sling-back pumps, the skirt made her average legs look long and sexy. And as if knowing the importance of today's hearing, Kay's hair had mercifully decided to cooperate.

On her best day, Sandy never looked this good.

Once again, Kay's emotions swung back in the direction of confident and sassy. But that ended the moment Dave's attorney shoved his arm between the closing elevator doors, forcing them open so he could ride up to the fourth floor too. She tried to make herself invisible, inching behind other passengers until she was wedged into one of the back corners of the car.

Seeing Bill McCaffree again after all these years transported Kay right back to the horror that was the first divorce hearing. Not that it was especially heated or nasty. It was just so surreal. The last thing Kay ever imagined was facing off against her best friend - the man she loved and the father of her children, in a court of law. Enduring the pain and humiliation of a legal proceeding brought about by Dave's public petition to have her officially removed from her own life was a true test of what one person could bear.

Given the fact Dave had come out on the losing end (financially, anyway) of the divorce, Kay was surprised he had, once again, retained the services of Mr. McCaffree. The attorney's dispassionate approach to lawyering left Kay with the impression he had seen it all, was bored, and merely going through the motions. Even the nasty barbs and blustering objections hurled at Kay and her attorney during the divorce hearing seemed like part of a well-worn script he'd been working from for a very long time.

Bill was short and squat, and the wrinkled, ill-fitting business suit he wore made him appear almost square. Like so many bald men Kay knew, he compensated for his receding hairline with a thick mustache and goatee which made him look like a younger Burl Ives.

After they reached their destination, Kay hung back, making sure there was plenty of distance between them as they got off the elevator. She walked slowly through the short corridor that led to the open double doors of the hearing room waiting area.

A tall, horseshoe-shaped receptionist desk was located on one side of the room, with the opposite side containing a neat, L-shaped placement of chairs against the wall. A sumptuous, matching ottoman sat in front of every third chair.

How nice of the courts to give people a place to put their feet up while they wait to have their wages garnisheed.

Mr. McCaffree, standing on the far side of the receptionist desk, had just checked in with the woman behind the desk when he looked up and caught Kay's eye. He smiled and said good morning as if they were old acquaintances. Kay couldn't bring herself to return the smile, but acknowledged his greeting with a polite head nod. She knew what awaited her behind the doors of the hearing room, and niceties would definitely not be observed.

Kay took a seat where she could see the elevator. She looked at her watch. 9:52. Where was Judith?

Retaining the services of Judith Klein, experienced family law attorney, had been one of Leslie's better suggestions. Not only was Kay more comfortable with a female attorney, but Judith's reassuring, non-judgmental assessment of Kay's case, left Kay feeling confident they'd be able to get everything back on track with a minimum of problems.

Once again the elevator doors slid open. It wasn't Judith, but Dave who stepped out, looking dashing in tan slacks, navy blue blazer, and light blue shirt. He wasn't wearing a tie and the top two buttons of his shirt were open in a casual, "which way is the bar?" kind of way. The moment Kay saw him her breath reflexively sucked in.

She sat up a little straighter in her chair and put an open, friendly expression on her face. He stopped and scanned the room, spotted Kay, but disavowed her presence with a quick skip of his gaze over to where his lawyer was sitting, briefcase open on an ottoman, shuffling through a stack of papers. He glided right past her with an air of indifferent dismissal. Just as quickly as it had rushed in, Kay could feel the air rush out of her body like a punctured balloon. But he must have changed his mind about acknowledging her, because he made a quick u-turn and headed straight for her. The look on his face was one she wasn't familiar with. She sat frozen in her chair, not knowing what to expect.

He stopped in front of her and bent his head down. For a nanosecond Kay thought he was going to kiss her on the cheek but it was only to deliver his message into her ear.

"I can't believe you're doing this to me," he said in a whispered hiss. "You know, Sandy said you didn't want us to be happy and it looks like my wife is right."

My wife.

Kay had always found it painful to hear Sandy's name come out of Dave's mouth, but those two words pierced Kay's heart with an especially-cruel violence.

Foul, foul! Kay wanted to loudly object to some invisible referee. *She's only your wife because she cheated!* as if she had lost Dave in some kind of school-yard game.

Before Kay could respond, Dave straightened up and resumed his walk over to where his lawyer was sitting. McCaffree jumped up and greeted Dave with a hearty, "let's-get-em" handshake. Already rattled and humiliated by Dave's angry earful, Kay could feel her knees go weak as she witnessed what she thought was an intimidating display of male solidarity.

With her eyes transfixed on the opposing team, Kay had failed to notice Judith's arrival. "Good morning, Kay," Judith said, startling Kay out of her uneasy trance. "Sizing up the opposition?"

"Oh. Good morning, Judith," Kay said. She rose to her feet and shook Judith's hand with a grateful exuberance, relieved the cavalry had arrived.

135

And what a cavalry it was! Stunning in a black and gold-trimmed, white-on-black Chanel suit, tasteful accessories and perfectly-coiffed hair, Judith looked more like a woman who lunched at New York's Russian Tea Room, than an attorney who went to battle for wronged spouses.

"I apologize for not being here sooner. I'm having the Mercedes worked on and the garage man was late picking it up. Have they called our case?"

"Not as far as I know," Kay answered. She was struck by how out-of-place the dazzling woman seemed in this depressing den of domestic strife.

"Good. I need to have a quick word with Bill," Judith said. With a stride as elegant as her designer ensemble, Judith approached opposing counsel and politely interrupted the conversation he was having with his client. McCaffree, obviously glad to see this vision of loveliness in front of him, grinned from ear to ear, took Judith's shoulders in his fat little hands and kissed both cheeks. He then introduced Judith to Dave, who greeted her politely, but like Kay, withheld any unnecessary friendliness, given the nature of what she had been hired to do to him.

Kay watched as Bill excused himself from Dave's presence and the two lawyers walked arm in arm, like old friends, over to a private corner where they could talk undisturbed.

Of all the things she disliked about lawyers, the thing she hated most was how they pretended to take their cases as personally as their clients. Especially insulting was the way they faked animosity toward the other attorney. The truth was, they were all a tight band of brothers/sisters, who could just as easily switch sides and argue the other client's case. They all worked from the same play book and the only genuine acrimony they ever felt was if a client was late making payments.

Kay had made this shocking discovery during her first go-round with the family justice system. At the invitation of friends who were, mercifully, trying to distract her from the stress of the hearing, she had gone out for drinks at a local sports bar. There she spotted her, then attorney, John Larabee, yucking it up, beer in hand, with Bill McCaffree. She felt confused and betrayed. Her friends were kind enough to enlighten her about the world of lawyers and how they worked all sides of the street. Since that time, Kay had remained quite jaded about the legal profession, but tolerated it as a necessary evil.

It was obvious the chat between the two attorneys had nothing to do with her case. Nevertheless, as soon as her brief confab with McCaffree was over, Judith walked back and pretended to be vexed by her colleague, apparently to make points with Kay. Kay wanted to tell her she needn't have bothered, but she just smiled and told Judith not to worry.

"You know, I have to say I'm a little surprised to see Bill McCaffree again. I assumed Dave would want to start fresh, like I did," Kay said.

Judith nodded in agreement. "Well, in my experience, most people, who've done the type of things your ex has, prefer to limit the number of people who know about it. Starting fresh means rehashing all the old dirt and then piling on the new. It's just easier working with someone who already knows the story. It saves on humiliation," Judith explained.

"Saving on humiliation is exactly the reason I *did* get a new attorney," Kay said, chuckling at the irony. "I was too embarrassed to let John see how I'd squandered all his hard work."

"Oh, now, now," Judith said in a practiced maternal voice as she patted Kay's hand. "Don't go there. Remember, you were just acting in good faith. Anyway, we're here to put everything right." Then changing the subject she said, "It's after 10. They should have called us by now. I'm going to see what the delay is." She walked over to the tall desk, elegantly leaned over the top and spoke quietly to the receptionist.

Kay's stomach was doing flip-flops. At this point she would have been happy if the judge had postponed the hearing all together. The only thing keeping her in her chair was the deep responsibility she felt for Corey and Mariah. None of this mess was their fault and she needed to correct her foolish mistake.

Judith walked back and took a seat next to Kay. "The receptionist just told me Judge Sommers is out on a family emergency so our case is going to be heard by her Special Master."

"Oh no," Kay said. This had to be a bad omen. As much as she hated going through this process, Kay remembered Barbara Sommers as being practical and fair.

"I'm not comfortable with this, Judith," Kay said. "Maybe we should put things off until Judge

Sommers can be here."

Judith knitted her brow. "I guess we could do that, but I don't recommend it," she said. "Look. The Special Master has been appointed by Judge Sommers, herself, to carry out her orders and rule on her behalf. I truly believe our case will be just fine in their hands. And keep in mind the meter is running and I'd hate to have to bill you for a wasted morning."

Kay opened her mouth to respond but was beaten to the punch by the receptionist who loudly announced, "Manning vs. Noland!"

It was too late now. Kay would just have to take her chances with this "Special Master" - whoever they were.

12

Donuts Can Be Good for You Too

"Hello, Mr. McNab? Kay Manning here from Salinger's. How is everyone getting along?"

Keeping in touch with families after the funeral was another important part of Kay's job. Although she was acting in a professional capacity, she couldn't ignore the special bond she felt after sharing the personal experience of a loved one's passing. Plus, making this phone call helped interrupt the broken record of the previous day's court hearing playing in her head.

The pain in Mr. McNab's voice was hard to miss as he described the deafening silence that had taken up residence in his home after the funeral once family, friends and neighbors returned to their regular routines. Kay knew there would be no such return for Mr. McNab. He would either have to carve out a new groove for himself, or keep the old one and make painful adjustments to accommodate Emily's absence.

Kay's heart went out to him and all her surviving male clients. Men seemed to have a much more difficult time of it than women. It was something about being alone they just didn't seem to be able to tolerate. It was amazing to Kay that so many of her male clients married within six months of their wives' deaths. Whereas, most of her female clients were still single years after seeing their husbands off to the Great Beyond.

Same with divorce, too.

'*Aha!*' Kay thought as soon as Kay heard Mr. McNab complain about all the unsolicited casseroles delivered to his front door by "concerned" widows from his church. That was a sure sign it wouldn't be long before there would be a new Mrs. McNab. If Kay had to guess, the lucky woman would be the one who, rather than just dropping the meal at the door, would stay to make sure it got heated properly.

"Hang in there, Mr. McNab. The next few months are going to be tough, but you have a supportive family and I know they're going to be there every step of the way. And if there's anything we here at Salinger's can do for you, please don't hesitate to call."

They ended their phone call with Kay reminding Mr. McNab that Emily's headstone would be delivered to the mortuary in approximately three weeks. "I'll call you when it's in so we can make setting arrangements at the cemetery."

***

Things were slow this week at the mortuary, so Ruth decided it would be the perfect time for pre-Spring cleaning. This morning the entire staff had been hard at work sprucing up the main chapel. As the self-appointed general in charge of operations, Ruth handed out assignments with a Patton-like intensity. Uncle O was in charge of cleaning and polishing all twenty-four oak pews. Ed and Leo were relegated to vacuuming and shampooing the carpet and Kay was assigned to cleaning all the light fixtures. Of course, someone had to man the front desk and answer the phone, and General Linton was happy to make the sacrifice for her troops.

Kay was shaking out, yet another, dried assortment of dead bugs from the glass globe of one of the ceiling fixtures when Ruth walked in and loudly announced, "break time!" Obediently, everyone stopped what they were doing and headed for the break room for some much-needed R and R (rest and refreshment).

To everyone's pleasant surprise, Ruth had brewed a fresh pot of coffee, and had an assortment of soft drinks icing down in a cooler. A platter of fresh fruit and cheese sat on the table waiting to be enjoyed.

"I take back every mean thing I said about you this morning," Ed said, as he reached for a can of his favorite soda.

"Don't we have any donuts?" Leo whined, turning up his nose at the arrangement of apples, oranges and bananas. Looking at his pencil-thin frame, you would have thought he'd never seen a donut in his life.

"Fruit is better for you, Leo," Ruth said.

"Yeah, but I'd rather have a donut," Leo said.

Ed pulled his wallet out of his back pocket, opened it up, took out $10. "Here, Leo. Run over to Gil's and pick up a dozen. I wouldn't mind having a donut myself." It was rare that Ed went over Ruth's head and it was apparent she wasn't too happy about it.

"C'mon Ruth. We're all working hard. Don't you think we deserve a treat?" He threw her his signature Chamber of Commerce smile and Kay watched as the slighted woman melted before his eyes.

Even though the smile wasn't meant for her, Kay felt a tingle watching Ed ply his charms.

He's got to get a lot of mileage out of all that charisma.

Considering his looks and charm, Kay was baffled by Ed's lack of a significant other.

"Oh, all right," Ruth said, "but take Uncle O with you and don't be gone too long. That chapel's got to be done before we start getting busy again. If we slack off for too long, we'll lose our momentum."

"Hmmph. Who's we?" Leo muttered under his breath as he hurried out the door, with a slow Uncle O trying to keep up.

"Get some glazed, jelly, and sour creams," Ed called after the two men.

Ed turned back to Ruth and Kay, shaking his head and chuckling. "Leo can be a pain, but he's a good worker."

Ruth and Kay nodded.

Ed pulled out a chair from under the table, turned it around, sitting backwards on the seat as he rested his arms across the top of the chair. Seeing Ed in this position reminded Kay of a heated argument she'd once had with Dave when she theorized he, and men in general, sat that way to call attention to their "junk," while protecting it at the same time. She called it her "best of both worlds," theory, to which her ex had taken great offense. For a brief moment she considered asking Ed his opinion of her hypothesis, but decided it would be inappropriate. Anyway, her premise had just been proved (to her, anyway) since now she was thinking about Ed's "junk."

But her indecent musings didn't last long. Ed's face took on a concerned expression and he asked, "So, Kay, how did things go at your divorce hearing yesterday?"

Kay almost choked on the section of orange she had just put in her mouth. She had no idea Ed was aware of what was going on in her personal life and she shot Ruth an irked, WTF glance.

Ruth ignored Kay's obvious aggravation. "Yes, Kay. I was explaining to Ed why you weren't able to come into work yesterday."

Ed continued to look at Kay with a sympathetic expression. Kay's feet fidgeted under the table.

"Uh...well...it wasn't really a divorce hearing...just some legal loose ends that needed to be tied up." Kay tried to sound nonchalant but she was deeply embarrassed.

Fortunately, the growing awkwardness of the moment was interrupted by the shrill, outdoor ringer of the phone sitting outside the break room window. ("...always have to be able to hear the phone," Ed would say.) Ruth took a hurried step toward the door, but Ed waved her off. "Stay there, Ruth. I'll get it."

As soon as Ed was out of earshot, Ruth turned to Kay. "I'm sorry Kay. I wasn't expecting him to ask, and I'm a terrible liar."

Kay knew it wasn't reasonable to expect Ruth to make up some lame story just because Kay wanted to protect her image as a smart, together, no-nonsense woman - and not some poor, down-trodden ex-wife.

"I'm the one who's sorry. I shouldn't have put you in that position in the first place," Kay said.

"Well, let's just forget about it," Ruth said with a reassuring smile. "Anyway, I worried about you all day. I almost called you last night, but I figured the last thing you wanted to do was rehash the whole ordeal."

"Yeah. It was a long day. But all things considered, the girls and I made out ok."

"So, if you don't mind me asking, what happened?"

Remembering the events of the previous day, Kay suddenly became choked up and an involuntary release of hot tears streamed down her cheeks.

"I was a fool, Ruth. An a-number one jackass. But you probably already surmised that when I told you about the stupid deal I made with Dave."

Ruth smiled and cocked her head to one side. "It's alright, Honey. Most women are fools at one time or another."

"Well *this* fool let her ex-husband bamboozle her into thinking he had changed. But you know the old saying, "The more things change..."

Kay leaned over the table and pulled a couple of napkins from the stack sitting next to the fruit platter. After a healthy nose-blow she sighed and continued. "Anyway, I found out, big surprise, his sob story about a pay cut was complete B.S. He's pulling in close to $100 grand a year, thank you very much."

Ruth's eyes grew wide and she said, "Oh my goodness. I can't imagine what your reaction must have been."

"I *didn't* react," Kay said. "I couldn't. My lawyer had been very adamant about that. And, all things considered, I did pretty well. That's until…"

"Until?" Ruth anxiously interjected.

"Until I learned his health insurance is part of his compensation package," Kay said.

Ruth scrunched up her eyebrows and just looked at Kay.

"Ruth, his company PAYS for his insurance. It doesn't cost him a dime. His entire family is covered free of charge. And when I say "entire" I mean him, his wife and his son."

"I'm still not following you, Dear," Ruth said.

"Look, the whole reason for me taking him back to court came about after I asked him to split Cory's therapy co-pay with me…which was part of our agreement. His part of the co-pay was only $7 and the bastard had the unmitigated gall to snap at me and say he didn't have it. You'd think I'd asked for $7000. It wasn't 'til a couple of days later, I found out he was throwing around $20 bills at the mall. But you have to understand, Ruth. It wasn't just the stupid $7. For awhile now he's been slowly, but surely, backing away from everything he promised. The co-pay was just the proverbial "last straw." Or so I thought until I found out about his free insurance."

Clearly caught up in Kay's heated retelling of

146

the story, Ruth breathlessly asked, "So, did you make a scene? I know I would have had to make a scene."

"I almost broke my neck snapping my head around to keep from coming unglued," Kay said. "I just stared out the window behind me, biting my cheek. If I hadn't, I might have lunged across the table for his throat. The great thing was the judge got it and demanded to know why Dave hadn't put the girls on his policy."

"And did Dave have an answer?" Ruth asked.

"Are you kidding? He *always* does. He made some lame excuse about how he was trying to spare me the hassle of transferring the girls from my policy to his; which seemed to upset the judge because he kind of yelled, "Did you ask Ms. Manning if she minded going through the "hassle" to change things?" Dave had to admit he hadn't."

"So what happened?" Ruth asked.

"Well, I guess at that point the judge had heard enough because he made his ruling then and there. Not only did he reinstate the original child support order, he ordered Dave to pay back all the money I haven't been getting. And he said the girls were to be put on Dave's insurance ASAP. "

"That's wonderful," Ruth said. "I imagine you're going to get a tidy little sum."

"10 grand tidy," Kay replied. "That's going to really give me a nice little financial boost."

She went on to tell Ruth how the judge surprised the battling exes by ordering them to mediation - something they were supposed to have done during the time of the original divorce.

147

"Our case must have fallen through the cracks somehow, because we never went," Kay said. "But I'm kind of glad because the judge wants the girls to be interviewed by the mediator. He thinks they're old enough."

Ruth frowned. "Is that wise, Kay? Isn't that a lot of pressure for young children?"

"That's what I thought too, but the girls will be interviewed separately, without Dave or me being there. They'll finally have the chance to have their say about things without being afraid of hurting our feelings or making us angry.

Then Kay chuckled. "You know, Ruth, I almost got out of there scot-free, but the judge told both of us, under the circumstances, he could have easily placed us in contempt of court because we'd been ignoring the original court order. My sister said it was his way of saying I'd been an idiot and Dave was an asshole."

Ruth let out a big laugh. "I think your sister may just be right."

"But all's well that ends well," Kay said with a sigh. "At the very end the judge told Dave, "I shouldn't have to tell you this, Mr. Noland, but your first family comes first."

"That's very true," Ruth said. "It really needed to be said."

Yeah," Kay sneered, "But, I'm not holding my breath. Dave's got a big handicap that'll always make it difficult for him to comply."

"You're referring to his wife, right?" Ruth asked.

Kay rolled her eyes.

"Damn it, Leo. You got glaze all over the door knob." Uncle Owen could be heard swearing from down the hallway. "You couldn't wait five minutes 'til we got back, could you?"

"Don't sweat it. I'll wipe it off." Leo griped back at him. The two men came into the room and Leo thrust the white bakery bag in Ruth's direction. The top of the bag was rolled so far down she worried she'd find the donuts smashed into a doughy blob at the bottom.

"Does the trip to the bakery count toward our break," Leo groused, "or does it start now?"

"Hey Leo," Uncle O butted in, "I think you're in the wrong job. You should work at the bakery. You could be their head loafer."

Leo pinched his lips against his teeth and said, "Hardee har har. I'd tell you to act your age, O, but you're so old you'd die."

These two usually went for the jugular with their insult slinging, but were obviously keeping it PG-rated in respectful deference to the females in the room. But Kay knew, first hand, how down and dirty they could get. All insults aside, though, it was evident the two men were best of friends.

"So what'd I miss?" Ed said, bounding into the room, eager to join the conversation.

"Not much," Ruth said, glad to put an end to the juvenile sparing. "But the donuts are here," she said, holding up the plate where she'd emptied the sugary contents of the bakery bag. She carried it from person to person like a server at a cocktail party.

Ed selected then dug into a blueberry, sour cream glazed beauty, and in between noisy sucks of icing off his fingers said, "By the way, O, it looks like we've got one on deck. Are you gonna be available later for a pick up?"

Owen looked down at the table, tapping his fingers while he thought. Then he looked up. "Well, I promised Addie we'd go to the casino tonight. There's a slots tournament she's been wanting to get into. Did they give you any idea how soon?"

"Nah. The hospice nurse said she was just giving us a heads up; it could be as late as tomorrow," Ed said.

"I'd be happy to be on call, Ed, but you know how loud the casino is. It'll be hard to hear the phone," Uncle O said.

'You've got "vibrate" on your cell,' everyone around the table thought at the same time.

"Don't worry about it, O," Ed said. "You and Aunt Adelaide go and have fun. We've got it covered."

Owen looked around the table, grateful no one had pointed out the obvious solution to the casino noise problem. He slurped the last few drops of coffee from his styro-foam cup, before bringing it down hard on the table. "Well, I'm gonna go finish the pews," he said as he rose from his chair. "I still have the whole left side of the aisle to do and they're not going to do themselves."

As he headed out the door, Ed kiddingly called after him. "Aren't you worried we're gonna talk about you?"

Uncle O just kept walking. "It's when people

150

stop talking that you gotta worry," he said. "Thanks for the goodies, Ruth."

Ed turned his attention to Leo, and inexplicably, brought up an old topic of conversation.

"Hey, Leo. Whaddya think of the job Kay did on the limo for the McNab service? Pretty good, huh. I bet you'd like her to be your permanent assistant."

The condom!

Kay looked over at Leo, who deliberately avoided her gaze. Kay figured Leo assumed she'd forgotten all about pursuing the answer to his closely-guarded secret. But thanks to Ed's weirdly-timed question, her curiosity had just received a reinvigorating boost.

"Hey, Leo, the Sigma truck just pulled up," Uncle O called, coming back into the hallway to announce the arrival of the weekly casket delivery. "I'll get the church truck and meet you outside."

Ed jumped up, almost knocking his chair over. "I got this, Leo. There's only one casket on the truck and I have to talk to the driver anyway. You just sit there and enjoy your break." Before he left the room, he snatched a can of soda, most likely to offer to the Sigma delivery driver.

Kay was unsettled by Ed's squirrelly behavior. His usual smooth, suave persona had been replaced by a nervous, hyperactive kid.

It's probably all the sugar in the donuts and soda.

Kay looked at Leo who had just helped himself to a third donut. If *he* was effected by the sugar, he didn't show it.

"So, Leo," Kay said with a Snidely Whiplash-tone in her voice. If she'd had a mustache, she'd have been twirling the ends. "I bet you were hoping I'd forget about our little conversation."

Leo swallowed the bite of donut he had just put in his mouth without chewing. He hurried to finish his soda and wipe off the crumbs from his place at the table.

"No. I haven't forgotten. But like Owen said, the chapel isn't going to clean itself. The sooner I finish shampooing the carpet, the sooner it's gonna dry. Thanks, Ruth."

He ran out of the room before Kay had a chance to say one more word.

"What was that all about?" Ruth asked watching Leo speed down the hallway. "It's not like him to cut his break short."

"Oh, it's nothing," Kay sighed. "It's just a little private joke between us."

Ruth slowly leaned against the backrest of her chair, folded her arms across her chest, and studied Kay's face.

"By any chance does it have something to do with a condom?"

Kay almost fell off her chair.

"You know?" she gasped. "I mean, how?…When?"

"Leo came to me not long after you found it in the car. He was worried you'd go to Ed. He thought you might have misinterpreted his silence as guilt," Ruth said.

Kay was insulted Leo thought she could be a snitch. Instead, she protested. "I never thought it was his…well…maybe just for a second; but he was being so mysterious, my curiosity got the better of me."

But something about Ruth's explanation didn't make sense. "If he isn't guilty, Ruth, why not go to Ed? Why come to you?" Kay asked.

Just then the light bulb clicked on in Kay's head. She locked eyes with Ruth and knew they were having the same thought.

"Oh my god," Kay said, "he's protecting Uncle O!"

Ruth poured out her anguish over trying to decide if she should talk to Uncle Owen; without solid proof the condom was his, a confrontation could put the mortuary in an untenable position.

"Owen isn't a paid employee," she said. "There's no formal disciplinary action Ed could take against him."

Nevertheless, if he was guilty, he had to be prevented from jeopardizing the propriety and reputation of Salinger's.

"It's an awful betrayal of Ed's trust," Ruth lamented.

"Ed's trust?" Kay shot back. She was indignant. "How about Aunt Adelaide's? If you ask me, in this scenario, I think the boss should be in the back seat, not the wife."

Ruth burst out laughing at Kay's unintended

backseat reference. Kay joined her the moment she realized what she'd said. But despite her laughter, Kay couldn't help feeling angry for Adelaide, given her own devastating experience with marital infidelity. Kay had only been around Adelaide a couple of times, but it was apparent the woman's world revolved around her husband - something to which Kay could relate.

"What I don't understand is what kind of woman would be attracted to an old fart whose nose and ear hair are so long you could braid them together?" Kay asked. "And what's the deal with the limousine? I mean, I'm all for status symbol sex, but this is ridiculous."

Ruth started to say something, then stopped. For a moment she debated the wisdom of spreading office gossip. But ever since Kay's pot intervention, the two had formed a bond that Ruth believed, supported the discreet discussion of delicate matters. Ruth looked at Kay, held up her index finger, while checking behind her to make sure no one was walking up the hallway.

"I have a pretty good hunch who O's paramour is," Ruth said in a hushed tone.

Kay wasn't sure she wanted to know - especially if it was someone she was acquainted with. It was going to be hard enough to face Uncle O from now on, without having to worry about how she'd act if she ran into the conniving tramp.

"Do the words "dehydrated chili okra" ring a bell?" Ruth said.

Kay thought for a moment, then gasped. "Oh no! You don't mean Mrs. Dash?"

Ruth made a pained expression and nodded slowly.

Having the name of a well-known salt substitute was the least of this woman's problems. Dorothy Dash - or Dot - as she preferred to be called, was a sixty-something, grossly-overweight, fashion-challenged woman who sported the worst blond dye job Kay had ever seen. Instead of trying to minimize its harshness, she teased it into a giant, bouffant page boy which framed a face made up with heavy amounts of blue eye shadow and black eyeliner. Garish red lipstick was her finishing touch of choice.

At least once a month Dot Dash would bring in a large Tupperware container filled with her "famous" dehydrated chili okra. Kay had to admit it was one of the most amazing snacks she had ever tasted.

"Were you aware she brings the okra specifically for Owen?" Ruth asked.

"No. I assumed it was for all of us - you know, because we handled her husband's funeral last year." Kay said.

Receiving edible goodies from grateful clients was quite common. In fact, it was unusual Leo had to go out for donuts earlier, considering that most days there was usually some home-made yummy waiting to be had in the break-room.

"From the first time she came in with that Tupperware container, she's always made it clear the okra is for O. She waits for me to page him so she can hand it to him personally. I feel like I'm speaking in Morse Code when I page him. "Dot Dash is here to

155

see you." "Then she wiggles and giggles and bats those mascara-clumped eyelashes at him. It's embarrassing, but O really seems to eat it up."

Kay recalled seeing Mrs. Dash the previous week in the front office, rolls of fat bubbling over the sides of a turquoise and brown tie-dyed halter top, pulled tightly over a turquoise mini skirt whose hem flounced over a pair of brown biking shorts. Kay assumed the flamboyant woman had probably been going for a Cyndi Lauper look but missed and ended up looking like a gay sumo wrestler.

Then she thought of Aunt Adelaide - slim, well-groomed and looking nice in one of those jogging suits that seemed to be the fashion for women her age. Not exactly exciting, but certainly not screaming at you like Dot Dash's crazy togs.

"I blame myself," Ruth said. "I was the one who asked him to return the container to her that first time. I pushed him into that women's pudgy arms. If Addie finds out I'll never forgive myself."

Kay thought Ruth was getting way ahead of herself. "Look, Ruth. We don't even know if it's a for-sure thing. Maybe it's time to talk to Ed. Owen is his uncle and it just might be easier for him to broach the topic with him, man-to-man."

"I think you may be right. I really don't think I could handle having that conversation."

Kay laughed and said, "Well, I happen to know someone who has the perfect remedy for getting through unpleasant chats."

Ruth gave Kay a fake look of disapproval and said, "Don't you have some light fixtures that need cleaning?"

Kay left Ruth to tidy up the break-room and made her way back to the main chapel, worried she may have unintentionally opened up a can of worms.

13

Mediation/Schmediation

The representative from the family court directed Kay to the room where the orientation video was going to be shown. The room was small and stuffy and was set up with four rows of eight chairs, accessed by a narrow aisle down the middle, and two narrower aisles on either side.

Kay wondered if it was designed that way to accommodate warring parties. But she really didn't care. Without thinking she took a seat in the front row - a habit she'd developed in college to avoid being distracted by her weakness for people watching. She credited this practice with helping her through college with a 3.8 GPA.

Of all the days for her car to break down, this had to be one of the worst. Not only did she hate having to take more time off work to attend to these annoying legal issues with Dave, now, instead of heading straight to the mortuary from here, she'd have to let Ed know she might be out the entire day.

Fortunately, she had managed to hold on to (create?) some good luck by getting an early start. The tow truck driver had honored her mom's automobile club membership, and since the court house was on his way, he graciously dropped Kay off at the front steps with time to spare. But now she was going to have to figure out who she was going to call to give her a ride to the mechanic's shop.

As the room slowly filled up, Kay fought the urge to turn around to see if Dave had arrived. She trained her eyes on the family court seal projected on the large screen facing the audience, and challenged herself to pick out all the images crammed into the little circle.

The first thing she saw was a horse-drawn stagecoach emerging from behind a lighthouse, heading at a full-gallop toward a blind-folded Lady Justice, scales in hand. She was lost in trying to figure out the meaning of the odd representation when she heard a voice say, "Is this seat taken?"

Kay turned and was stupefied to see her ex-husband smiling, affably, down at her. For a moment she thought she was hallucinating - so good was her little attention-focusing game. A quick over-the-shoulder scan of the room revealed numerous empty chairs, scattered here and there; she couldn't imagine why he had chosen the seat next to hers.

Danger, danger, Will Robinson!

The impulse to move (run) to another chair nearly overwhelmed her, but that would have been too awkward; so she just squeaked out, "No. Go ahead."

"Can you believe the parking in this place?" Dave asked, jostling her a couple of times as he tried to make himself comfortable on the under-sized, metal folding chair. She was offended by his physical touch - offended because it felt so pleasantly familiar after all these years but was no longer hers to relish or return. She wondered if he knew and bumped her

159

on purpose.

God, I HATE second-guessing everything this guy does.

But that's exactly what experience had taught her. And she'd learned it the hard way.

Does he expect me to answer?

This jolly Dave was a far cry from the man who had almost knocked her down storming out of the hearing room after getting his hat handed to him by the judge. After that horrible day Kay assumed he would never speak to her again - save for today's court-ordered mediation. Given his unexpected good mood, Kay couldn't help wonder if Sandy hadn't sent him off for the day with a confidence-boosting blow job.

Dave's attempt at friendly chatter didn't stop - not even through the 17 minutes of the video. Yes, it was old times for Kay, as she listened to Dave make hilarious comments at the amateurly-produced instructional video. This was the old Dave - the one with a natural sense of humor who knew how to make her laugh. And laugh, she did. But despite the hilarity Kay couldn't help resenting how easily he slipped back into that persona she had fallen for so long ago - the one that brought out the best in her. She hated him for taking that away from her. Most of all she hated him for wasting it on the humorless, wet-washrag that was Sandy - the old-before-her-time hag who disapproved of watching Seinfeld and insisted they sit through mind-numbing episodes of "Murder She Wrote" and "Matlock."

160

If you gave her another million years, Kay would never be able to understand why Dave had sold his soul to this musty, uninteresting, dull, controlling shrew of a wife.

Why, why, why? I mean, even blow jobs have their limits.

The video ended, and a representative from the family court stood at the front of the room and asked if there were any questions. There weren't any and most of the people had already begun filing out of the cramped room. Dave stood and hung back apparently waiting for Kay. She bent her head over her purse pretending to look for some badly-needed, but elusive item hiding at the bottom. She didn't want to walk out with him, or take a seat next to him in the waiting room. The faux twosome-ness was unnatural and painful. Fortunately, Dave took the hint, and walked away without saying anything.

Out in the waiting room, people nervously milled around waiting for their cases to be called. With her own sad and confused feelings reflected back at her, Kay knew she fit right in. She recognized the inner struggle of trying to come to grips with being a divorced person.

Even though it had been seven years, Dave's loathsome actions made it seem like seven days. And while she was happy today's session was aimed at settling things with the girls, she wished there was some sort of mediation that could help her move forward, once and for all.

Kay watched Dave on the other side of the

room, pacing nervously while he talked on his cell phone.

Probably reporting to the warden.

Kay pictured Sandy on the other end of the line, demanding a thorough accounting of the morning's events. As soon as he finished he searched the room for Kay and headed straight for the bench where she was sitting. She wanted to wave him off before he came in for a landing but just sat there helplessly as he wedged himself into the breath of a space separating Kay and a petite, foreign-looking woman praying the rosary. Kay wanted to lean over and request a couple of Hail Marys for herself.

Oh, by all means. Make yourself comfortable.

"This is bullshit," Dave complained as he forcibly widened the space with his elbows, his touch was much less pleasant this time. "I've got a pile of work waiting for me at the office."

"Crap!" Kay said. She had forgotten to call work. "Thanks for reminding me." She pulled out her cell phone and looked around for someplace else to sit so she could talk with privacy; every available seat in the room was taken. She would just have to speak as softly as possible.

Kay filled Ruth in on her transportation situation and said she'd be in as soon as she could get to her car - assuming it would be ready.

"Are you ok? You sound strange." Ruth said.

Strange? That's an understatement.

Kay just brushed off her friend's concern. "I'm just trying to keep my voice down. I'm in a room with a lot of people."

"Manning/Noland," came a voice from behind the check-in counter.

"Gotta go, Ruth. They just called our case."

Kay and Dave answered the summons and were directed over to where a tired-looking woman stood waiting, clipboard in hand. Her eyes never left the clipboard as she offered her hand and introduced herself.

"Hello. I'm Lucinda Portelli. If you'll please follow me…"

She led them down a long corridor to a surprisingly large office. In addition to Ms. Portelli's work space, the room contained a play area for children filled with an assortment of toys and stuffed animals. The walls of the office were decorated with numerous drawings, presumably by the social worker's younger clients.

"Please have a seat," Ms. Portelli said, motioning to three metal folding chairs configured in a loose triangle. Once everyone was settled, Ms. Portelli smiled as she looked at Kay and Dave over the top of her reading glasses and launched into her mandatory spiel about the goals of mediation. Before she got past the first goal (set up a co-parenting plan), Dave interrupted and snidely said, "We already have a co-parenting plan."

Unruffled by his rude cut-off, Lucinda smiled

and said, "I'm aware, Mr. Noland. The judge believes your plan needs review and revision, or there'd be no need for you to be here, would there?"

A derisive gust of air escaped from Dave's lips as he crossed his arms over his chest.

Kay was loving this. It was wonderful to have a bona fide authority confirm to Dave what she had tried to tell him that day in her driveway. But as all things happen for a reason, Kay realized his unwillingness to cooperate was turning out to be a blessing.

Lucinda continued. The plan is supposed to be in the best interest of the children and should respect their right to have a continuing relationship with each parent. And finally, both parents should seek ways to reduce conflict in front of the children.

With her opening recitation over, Lucinda didn't waste any time jumping right into the girls' interviews. Kay wasn't sure if she was being sincere when she complimented her and Dave on how polite and engaging the girls were, or if it was just a way to lead into bad news.

Ms. Portelli looked at Kay. "The girls have no issues with you, Ms. Manning." Then she turned in her chair toward Dave and launched into a list of complaints and concerns that went on for three, 8½" x 11" yellow pad pages. Most of the grievances Kay had already heard - numerous times:

Mariah is not allowed to have milk or other dairy because Sandy (contrary to the pediatrician's diagnosis) decided Mariah's soiling problem stemmed from an allergy to milk.

Sandy nags Mariah about how much she eats and controls her food. Little Dave has free access to the "treat cabinet" but Mariah has to ask permission.

The girls are not allowed to keep personal belongings at Dave's and have to carry a bag back and forth.

The girls want their own room at their dad's but Sandy insists they stay in the "guest room."

Sandy forces the girls to accompany her to church while Dave stays home.

The girls object to Sandy introducing them as, "my daughters," letting people believe she is their mother.

Sandy makes disparaging remarks about Kay "letting the girls run wild."

Mariah overheard Sandy tell Dave (without one shred of evidence) she suspects Cory is smoking pot and shoplifting.

Sandy hurt Mariah's feelings with a denigrating remark about her sister. "Cory doesn't need to be your role model."

Cory resents not being trusted to babysit her little brother even though she has regular babysitting customers.

Lucinda stopped reading, looked up and quietly asked Dave, "Mr. Noland, are you aware

Mariah is not allowed privacy in the bathroom?

"I don't understand. What do you mean?" Dave asked. He truly seemed to be at a loss.

"Well, Mariah told me when she's in the bathroom, your son kicks at the door until his mother insists Mariah let him in."

Dave was unfazed. "Is that really so terrible? They're just kids," he said.

"Mr. Noland, that so-called "kid" is menstruating. She said the last time your son barged in she was changing her pad and he got an eyeful."

Dave sat there looking like he'd been hit in the face with a bag of quarters.

"My wife told me Mariah had gotten her period, but she didn't mention Little Dave saw anything."

"Well, according to Mariah, your wife got upset with her for possibly traumatizing your son."

This was the first time Kay had heard about this new humiliation. Why hadn't Mariah said anything to her?

"Oh please," Dave scoffed. "Mariah doesn't even know what "traumatizing" means."

"You're missing the point, Mr. Noland. Your child is being denied the simple dignity of privacy each of us deserves as a human being."

Dave brushed some imaginary lint from his

166

pant leg, avoiding Ms. Portelli's disapproving gaze.

Kay was softly crying, devastated for Mariah. She wanted to throttle Sandy.

"What really concerns me about this, Mr. Noland," Lucinda went on, "and everything else I've related to you, is you either seem to be absent or unwilling to intervene when your daughters are being subjected to this negativity."

Lucinda turned to Kay and said, "The girls said they've told you about this. Have you said anything to Mr. Noland?"

"I have," Kay said, muffling a sob. "He either denies it or just brushes me off saying the girls are exaggerating. But I had no idea, whatsoever, about the bathroom situation. Mariah never said a word." Kay turned to Dave. "How could you let this happen? For, chrissake, you're her father! "

Dave looked at Kay with a deer-caught-in-the-headlights expression.

"Look Mr. Noland," Lucinda said. My job is not to admonish you, but to bring some things to your attention so we can serve the best interests of your children. First and foremost, you have to understand parenting your girls is *your* responsibility. You cannot relinquish this to your wife."

Much to Kay's surprise, Dave looked Lucinda in the eye. "Well, I guess I do have a tendency to be a little passive," he said.

"I'm not entirely unsympathetic. I know it's

difficult to blend families," Lucinda said. "You're not the first client I've had who feels more comfortable letting their wife take the primary parental role. But a step-parent's role should always be secondary."

Even though Dave was nodding, Kay knew he would always be helpless in the face of Attila His Honey.

"You have to remember, this was *your* choice. Your daughters didn't ask for any of this and it's up to you to make your - THEIR - home a place where they feel wanted, protected and free to be who they are."

Dave nodded again, looking like an eight-year old who promised not to play baseball in the street anymore after breaking a window.

Kay was still crying. Part of it was anguish over her children's pain but a bigger part was the relief of having someone in authority say Dave's behavior was not ok. From Day One he had run roughshod over her and the girls while denying, diminishing and defiantly daring anyone to say his actions were dishonorable. He might be able to dismiss Kay's objections with flimsy justifications, but the family court representative, who had heard and seen it all, was not going to let him get away with making his kids the scapegoat for his sins.

Kay tried to concentrate as the review of their parenting plan continued, but the endless flow of tears was a distraction. Of course, Dave ignored her emotional blood-letting; Lucinda was becoming concerned. "Do we need to stop so you can get a drink of water, Ms. Manning?"

"Oh. Just ignore me. I'll be ok," Kay choked out. "Please continue."

But her sobs kept coming and so she did her best to stifle them with a cupped hand and several tissues over her mouth. This just re-routed them to her shoulders making them dance up and down with liberated emotion.

The rest of the review was fairly straightforward, with few, if any changes made. After seven years, the well-written plan still held up. Lucinda hurried through each stipulation, asking the couple if they agreed, and both nodded without comment.

When Lucinda was finished she said, "You know, you two did a very good job drawing up a fair and workable plan." Then she chuckled and said, "it sure makes my job easy.   And if you work together, there's no reason why it shouldn't make your job easy too."

Mercifully, the meeting came to an end and Lucinda Portelli walked Dave and Kay to the door, thanking them for their cooperation and wishing them the best for the future. Before Kay made it out the door, Lucinda stopped her and asked her to hang back a moment. She closed the door on Dave and addressed Kay, who was still crying. "Ms. Manning, I think you could really benefit from some counseling. It's obvious you have some serious unresolved issues with your ex-husband. For your sake and the sake of your girls, I highly recommend seeing someone."

Appearances to the contrary, Kay was happy.

She'd gotten what she'd come for. Her only regret was her tears of gratitude for being validated were being misinterpreted as a cry for help. She briefly considered telling the concerned social worker she'd already had two years of therapy, but since she'd probably never see Lucinda Portelli again, she just nodded in agreement. All she could think about now was getting out of there and finding a ride.

* * *

Kay hurried toward the elevators to join the small group of people getting into the open car. She had just stepped in when she heard, "Hey, Kay. Hold the doors." It was Dave. He reached the front of elevator just as the doors were sliding shut. Kay was about to give him a helpless shrug and "sorry" look, but at the last second something compelled her to push the Open Door button.

Maybe therapy isn't such a bad idea. I need to figure out why I can't say no to Dave.

"Thanks," he said breathlessly as he jumped in and turned in the obligatory, everyone-face-forward-pirouette. "I was looking for you back there, but I guess you got away from me."

Apparently, not fast enough.

Dave leaned over and quietly spoke out of the side of his mouth. "Where's your mechanic's garage?"

His cloak-and-dagger delivery made Kay want to respond with a silly, "the pellet with the poison's in the vessel with the pestle." But she decided against the Danny Kaye patter. "On Parsifal, near the horse arena. Why?" she said.

"I go right past there. I could drop you off." Then he added, "I overheard you say you needed a ride when you were talking on the phone."

Immediately, Kay became suspicious. The whole reason they were even standing in this elevator, descending through bowels of the Family Court Building was because Dave had demonstrated his deep dislike for doing favors for Kay. But she had to be practical. There was no one she could call, and a cab ride would be at least $15.

Maybe I should ask him for half the fare.

"Well, if you're sure it's not an inconvenience."

"The only inconvenience is my parking spot. I hope you're wearing comfortable shoes, cuz we gotta walk about six blocks to get to my truck."

And so the strange togetherness of the morning continued. The only way Kay could abide their temporary coupledom was to walk three paces behind Dave. Apparently, this annoyed him because he turned around to her and said, "What? Are we in India now?"

He probably hadn't meant to be funny, but Kay laughed anyway. She had always been his best audience.

The ride reached every level of weirdness. Her place in the front passenger seat alongside him was so natural, so familiar - yet it was no longer hers. Kay pictured Sandy giving the leather upholstery a good going-over later to remove any traces of First Wife's female essences.

Their small talk was excruciating. With all the foul water that had passed under the bridge, especially over the last few weeks, their efforts at nonchalant friendliness were total phony baloney. Kay thought it was a shame, too, because it would have been the perfect opportunity to have a frank heart-to-heart, if only to put some closure on a wound that had remained open for the last seven years. But Kay knew Dave was incapable of having such a conversation. That depth of honesty could only be accessed by an adult who was in touch with his inner thoughts, feelings and motivations. Long before Kay ever met Dave, she suspected something had stunted his emotional growth, causing him to run whenever life became too real. Kay had always believed he'd left their marriage when she'd asked for more from a relationship stalled in second gear.

"Did the girls mention we're moving my mom to an assisted living facility?" Dave asked.

"You mean in between telling me what a bully your wife is?" Kay said. She couldn't resist stirring Dave's simmering pot of embarrassment over the girls' "big reveal."

"Oh, come on, Kay," he shot back. Kay was well-familiar with his tactic of trying to make her feel guilty for making things seem worse than they really were.

Satisfied she'd hit her intended target, she returned to the subject at hand. "No. No, they didn't.

172

Helen in a nursing home...I just can't picture it." Kay said, shaking her head. Even though there was no love lost between her and Helen Noland, she was still sad her ex-mother-in-law had reached that inevitable point in life which most people hoped to avoid.

"Assisted Living," Dave corrected. "She'll have her own apartment with a full time medical staff on the premises. We think it isn't safe for her to live alone anymore."

"I can't see your mom as a dependent, old woman. She's always been so feisty and self-sufficient."

Kay laughed, turned to Dave. "Do you remember that time..." He was crying. She had rarely, if ever, seen Dave Noland cry - and he wasn't doing anything to try to hide it.

Kay thought it was to his credit that he could shed tears for his mother. She knew from dealing with her clients at work, how gut-wrenching these decisions were. Her heart broke for him, but she sat there frozen. Something inexplicable blocked her from reaching out and showing him any sign of sympathy. It was just like that day in her doorway when he moved to hug her and all she could do was shrink back.

"My sisters insisted on a pricey facility on the east side of town. They're putting her in a big apartment with two bedrooms," Dave said. Large tear drops were falling from both sides of his jaw, spotting the lapels on his suit coat.

"That's great!" Kay said, trying to sound

supportive. "Having her own private living space ought to make the transition easier."

"Yeah. But I think she could just as easily transition to a one bed room - or even a studio. These jokers are asking almost $7000 a month! My sisters don't care. They're married to doctors."

"So you guys are divvying up the expense?" Kay asked.

"That's the plan," he said with a heavy sigh.

Kay jumped when Dave suddenly slammed the heal of his palm on the steering wheel. "Jesus. I can't ever seem to catch a break."

Kay sensed he expected her to ask what was going on, but that same inexplicable block prevented her from uttering a sound.

Dave shot a sideways glance at Kay to see if she was still paying attention. Her gaze remained fixed on the road ahead; he forced out a little sob to see if he could re-engage her in the conversation. Kay continued to give him (herself?) space.

So Dave upped the ante. "I know you think I screwed you on the whole child support thing. But, you have no idea the financial load I'm under."

Now she shifted her gaze from the road rapidly passing under the carriage of the truck and looked at Dave.

"What are you talking about?" she asked indignantly. "You make almost four times the salary I do. AND you get free medical." She decided to throw that last part in to show her disgust at his bonus perk.

"That's right. I do. But I'm still paying off creditors from the old business, including the IRS. I had to use up my savings to cover the cost of moving here."

"So why didn't you just tell me that in the beginning? Why the song and dance about a salary cut?"

"I was embarrassed," Dave said quietly. "I didn't want you to know about the mess I'm in. Anyway, with all the money going out, it might as well have been a cut. I was desperate to find some relief somewhere. I had no choice. I didn't know what else to do. You have to believe me."

Kay's eyes narrowed and her throat tightened. "I have to believe you?" Kay said. "I have to believe you?" she repeated, louder this time. "That's rich. Let's see… I believed you when you said you weren't having an affair with Sandy. I believed you when you said you'd never leave us. I believed you when you said you weren't leaving me to go to her - that you didn't know where she was. I believed you when you said you'd never marry her." She stopped and looked hard at Dave. "Shall I go on?"

Dave didn't respond. He just looked straight ahead, tears still streaming down his cheeks.

"Look. Why don't you cut to the chase and tell me what it is you really want? It must be pretty important if you've gone to the all the trouble of staging today's comedy-tragedy show."

This time he didn't hesitate a moment to answer her question."There's no way can I afford to pay you the ten thousand right now. With my legal fees, mom, and your full child support added to my debt, I'll be lucky to put food on my table. For godssake, Kay, I haven't had a new pair of fucking underwear in two years."

Kay couldn't believe what she was hearing. Or maybe she could.

Kay extended her palm toward Dave's face. "Whoa, whoa, whoa, Mr. Rotting Fruit of the Loom. I seem to remember hearing about a recent trip to the mall involving the purchase of big screen TV. Maybe you should have held on to a couple of those twenties you were brandishing about and spent them on some new tighty-whities," Kay said. It gave her great pleasure to tell him she knew about his little spending spree."

"That was a gift from Sandy's mom," he snapped. "It was a house warming present…not that it's any of your business."

"So what are you saying? After all the lies, deceit, mistreatment and noncooperation, you expect me to forgive what the judge says you legally owe me and the girls?

Right on cue came his signature, "Oh, come on," as if Kay had said something ridiculously unreasonable. "I have every intention of paying you. I just want to defer it until Cory turns 18."

Dave pulled into a parking spot in front of the mechanic's shop, put the truck in Park, and turned to

Kay. "I'll give you 10% interest. That's better than you'd get from any bank."

Kay couldn't think, let alone speak. All she knew was she had to get out of the truck. She opened the door and slid down to the pavement. She was just about to push the door shut when Dave said, "Wait, Kay. At least tell me you'll think about it."

She nodded just to get rid of him, knowing she wouldn't be able to think about anything else.

14

Ignore Isaac Newton

at Your Own Peril

Twenty minutes after two.

Fine time to be getting to work.

Under normal circumstances, Kay would have just gone home and blown off the rest of the day, but being at home alone with her thoughts was not an attractive prospect. And the inevitable, interrogating call from Leslie was something she wasn't ready to face.

Ruth saw Kay pull into the parking lot and hurried back to Kay's office to greet her. The look on Kay's face was one Ruth wasn't familiar with so she decided not to ask any questions.

"I'm glad you're here," Ruth said. "I think Ed is going to need you here pretty soon."

Just then, the mortuary's white pickup van pulled up right outside her window; Ed got out and headed inside.

Oh, I'm going on a pick up.

Kay was grateful she was going to be occupied with a mindless task.

"Hey, Kay. Glad you could make it," Ed said.

Kay opened her mouth to explain about her car, but changed her mind.

"We've got a contract case at O.M.I. that's going to be released in an hour or so. As usual, Uncle O is incommunicado so I'm going to have send you and Leo," Ed said.

Salinger's had a contract with the state to handle final disposition of indigent cases and any John Does who had no next of kin.

"Why the two of us?" Kay asked. She was a little miffed Ed didn't trust her to handle the pick up on her own.

"The body weighs over three hundred pounds," Ed said. He talked over his shoulder as he impatiently opened and closed filing cabinet drawers, unable to find his requisite forms.

Ruth smiled, shook her head and gently nudged him out of the way, knowing exactly where to locate what he was looking for. Ed deferred to Ruth and straightened up. "It's going to take two people. I'd go, but I'm headed to Memorial on another case."

"Why don't I take that one for you," Kay offered. "I mean, wouldn't it be better if you and Leo handled the O.M.I. case?" Kay had never worked with a body that heavy.

"Yes, it would be better," Ed said, obviously irritated. "But the family at Memorial has specifically requested me to be there. Don't worry. The body will

179

be on a gurney and you'll get help from O.M.I. staff to load him into the station wagon. And I should be here to help you unload when you get back."

Kay had never driven the station wagon before. It was a customized, 1967 Ford Country Squire and something of a curiosity. Ed's dad had purchased it new and it had served as a real work horse for the mortuary. Pick up vehicles had come and gone over the years, but Ed couldn't bear to part with his dad's car and kept it in tip top running condition. Good thing, too, because it came in handy on occasions like this.

"Didn't I hear you say you could drive a three-speed on the column?" Ed said.

"That's right," Kay said with pride. She was glad her dad had insisted she master the, largely obsolete, transmission.

"Good. I've sent Leo to gas it up," Ed said. "As soon as O.M.I. calls, you guys can take off. I want you to drive. Leo still has problems with the clutch."

Forms in hand, Ed made his usual dash for the door, muttering, "Why did I ever bid on that contract...more trouble than it's worth."

Kay picked up the phone to let the girls know she'd be late.

* * *

"So, what was wrong with your car?" Leo asked. He pushed Kay's purse toward her with the back of his arm across the long bench seat, trying to make room for an enormous stash of gas station junk food.

Kay looked at the colorful pile and chuckled. "We're not going to be gone that long, Leo. It's only thirty miles each way. You've brought enough provisions to last three days."

"Car trips always make me hungry," Leo said. He talked through his teeth as he used them to tear open a bag of corn nuts.

"Everything makes you hungry," Kay replied.

The forty-six year old, Ford hummed along as if it had just come off the showroom floor.

It's true. They really don't make things the way they used to.

Just as if she'd driven the car yesterday, Kay smoothly slid each gear into position with a coordinated push and release of the clutch. If it wasn't for the smell of corn nuts, Leo's loud, open-mouth crunching, and the heavy burden weighing on her mind, Kay would have almost enjoyed herself.

Air. I need air.

She cranked down (literally) her window, part way, reached for the large chrome radio knob and turned it on. Noisy country music accompanied by lots of crackling static blared out of the single speaker in the dash. She fumbled for an FM button and realized the old radio only picked up AM stations. Disappointed, she turned the radio off. Anyway, Leo had polished off his corn nuts and was already working on a quickly-melting, but quieter ice cream sandwich.

How does he stay so skinny?

"So, what was wrong with your car," Leo asked again, licking the sides of the sandwich to catch the melting ice cream.

Kay was embarrassed to tell him. In her frazzled state of dread of the morning's mediation session, she had misread the illuminated "Check Engine" symbol as the "Oil Pressure" indicator. She'd called roadside service only because Dave had always told her never to drive the car if the oil pressure light was on. She'd felt like an idiot when the mechanic told her the only problem was that she had failed to tighten her gas cap completely.

"Oh, nothing too serious," she said. "Something to do with the car's emissions system," which was true.

"Yeah. We've had that issue with the lim...," Leo stopped himself before he completed the word. He looked over at Kay to see if she was going to pick up and run with the loose end of his incomplete statement.

Kay stayed quiet. She was still thinking about the mechanic and how nice it was that he hadn't charged her for tightening her gas cap.

"Look, Kay. I hope you don't think I'm avoiding you about the...the...well, you know what, on purpose," Leo said, deciding to beat Kay to the punch.

Given her pressing personal priorities, Kay was unable to muster any enthusiasm for talking about Uncle O's attempts at spicing up his life with Mrs. Dash - or any other topic, for that matter.

"It's fine, Leo. Don't worry about it," Kay said.

Leo was completely thrown off by Kay's dispassionate answer. He eyed her with suspicion and after a few unsure moments said, "I know what you're doing. You're pretending not to be interested so I'll tell you everything. Well, nice try. It's not gonna work."

Kay was too preoccupied to argue. "You caught me Leo," she said with a sigh. "There's no getting anything past you."

For the remaining twenty minutes of their drive, the two sat in silence, broken only by the occasional rip of a potato chip bag or crackle of a cellophane Ding Dong wrapper. Even during the quieter lulls, Kay's attempts at organizing her thoughts were proving to be futile. She was glad when they finally reached the loading area of the Office of the Medical Investigator building. Kay backed up the station wagon to the open bay door and then she and Leo went inside to claim their weighty charge.

In all her many visits to OMI, the putrid odor that hung inside like an oppressive cloud was something Kay had never been able to get used to. She looked over at Leo, amazed he could keep all that junk food down in light of the nauseating smell.

The desk attendant didn't waste any time checking Kay's paper work and then calling down to the morgue to have the body brought up.

Kay was delighted things were moving along so quickly. They'd be out of there and back on the road before it got dark.

"I hope you don't mind," the desk attendant started. "We didn't have a body bag that would fit. I'm afraid he's going to have to be happy with the "ole" white sheet," he said. "Make that two ole white sheets," he added, clearly amused at his own stupid joke.

Forty-five, interminable, nose-holding, mouth-breathing minutes later, the elevator doors finally opened and two workers from the morgue rolled out what appeared to be a small white mountain rising from a gurney. Kay was stunned at just how large 300 lbs. really was.

"Can we please get those sheets tucked under the body?" Kay officiously requested, worried a sudden gust of wind might lift them up, off and away.

Back at the car, Kay opened the tail gate, stepped out of the way, and let Leo assist the men with the loading. Sitting in the driver's seat, Kay could hear them, in typical guy fashion, snicker and giggle as they speculated about the enormous man's sexual challenges. Leo had just made a joke about the guy having to use a hoist to lower himself on to his partner, when Kay finally heard enough. She gave the horn a quick, sharp blast. "C'mon, Leo. Ed's waiting."

* * *

Night had completely fallen by the time they

were back on the road and it wasn't long before Leo's junk food binge put him into a deep, peaceful sugar-induced coma. Kay was happy for the silence. With their task out of the way, she might just be able to get some serious thinking accomplished.

The gurney straps! Right there, direct evidence of her muddled brain popped into her head. If she'd been on her game, she would have had the attendants tie down the sheets with the gurney straps.

Oh, well. I'll remember next time. Back to the matter at hand.

Dave was going to want an answer soon, and she had never before been so conflicted. There was one thing she was sure of, though. She was in a rare position of power and she didn't want to waste it.

Kay decided the best way to reach a decision was to approach it logically and methodically, removing as much emotion as possible. So she asked herself, "What's the bottom line in this situation?"

Les would have said it was the girls and their well being. But Kay believed she'd already addressed that by taking steps to have their full child support reinstated. Dave's dressing-down by the mediator had been an added bonus.

Again, she asked herself, "What's the bottom line here?" This time the answer came immediately. "I need to prove to myself I'm over Dave and ready to move on."

So, in an effort to be logical and methodical she decided to make a mental list of the pros and cons associated with saying no, then yes

No - Pros

1. $10,000! 'Nuf said.

2. Kay was not a bank. Let him use the proper channels to get a loan.

3. If history was any indicator, he was trying to pull another fast one.

4. Dave would learn to think twice before approaching her with absurd requests.

5. She'd have the undying admiration of Leslie and Ruth

No - Cons

1. No matter how solid her reasons for saying no, Dave and Sandy would interpret it as retaliation.

2. Her relationship with Dave might not ever normalize.

Yes - Pros

1. Dave seemed to be in a truly-dire financial situation. She'd be helping the girls' father.

2. The reinstated child support had restored the "comfortable" factor in her finances. She didn't need the $10,000.

3. $10,000 back pay was an unexpected bonus. Kay hadn't requested it. (*hmmmm...neither had her attorney*)

4. $10,000 deferred for five years at 10% interest would come to $15,000! 'Nuf said.

5. Saying yes would prove to herself she was over Dave and ready to move on. (*Would it?*)

Yes - Cons

1. Dave and Sandy were incapable of appreciating her magnanimous gesture. She'd still be the "bad guy"

2. Ruth and Leslie wouldn't be shy about expressing their disappointment and disapproval.

There it was. Logical and methodical. But it was evenly split. Kay was no closer to a decision. It was clear she was going to need more time. Yes. She'd take her time.

Let Dave cool his heels awhile.

Feeling a little better, Kay allowed herself to relax into the bench seat. She leaned her head back, arching her neck in search of the head rest that was still about three years away from being invented.

Never mind. We're almost there.

Kay straightened up, reached over and shook Leo's arm. "Leo. Hey, Leo, time to wake up."

The car rounded the last curve and began its climb up the moderately-steep hill that stood at the edge of town. Kay turned to see if Leo was responding when out of the corner of her eye she thought she saw the gurney rolling back away from her. Horrified, she snapped her head around to get a look. Sure enough, the foot of the gurney and the feet of the deceased were resting against the car's tail gate.

Kay shook Leo's arm again. "Leo…LEO! Wake up! You didn't lock the gurney wheels!"

She looked back again, terrified the old tail gate might come open with all the weight pressing against it. It appeared to be holding.

So far, so good.

As the station wagon crested the hill, she could see the mortuary's lighted marquee in the far distance. She let out a sigh of relief. They began their descent.

Oh no. It's gonna roll back this way.

Right on cue, Kay heard the creak of the wheels as the gurney began to roll forward. She took her foot off the gas pedal to reduce her speed, hoping to guide the gurney to a gentle stop at the back of the seat. But before she had a chance to slow the momentum of the rolling stretcher, something (*a dog?*) streaked past the front of her car. Kay slammed on the brakes, propelling the gurney at top speed into the back of the seat, sending three hundred pounds of unsecured dead weight flying at 30 mph across the top and slamming into the AM radio on the dash.

With only the waist-style seat belts of the old car to strap him in, Leo's body whiplashed forward and back like a cooked spaghetti noodle. Amazingly, he stayed asleep.

"*Sixteen tons and whadda ya get...*" Tennessee Ernie Ford's deep baritone wafted out of the dented radio speaker.

It was the music that finally roused Leo back to consciousness. "Hey. I like that old song," he croaked, completely oblivious to the calamitous chain reaction of the previous 10 seconds. That is until he realized there was a dead body separating him and Kay.

"What the eff?" Leo said. He rubbed his eyes, trying to make sense of what he was seeing.

Kay's heart was pounding and her hands were drenched with cold sweat. The station wagon had stalled in the middle of the road and she knew she had to get it moved out of the way - preferably to a level area where she and Leo could push the body back on the gurney.

Kay's legs shook uncontrollably against the clutch and gas pedal as she attempted to restart the car and move out of first gear. After a couple of beginner-like hops, the station wagon slowly moved forward and she quickly found a suitable spot to pull over. As soon as she brought the car to a stop, she barked at Leo. "Get in the back. I'll push from his shoulders while you pull from his legs." Leo didn't waste a moment obeying Kay's urgent command.

Flashing red lights and short burst of BWEEP bip bip BWEEP announced the unwelcome arrival of the police to the scene.

Kay shook her head.

I really need to start checking my horoscope before I leave the house.

"Pull, Leo, pull," Kay said frantically, as she pushed as hard as she could. Maybe they could get the body back on the gurney before the officer made it to her window.

The body didn't budge.

She glanced at the side view mirror and saw the beam of a flashlight growing more intense as it neared her driver's side door.

"Ok, Leo. One more time. On my count. One, two, three. PULL!"

Kay was pushing with all her might when the beam from the flashlight landed on her hands pushing against the body's shoulders. Kay looked over to see the horrified face of a young, female police officer. Just as Kay reached to roll down the window to explain, the woman's eyes rolled back in her head and she wilted to the ground in a dead faint.

"Oh God, Leo. She's passed out."

With a graceful agility Kay didn't know Leo possessed, he leapt back into the front seat and yelled. "Hit it, Kay, Hit it! Let's get outta here before she comes to."

Kay sat there frozen.

"What the hell are you waiting for? Go, go go!"

"Ohmagodohmagodohmagod." She peeled out, fishtailing and sending a hail of gravel over the fallen officer.

"What if she's dead?" Kay shrieked in panic. "Oh god. *We're* dead. Ed's going to kill us and we're going to jail."

Kay looked over to Leo who had buried his face in his hands. He appeared to be crying.

"Leo? Are you ok? Please don't fall apart on me now," she said.

Kay pulled one of his hands away from his face and a rollicking "Bwaa ha ha ha" exploded out of his mouth. He laughed and laughed until finally he made himself gag. His eyes grew wide as the remnants of his grease, salt and sugar bender threatened to come back for a return engagement.

"Don't. You. Dare. If you throw up, I'll…I'll…" Kay stopped, because she didn't know what she'd do…or what she was doing, for that matter. "Roll down your window and take some deep breaths."

Kay turned on to the first available street and parked the car. After a few stomach-settling gulps of fresh air, Leo turned to say something to Kay. But as soon as he saw the head of the body resting against the dash of the car, radio knobs embedded in its head, his raucous laughter started up again. "Bwaa ha ha ha…wait'll I tell O about this. He's gonna shit his pants laughing. Bwaa ha ha ha."

Yeah," Kay said flatly, "especially when he finds out it was you who didn't lock the gurney wheels."

That shut Leo up.

"Not so funny now, huh, Leo," Kay said. She was angry because she knew Ed was likely to hold her equally responsible for the unlocked wheels and unstrapped body.

"Look. I have an idea," Leo said in take-charge voice. "We'll drive to my brother's. He's just a few blocks from here. There's always a bunch of guys hangin' around, drinking beer. They'll help us move this guy."

With no other viable option on the horizon, Kay turned the car in the direction of Leo's brother's house. There was no argument from the corpse.

Leo knocked on the door and the porch light came on. After a quick explanation, Leo's brother, Frank, and two other men Kay didn't know, came bursting out the front door to verify Leo's unbelievable story. After seeing the corpse resting against the dash, one of the men suspiciously looked up and over the car, then up and down the block. "Are we on TV?" he said with a loony laugh. "Are we getting punked?"

"No, you asshole," Frank said. "Stop being an idiot and let's help these guys get this body back on the stretcher.

Kay stood out of the way as the four men, using their combined leverage, easily guided the dead weight back on the stretcher.

"So, if you don't mind me asking, what happened?" Frank said to Kay.

"Newton's First Law of Motion," Kay said.

"Sorry?" Frank said.

Kay laughed. "I braked for a dog on the hill and the gurney wasn't locked down."

"It must have been moving at quite a clip if the body broke out of the gurney straps," Frank said.

Kay and Leo looked at each other, neither one willing to admit to their other big boner.

Finally Leo piped up, "Actually, the straps weren't long enough to go around the guy."

Yeah. The straps weren't long enough. That's the ticket. I'll have to remember that one.

* * *

Five minutes later, Kay was backing up the station wagon to the embalming room door, gurney properly locked down and the body squarely on top.

Ed, already embalming his pick up, opened the door when he heard the distinctive hum of his favorite old car. "There you are. I was starting to get worried," he said.

"Oh you know how those guys are at O.M.I. It's always hurry up and wait," Kay said.

"Ok. Let's get this guy in here and ready for the crematory. Jerry's hanging back to wait for him." Ed said.

Using big, deliberate moves that were obvious

only to Kay, Leo unlocked the gurney wheels. With relative ease they rolled the massive corpse out of the car and into the embalming room, where Ed had already prepared the mortuary hoist. With Ed at the shoulders, Leo at the waist and Kay at the knees, the body was quickly secured, lifted off and suspended high over the gurney.

"You two go grab the air tray. It's in the hall." Ed said.

"Air tray?" Leo said, referring to the receptacle used to ship casketed bodies by air. "Aren't we putting him in a cremation tray?"

"He'll never fit." Ed said. "It's an air tray or nothing. And Jerry won't take him that way."

Working quickly in team fashion, Kay and Leo set the plywood bottom on top of the gurney and then Ed pushed the button to lower the body on it. Kay was thinking about Leo's hoist joke, when Ed suddenly stopped the lift.

"Hey. Check out these weird round dents in this guys head." Ed thumbed the deep impact impressions from the radio knobs. "I wonder if that's what killed him?"

"Yeah…we were wondering about that too," Leo said with a straight face.

"I guess we won't know 'till the death certificate comes," Kay said. She managed to remain equally composed.

Kay did her best not to lock eyes with Leo, lest

she trigger another round of bwaa ha ha has.

It was a tight squeeze, but the lid finally went over the tray and the gurney was rolled back into the station wagon.

"Do you have the cremation order?" Ed asked Kay as he walked her to the front of the car.

Kay nodded.

Leo and Kay opened their doors simultaneously and the breeze that blew across the front seat picked up some of the wrapper evidence of Leo's junk food binge and deposited them at Ed's feet.

"Jesus Christ, Leo! Clean this up - and anything else that's still in the car. I don't want Jerry seeing it." He turned on his heel and stormed back to the embalming room.

"Why does he assume it's me?" Leo muttered as he snatched up food wrappers from the seat and the floor. Kay rolled her eyes, started up the car and waited for Leo to take his armful of trash to the dumpster behind the building.

They completed their delivery without further complication and soon were headed back to the mortuary.

"What are we gonna do about that cop, Leo?" Kay asked. She was sick with worry. "I wouldn't be surprised to see her waiting and ready to slap the handcuffs on us when we get back."

"Oh, I'm quite sure that's not gonna happen,"

Leo said with the same juicy-secret smile she'd seen that day back in the break room.

"Oh please," Kay scoffed. "You can't possibly be that naive."

Leo smiled again, this time rubbing his palms together. "Ever hear the words "situational syncope?"

"I'm afraid this is more than just bad timing, Leo," Kay said.

Leo threw his head back and laughed. "No. Situational syncope. It's a medical condition that causes people to faint when they're shocked or stressed. That's what happened to Lindy back there."

"Lindy? You know her?"

It seems Leo and Melinda, aka "Lindy" O'Malley had dated a couple of months before she entered the police academy. She confided to Leo she was going to keep her strange medical affliction a secret because she didn't want it keeping her from realizing her life-long dream of becoming a police officer.

"Believe me, Officer O'Malley is going to put the incident far behind her, as if it never happened. It's your, my and her secret."

Now it was Kay who was smiling.

Kay dropped Leo off at the embalming room door and went on to park the station wagon in the special garage Ed had built to house his prized possession. She was walking back to the main building when she noticed the door to the main garage was open. As she came nearer, she heard the slam of a door then almost crashed into Uncle O as he hurried out of the garage.

"Oh. Hello, Kay," Owen said, shaken by surprise. "I was just bringing the limo back from Mike's. Six month servicing time, you know," he said with a little laugh.

Do I have Stupid written across my forehead?

Kay made a point of looking at her watch. "Mike kept the car a little later than usual, don't you think?" Kay knew it was mean, but she couldn't resist putting O on the hot seat and watching him squirm.

"Heh, heh. Yeah. He's a pretty busy guy," Owen replied. "I noticed the lights on in the embalming room. Is Ed working?"

"Yes he is. By the way, he tried to reach you earlier. He needed help with an extra pick up. But not to worry. Leo and I took care of it," Kay said. She was trying to ramp up his discomfort.

Owen slowly pulled the garage door down, his face telegraphing the mental frenzy taking place in his head.

Kay resumed her walk to the building. She wondered if Ruth had ever talked to Ed about the condom situation. Uncle O hurried to catch up.

"Look, Kay. I was supposed to take the limo in last week. Ed's going to be mad if he finds out I waited 'til today. I'd appreciate it if you didn't saying anything to him about running into me at the garage."

Kay looked at Owen with a fake look of shock. "Uncle O! Are you asking me to lie for you?"

If this old man is up to no good, I'm not going to make it easy for him.

Owen stopped in his tracks. A look of panic came over his face. "I'll buy you something," he offered breathlessly. "Anything you want."

The fun had suddenly gone out of Kay's little game. The conversation had turned scary.

"Calm down, Uncle O," Kay said patting his arm. "You don't need to bribe me. I was just having a little fun with you."

Owen pulled out a handkerchief from his pocket and mopped imaginary sweat from his forehead. "It's just…well… you know how mad Ed gets. I'm going to catch it anyway for not going on that call."

"It's all ok," Kay said, giving him a final reassuring pat. "I've gotta get going and so do you." She smiled and continued on her way, leaving Owen standing in the middle of the parking lot.

* * *

Ed was putting the finishing touches on his deceased when Kay walked into the embalming room. Leo was busy cleaning up, returning chemical bottles, instruments and cosmetics to the glass case in the corner.

"If there isn't anything else you need from me, I think I'll head home," Kay said.

198

Ed looked up at Kay, smiled. "No that's it. Go ahead and go."

She was almost through the door when Ed stopped her. "Oh. By the way. I took a message for you this afternoon that sounded pretty important. You might wanna have a look. I left it on your desk. "

"Ok. Thanks." Kay said. She detoured back to her office.

"Great job today," Ed called after her. "Thanks for all your help."

As she approached her desk, Kay could see the little pink memo paper taped to the handset of her phone. She peeled it off and shuddered when she saw it was from Dave. *Call Back* and *Urgent* were check-marked prominently in black Sharpie-sized ink.

Urgent, my ass. I will not be rushed, Dave Nolan. You'll get my answer when I'm good and ready.

She crushed the message into a little pink ball, tossed it in the trash and headed for the door. It was going to feel good to drive away and put this day of manipulation, mishaps, and mayhem behind her.

15

Percolatté

DATE: April 18th, 8:44 a.m.

TO: Kay_Manning

FROM: Dave@dnoland.com

SUBJECT: Hi!

Hi? Are you kidding me?

It had been three days and Kay had yet to respond to Dave's phone message. Kay knew he had to be getting anxious because this was the first and only time he'd ever emailed her - not to mention the breezy subject line. It was a dead giveaway.

She was tempted to delete the email without reading it, but decided it might be worth seeing how far he'd abase himself to get her to give him a "yes."

Hey Kay,

Not sure if you received my phone message the other afternoon. I know how busy you guys are over there, with everyone dying to get in. LOL.

Oh, brother.

I was just wondering if you'd given any thought to my little proposition. No pressure, or anything. I'm just doing a little financial planning, and it would be helpful to know what type of arrangements I need to make. Financial, not funeral. Ha ha.

I look forward to hearing from you.

Dave

200

A little thrill passed through her as she imagined making Dave's funeral arrangements with Sandy, crazy with jealousy, after being told, "*Ms. Manning will be handling Mr. Noland's bathing and dressing.*"

She quickly deleted the fantasy from her mind.

What am I thinking? Salinger's is the last place Sandy would bring Dave.

Kay reread Dave's email, shaking her head at his pathetic attempt to disarm her with cliché funeral humor. She was especially insulted by the characterization of his nervy request as a "little proposition."

She wasted no time drafting an answer, but scheduled its delivery for three hours later. If she hit the Reply button now, he was sure to read something into her quick response and she didn't want to give him any undue encouragement.

I hate playing these stupid games.

DATE: April 18th, 11:47 a.m.

TO: Dave@dnoland.com

FROM: Kay_Manning

SUBJECT: Re:Hi!

Your "little proposition" is too important to discuss through email or on the phone. I would like to arrange a face to face meeting. How's 10, Saturday morning at Percolatté on Sixth St.?

There are a few things I need to know before I decide to help you with your financial arrangements. Now, if it was funeral arrangements… Ha ha.

```
       No  need  to  reply  if  you  plan  on  being
there.
       Kay
```

Kay decided she wasn't going to reinforce his weaselly modus operandi by allowing him to deal with her via safe, remote methods of communication. The issue really was too important. Even more important was being able to keep a cool head so she could make certain she'd covered all her bases before giving him her decision.

By the end of the day, she hadn't received a response, so she relaxed and turned her attention to finishing her work day and going home.

* * *

Dave was already seated at a table when Kay walked into the coffee shop. She noted, then dismissed her heart's usual skip-a-beat thing, having finally resigned herself to the fact Dave would probably always have that effect on her.

…something chemical beyond my control.

Kay took Dave's early arrival as a good omen. She knew the "waitee" usually establishes the advantage over the "waitor." If he was, at all, nervous, she was about to sharpen his pins and needles with a self-assured stride and a stunning picture of beauty in her slim-fitted white jeans, white and navy striped tee, casual navy blazer, and a sassy splash of color from her red ballet flats. The first four tiny buttons on the tee's v-neckline were strategically opened to project just the right amount of flirty boobitude.

Her goal, as always, was to remind him of the

stark difference between her and Sandy.

Heads turned as Kay gracefully serpentined between tables making her way to Dave's chosen location at the far corner at the back of the coffee shop.

Probably doesn't want anyone he knows to see us together.

He jumped up when he saw Kay and hurried to pull out a chair for her. Kay tried not to let any smugness show as she watched him struggle to keep his eyes off her chest.

Always know your audience.

"You must have gotten here early," Kay said, looking at her watch as she scooted closer to the table. *10:00 straight up.* "I hope you haven't been waiting too long."

"Nah. I had a few things to take care of at the office this morning and I finished sooner than I expected," he said.

"Has someone taken your order yet?" Kay asked, looking around the room for an available server.

"Actually, you have to place your order at the counter. Tell me what you want and I'll get it for you."

I want you tell me you're sorry for all the dirty, rotten things you've done to me and that you're ready to be my friend and a reliable dad to Cory and Mariah. Good luck getting that at the counter.

"Oh. Thanks. Let me see." Kay squinted to read the chalk board menu behind the counter. All the selections were written in difficult-to-read pastel

203

colored chalk. "Just get me a medium regular coffee with a splash of half and half." There wasn't anything on that board that was worth straining her eyes for.

Kay pulled her wallet from her purse but Dave waved her off. "No. I've got it. I'll be right back."

Dave was being gracious now, but Kay knew that was likely to change once she told him what she had come to say. At any rate, it was fun watching him trip over himself to get in her good graces.

It wasn't long before he was back with a tray carrying two cups of steaming coffee along with a cheese Danish and thick slice of banana bread. "I didn't have time to eat before I left the house. I know you like banana bread, but if you don't want it, I'll eat it."

Dave seemed to be pulling out all the stops and it was working…sort of. Kay couldn't help but be flattered by the fact he'd remembered her fondness for banana bread. But she had to take his gesture with a grain of salt since he was, after all, the king of ulterior motives.

"How sweet," Kay said insincerely. "Looks half - I mean, fresh-baked." She cut a brown, moist corner with her fork, put it in her mouth, and smiled at Dave as she chewed.

Dave ignored her cattiness and dug into his own pastry with gusto.

They both sat there eating and sipping - neither one having much to say in the way of polite chit chat. So Kay decided to lead the charge with a statement sure to provoke and embarrass her coffee-mate.

"I bet you've caught a lot of shit from Sandy over all these meetings with me."

His face instantly turned red, followed by a classic denial. "Sandy knows settling these issues is just as important for our family as they are for yours."

Does he hear himself when he's talking?

"See," Kay said, stabbing the air in front of Dave with her fork. "Right there. That's part of the problem. You've allowed Sandy to classify the girls as *my* family and not yours. Maybe if you claimed them these money issues wouldn't be such a big deal. I mean, I'm sure you don't have to cut deals with Sandy every time she needs something for Little Dave."

"Yeah, but you..."

"But me, nothing. This has been your trip from the beginning. The girls and I were never consulted. We just got caught under your wheels, dragging us along as you made your hasty get-away. Now, I can understand you cutting me loose, but I'm not going to let you do it to the girls."

Inside, Kay was quite riled up; outside, she was the picture of calm.

Dave shook his head. "Ever the drama queen."

Kay leaned forward, looked directly into his eyes. "I callz 'em as I seez 'em."

She wasn't trying to be funny, but Dave laughed.

I think he's starting to show cracks around the edges.

Kay had fired the first shot across the bow and was satisfied she'd set the tone for the rest of the conversation. Not surprisingly, Dave responded by calling a time out. "I'm going for a warm-up. How 'bout you?"

"Nah. I'm good."

Kay sat gazing out one of the coffee shop's big picture windows taking in the intoxicating beauty of the late-April morning. Passersby's steps seemed to be buoyed along by the lightness of the soft, warming season. A young couple kissing as they waited for a green light at the cross walk had captured her attention. She was lost in the sweetness of the moment when a loud tap on the window woke her out of her reverie. She turned to see Ed, looking smokin' hot in his tennis whites, grinning at her from the other side of the glass. He was saying something to her, but Kay pointed to her ear and shook her head. Ed gestured toward the entrance and headed in that direction.

He's coming in. Oh no. I'm going to have to introduce him to Dave.

"Well, fancy meeting you here," Ed said as he briskly strode over to her table. "I didn't know you were a Percolatter," pronouncing it like the coffee brewing appliance.

"Yeah. I probably seem like more of a slow dripper," Kay said.

"Huh? Oh right. Cute," Ed said. He helped himself to Dave's chair before Kay had a chance to extend a courteous invitation. "You look too pretty to be sitting here by yourself," Ed said, smiling as he

206

took in Kay's vision of loveliness.

Kay wasn't used to being the recipient of Ed's legendary charm. His compliment made her blush and giggle, as if the rest of her buttons had suddenly popped open.

Two seconds later Dave was back glowering at the handsome stranger occupying his chair and making his ex-wife laugh.

Oh, please, oh please. Don't let Dave embarrass me.

Ed jumped up. "Oh. Excuse me. Is this your seat?"

With some awkward back-stepping and criss-crossing, the two men switched positions. Dave reclaimed his seat with an air of self-importance, like he had rightly ousted a pretender to his throne.

"Ed, this is Cory and Mariah's dad, Dave Noland," Kay said, unable to introduce Dave with the words "ex-husband."

Ed's eyes flew open wide and was first to extend his hand. "Ed Salinger. Good to meet you."

Begrudgingly, Dave took Ed's hand, gave it a cursory single pump. "Oh. Right. We spoke on the phone the other day. Somehow I pictured you much older."

Ed let out a good-natured laugh. "Yeah. I get that a lot. I'm the junior."

"Sorry?" Dave said, clearly oblivious to the meaning behind Ed's explanation.

"Oh, nothing. I better let you two get back to

your coffee. I'm gonna be late for my set. See you Monday, Kay. Nice meeting you, Don."

"Dave," Dave corrected. But Ed didn't hear him. In typical Ed fashion, he hurried to the counter to get his coffee, shaking his head and muttering to himself.

Kay wanted to laugh at Ed's deliberate insult. He had a stellar reputation for never forgetting a name or a face so she couldn't understand why he felt the need to dis Dave. It was out of character for the man who was a stickler for holding to the principals of the Dale Carnegie How To Win Friends and Influence People program, of which he was a proud graduate. Nevertheless, she was disappointed to see him go.

"What a jerk," Dave sneered. "You know he's got a thing for you, don't you?"

Little sparkles of delight tickled Kay's insides at Dave's cynical observation. But she quickly dismissed the idea when she remembered Dave's history during their marriage of accusing any male crossing her path as "having a thing for her," and referring to them as either a "jerk," "joker" or "clown." As tempting as it was, she knew better than to entertain feelings for her boss. She let out a derisive snort.

"No really. Trust me. It's a guy thing."

"Whatever," Kay said, sounding just like Cory. "Are we ready to get down to business?"

With a look of hope and dread on his face, Dave nodded.

Kay inhaled deeply. "So here's the deal. I'm going to do the talking and I want you to sit there and

208

listen without interrupting. It's important I get through this because I may never get the chance again. Agreed?"

"Agreed," Dave said.

Dave shifted uncomfortably in his seat waiting for Kay to begin. The cold, hard stare she was giving him seemed to last an eternity.

"First of all, I want to say that in light of all your previous failed arrangements with me - marital, parental, financial and otherwise, I think you have a lot of balls asking me for, yet, another pass for your unacceptable behavior."

Kay could tell he was fighting an impulse to look away, but somehow, managed to hold her unrelenting gaze.

"You have proved to be cruel, dishonest, unreliable and untrustworthy. Not exactly the most desirable traits to bring to the table when making the type of proposal you've presented me with."

"I know you thought I was stupid and gullible last September when I jumped at your original offer without giving it the due diligence it demanded. But I did it for a reason, Dave. After seven years I thought we had an opportunity to build a new relationship based on our old friendship." Then her voice got quiet. "You see, even though I'd accepted the end of our marriage, I just couldn't wrap my brain around never being friends again - that the only role you'd play in my life would be adversarial. Up until the time you met Sandy, we were pretty good friends, don't you think?"

Dave looked blankly at Kay. She felt slighted by his non-response, but pushed on.

"Knowing me like you do, I believe you took advantage of my unresolved feelings."

Dave started to object, but Kay put up her hand.

"Come on now, Dave. Give me credit for knowing *you* like I do."

"It's taken me awhile, but I've finally realized my hope for any new alliance with you just isn't going to happen. Sandy will never allow it and, let's face it, you're just not that into it either.

Kay had been resisting these thoughts for some time, and giving voice to them only underscored their difficult truth.

"You asked me to think about it and I did. In fact, it was all I could do. For days, now, I've wracked my brain and searched my soul and the only conclusion I could come to was I've earned the right to be selfish."

Dave crossed his arms across his chest and finally took his chance to look away. Kay waited for a moment said, "Dave? Dave, are you listening?"

He looked back at her like a sullen teenager, and quietly said, "yes," then looked away again.

"As I said, I decided it's my turn to be selfish - but probably not in the way you're thinking."

That got his attention.

"I've decided it's time for me to take matters into my own hands."

Dave slowly sat up in his chair as he watched Kay feel around under the table for her purse. A look of terror passed over his face when he realized she'd found what she was looking for and began to slowly pull it out.

"Kay, please don't do this," he pleaded. "I think we can resolve our issues without resorting to violence."

He ducked when her arm flew out from under the table. A white, letter-sized envelope sat in the pinch of her thumb and index finger.

Dave looked as if he was going to have to excuse himself to go home and change his underwear.

Kay roared with laughter. "Violence? Oh my god. Did you think I was going to shoot you?"

Dave managed a wimpy shrug and a sickly smile.

"Either your conscience is really hurting, or you see me as one crazy bitch." The laughter continued.

For the next few moments Kay enjoyed a good laugh at Dave's expense, until he'd had enough. "Alright, Kay. You've had your fun. Like you said, let's get down to business." He reached for the envelope that had dropped on the table, but Kay slapped it down before he had a chance to pick it up.

"Hang on a minute," she said. "Before I show you the counter-proposal I've drawn up, it's important for me to explain my whys and wherefores."

This time Dave couldn't control himself. He rolled his eyes.

Kay snatched the envelope from the table and

got up from her chair. "Ok. I can see we've wasted each other's time. If you can't keep your agreement to hear me out, why should I believe you'd stick to any new arrangement? Maybe it'll be better, all the way around, to just abide by the judge's ruling."

"Wait, Kay. Please," Dave said with alarm. "It was just a reflex. I shouldn't have done that. Please sit down. I really do want to hear what you have to say."

Kay's heart was pounding and tears were stinging the corners of her eyes. She hated his ability to cut her to shreds with the smallest of gestures. But today, for some strange reason, she was able to hold on to her composure. Maybe it was because she was bolstered by her rare position of power.

Even though every bone in her body was screaming at her to walk right out of that coffee shop, she just couldn't resist playing out the rest of her hand. For dramatic effect, she hesitated a moment or two, then slowly sat back down. She picked up her coffee cup, peered inside and said, "I need some more coffee."

Dave jumped up. "Sure. No problem. Let me get it for you." He took the cup from her hand and rushed to the refill station. Kay smiled to herself, letting the thrill of her new-found authority deliciously cascade over her.

Setting a record for all-time fastest coffee refills, Dave returned to the table and carefully placed the cup in front of Kay. He took his seat with a look on his face that reminded Kay of a cocker spaniel waiting to be petted and praised after returning a tossed stick. Unfortunately for him, a polite, "thanks," was his only reward.

All it took was a quick sip for Kay to realize she was coffeed-out. She banished the cup to the far side of the table without regard for her eager server's feelings. If Dave took any offense, it was undetectable.

"So…you were getting ready to tell me about your selfish proposal," an anxious Dave prompted, then quickly corrected, "I mean, about how and why you came up with a counter proposal."

Kay found his reddening cheeks quite gratifying.

"Yes…well," she began, clasping her hands together and placing them on the table. "As I said, I decided it was my turn to be selfish. But the more I thought about it the more I realized it wasn't as straightforward as all that. It's true a selfish "no" would get me a pile of cash and some delicious, vengeful satisfaction. Not to mention I'd avoid looking like a first-class chump in front of my family and friends who want to see me stick it to you."

As quickly, but casually as he could, Dave put his hand over his mouth and nose to stifle a derisive snort.

Good boy.

"But then I realized saying "yes" would also be selfish. I'd get a big fat ego stroke by swooping in to play the hero to my poor, floundering ex-husband - not to mention an even bigger pile of cash after five years."

Dave continued to sit and listen, while doing his best to control his reactions.

213

"But the more I thought about it, the more I realized both selfish choices leave a lot to be desired. They just aren't selfish enough, if you know what I mean."

Dave sat back. "No, Kay, I don't know what you mean. In fact, I'm completely lost."

"Well, the thing is, I'm still a single parent with two girls who require a lot of time and attention. The help I asked you for back in September hasn't gone away." Kay let out a little chuckle and said, "You probably don't realize it but I got spoiled by how well our original agreement worked in the beginning. It really made my life so much easier." Then she sighed and said, "If only you'd stuck to it, we wouldn't have had to go through all this crap and we wouldn't be sitting here right now."

Now it was Dave's turn to sigh. "Kay, I wish you could appreciate my situation. I have demands pulling me from twenty different directions."

Kay just shook her head. "How the hell do you expect me to appreciate your situation when all I get are lies and half-truths? Look, I did my best to work with you until you went and shit on everything. It's not my fault you have a habit of ruining the good things in your life."

It wasn't Kay's intention to go down the road of, once again, defending their marriage. She knew she had to keep things on track; she picked up the envelope, opened the flap and pulled out a one page, double-spaced, type-written form. "I've drawn up a counter-proposal, that I believe, not only meets my parental assistance needs, but satisfies my selfish desires, as well."

She handed the paper to Dave, who snatched it out of her hand.

"I realize I'm taking a big a chance by not having it drawn up by my attorney and I'm sure your lawyer wouldn't be too keen on having you sign this without his review and approval. I just couldn't see adding anymore to our already-bloated legal bills.

Kay stayed quiet and allowed Dave to read all the stipulations she'd laid out in exchange for her acceptance of the deferral of his outstanding back child support.

THIS AGREEMENT (the "Agreement") is entered into effective as of _____ _____, 20__ by and between <u>Dave Noland</u> ("Party#1") and <u>Kay Manning</u> ("Party#2").

In consideration of the mutual covenants set forth herein and other good and valuable consideration, the parties agree as follows:

I. {Fees, Payments, etc.}. Party#1 agrees to pay Party#2 <u>Ten thousand dollars ($10,000) at twelve percent (12%) interest deferred over five (5) years</u>.

"**TWEL**..." Dave started to shout, but looked around the room and quickly got control of himself. "Twelve percent?" he said, slightly choking on the words.

Kay knew her demand for more interest was going to piss him off, but she knew she had nothing to lose. If he wanted her cooperation it was going to cost him.

Dave's eyes went cold. "Looks like your

friends and family are going to get their wish. You just love sticking it to me, don't you?"

"No. What I'm loving is finally standing up to you and not being the push over you were counting on. If you choose to see it as me "sticking it" to you, I guess there's nothing I can do about that. Please continue."

The rest of the agreement was basically a written statement of their original agreement with a few new stipulations:

II. {Other terms/conditions}. 1. Party #1 agrees to pay one half of Cory's tuition for her school's Summer Honors program.

Kay knew she should have asked for the whole amount, but her over-developed sense of fairness overruled her.

2. The reduction in child support during the summer visitation will be reduced by 1/3 instead of the court ordered 2/3, since Cory is not participating.

3. Party #1 agrees to make arrangements to have Cory picked up from summer school and driven home.

5. Party #2 reserves the right to ask for Party #1's financial assistance with any unexpected expenditures relating to the children.

6. The parties agree to meet on a quarterly basis to review the agreement and make changes as needed.

> 7. Any egregious breach of the agreed stipulations by Party #1 will render this agreement null and void and the original court order will be reinstated.

"Well?" Kay asked, beginning to get a little anxious.

"Why didn't you ask for this stuff when we were in mediation?" Dave said.

He's got a point there.

"I don't know," Kay said with a shrug. "I guess it was because I was so upset over what the girls told the mediator."

Invoking the girls' interview was a convenient dodge - and a low blow. The truth was Kay hadn't even formulated the requests until after Dave had asked for the deferment.

With his resolve to be good wearing off, Dave looked back at the paper in his hand. "Well, it's obvious you never went to law school...Applicable Law... Construction...Counterparts...Parties Bound...Mutual Understanding...Force Majeure," Dave read under his breath. "Where did you come up with this cheesy form?"

He was trying to embarrass her, but it wasn't working. "It's a template I downloaded from the internet," she said matter-of-factly, "and it suits the purpose just fine."

Dave continued to look at the paper as if he was giving it serious consideration; Kay knew he was stalling. Since there wasn't anything he could reasonably object to, he tried the only delay tactic left to him. Patting his chest with both hands he said, "I don't have a pen."

"Not necessary, " Kay said. "We're going across the street to the bank to sign it in front of a notary."

Kay returned the form to the envelope, gathered her purse and with a clear sense of purpose, set out to lead a two-person parade toward the exit of the coffee shop.

"Hold up, Kay" Dave said, looking at his watch. "I didn't realize it was so late. I promised Sandy I'd watch Little Dave while she ran some errands. Look. Why don't I meet you at the bank first thing Monday morning?"

Kay cocked her head, ever so slightly, to one side and smiled. *Gotta run it past Mommy first?*

The red tinge from a few minutes earlier made a reappearance across Dave's cheeks.

"Alright, "Kay replied. "Except let's meet at the south side branch of Community Fidelity Credit Union. It's on my way to work. Say 9:00?"

"I'll be there," he said. The relief in his voice was difficult to miss.

With nothing more to say, Kay simply gestured "good-bye" and hurried to the Ladies room to give her bursting bladder some much needed relief. When she came out she was glad to see Dave was gone. She headed for the door, anxious to get home, but was stopped by a worker behind the counter.

"Excuse me Ma'am," the young woman said.

"Yes?" Kay replied, wondering if Dave had

218

forgotten to pay for the coffees. *Wouldn't put it past him to stick me with the bill.*

"The man you were sitting with asked me to give you this." She picked up a small, white styrofoam to-go box and held it out to Kay. Kay took it from the woman and looked inside. It was piece of banana bread.

It was all she could do to keep from melting, right then and there, into a big puddle of delight - not because she was going to get to eat another piece of delicious baked goodness, but because Dave had done something thoughtful and personal just for her. And this time it couldn't be about ulterior motives. She had been clear and tough about what it was going to take to get her cooperation. This had to be a gift from his heart.

We really are still friends.

Kay hurried toward the corner cross walk with a lighter step, but fighting with the top of the styrofoam box to keep it from popping open. She had almost reached the small group of people waiting for the light to change when she spotted Dave at the front of the pack. There still time to catch him and thank him for his sweet gesture.

Trying to be as non-intrusive as possible, she carefully inched up through the tiny gathering until she was standing directly behind him. She was about to reach up to tap him on the shoulder when she realized he was on his cell phone.

"Yeah...I finished sooner than I expected. How does an early lunch at Le Chantecler sound? Say 11:30?" Dave said. His voice was dripping with syrupy sweetness.

Hmmm…French food as penance for spending time with me. Très veule.

Pause, then a chuckle.

"Wait'll you see the stupid proposal she wants me to sign. You're right. She really is an idiot."

Pause.

Dave laughed. Then he lowered his voice and said in a throaty whisper, "Me too."

The light turned green and everyone made their way across the street. Everyone, that is, except Kay. She just stood there staring at broken pieces of banana bread and the empty styro-foam box lying at her feet.

16

Aloha Oe

"Mom," Cory yelled from upstairs. "Are you finished with my bibbers yet? Violet's gonna be here any minute."

Kay had just tied the finishing knot on the hem of Cory's band uniform and was cutting the thread with her teeth. She looked up just in time to catch sight of Cory coming down the stairs dressed only in her band uniform jacket and shako, knees bent in full plié, attacking each step with alternating feet.

"I think you should go dressed like that," Kay kidded. "Your band would win first prize for sure."

Mariah, who was sitting on the floor at the coffee table eating a bowl of cereal and watching Saturday morning cartoons, looked over at her sister. "Eeew, gross," when she saw Cory's state of half-dress. "Her teacher would kick her out of the band for sure."

"He's the band director, not the teacher, Stupid," Cory snapped.

Kay turned the newly-hemmed bibbers right-side-out and gave them a quick inspection before tossing them at Cory.

"I'm the one who made the joke, Cory. Do you think I'm stupid?" Kay asked.

Cory shot her sister a dirty look before contritely answering. "No. She just drives me crazy with all the stupid stuff she says."

Kay frowned. "You know, I'm getting real tired of that word. Genuinely smart people choose better vocabulary or know when not to say anything at all."

In true teen-age fashion, Cory ignored her mother's admonishment and busied herself with removing her jacket so she could slip into her bibbers.

"Do you think Dad's gonna come today?" Cory called out from the bathroom, double-checking her mom's handiwork in the full length mirror.

"I asked him when he dropped Mariah off last Sunday, and he said he was planning on it," Kay called back.

Ever since they'd signed the agreement a little less than a month before, Dave had remained steadfastly-cooperative and friendly, even making a point to hang back for a few minutes of conversation every time he picked up and dropped Mariah off. It was surprising since Kay had angrily rebuffed his attempt to negotiate a lower interest rate and reduce his child support payments by pushing Cory to spend the summer with him.

Truth was, after hearing his disparaging comments that day on the street corner, Kay had agonized over whether it was wise to go through with signing the agreement at all. She had always known Dave and Sandy talked about her in denigrating terms; to hear it first-hand was a whole new kind of "ugly." Her humiliation was such she was tempted to invite her old friend, Denial, back to put a comforting spin on the whole distasteful situation. Fortunately, Kay discovered the phony psychological device was no longer effective - which could only mean she really was moving forward. Humiliation wasn't fatal and, banana bread gifts aside, Dave was not, nor would he ever be, her friend again. Getting the agreement signed was the important thing and was in the best interest of everyone involved.

It was ironic now that Kay had finally gotten her wish for a more amiable Dave, she could barely stand to look at him, let alone allow him to chat her up. A recent cancellation of Mariah's weekend visit because of an out-of-town trip, almost caused Kay to do an impromptu jig knowing she wouldn't have to see or talk to him. These days, the only satisfaction she derived from their "relationship" was his adherence to the agreement.

The door bell rang and Cory tore for the door to greet Violet. The two friends stood there, talking a mile a minute, gushing compliments and assessing each other's level of nervousness. Violet's mom honked the horn.

"Bye, Mom," Cory said, starting to close the door. "Wish us luck."

"Aren't you forgetting something?" Kay asked.

Cory stood there for a second then snapped-to. "Oh my god. My horn!" She dashed up the stairs and just as quickly returned with her instrument case.

Kay held the door for her daughter. "Be sure to thank Bonnie for me and tell her we'll bring Violet home after the competition."

"Mom," Cory said, drawing out the vowel in a whiny sing-song. "She already knows that."

"Tell her anyway. We'll see you later. I know

you're going to do just great!"

"Bye, again." Cory ran to jump into Violet's mom's waiting car.

"Watch your plume!" Kay shouted to her excited daughter.

Kay closed the door and looked at the clock. "If you're finished with your cereal, Mariah, turn the TV off, and go take a bath. We have to be ready to leave in about an hour."

"Can I please finish watching Hannah Montana? It's almost over." Mariah whined.

"It'll be on again next Saturday. You can watch it then."

Mariah made a face as she picked up the remote and switched off the TV. "Nah ah," Mariah contradicted. "I'll be at dad's next Saturday. Sandy makes me watch Blues Clues with Little Dave. I never get to watch what I want." The little girl walked over to Kay, threw her arms around her waist and buried her face in Kay's chest.

Kay lifted Mariah's chin and looked down into her perturbed little face. "I'll put in a good word for you next time I see Dad. Ok?" After all, Dave seemed to be going out of his way to be amenable to Kay's requests and suggestions.

"Ok," Mariah said. "But I don't think it'll do any good."

Kay pulled Mariah's arms away and playfully smacked her on the butt. "Get a move on, young lady. We're gonna go see your sister march."

* * *

224

The District Pageant of Marching Bands couldn't have asked for a more perfect day to hold their year-end competition. Supporters and spectators crowded the stands waiting to be dazzled by Lymon Stadium's transformation into a giant kaleidoscope of stunning symmetrical formations timed to rousing music selections

Kay and Mariah arrived early enough to find seats at the 50 yard line, but up high-enough to provide a superb vantage point. Brightly-colored uniformed kids rushed this way and that, running scales to tune their instruments as they waited for their cue to line up on the field. The excitement was contagious.

This was Cory's first band competition. She was a freshman, but a year younger than most of her classmates, having skipped first grade because of her advanced reading and math skills. Even though she had been first chair trumpet in her middle school concert band, Kay was concerned Cory might not be ready for the rigors of marching band; she needn't have worried. Cory took to it like a duck to water. She told Kay she hoped to be Drum Major by her senior year.

"Mommy, look. I found Cory," Mariah said, pointing to her sister's smiling face in the pageant's glossy program photo. They were busy trying to identify other kids they knew when their concentration was broken by a child's loud tantrum.

"Lemme go. Me lee lone. I want Riah. I want Riah."

Kay and Mariah both turned and looked over and up about ten rows to see Dave and Sandy trying to calm a kicking and screaming Little Dave.

Kay had prepared herself for the probability of running into Dave; she never expected to see his wife and little boy. This was the first time she'd seem them together in family formation; it caused little ripples of nausea to rise up from her stomach. She forced herself to swallow the rush of saliva in her mouth, and plastered a friendly smile on her face.

You can do this.

She waved hello.

"It's ok if Little Dave wants to come and sit with us," Kay hollered up to the fussing boy's parents. What she really wanted to do was call security and have them all forcibly ejected. Anyway, it was highly unlikely Sandy would allow her precious little child anywhere near Kay's vicinity.

Not surprisingly, they ignored Kay's greeting.

Kay turned to Mariah. "Do you want to go up and sit with your little brother?" She hoped Mariah would say no. But the little girl, always happy for any chance to be with her dad, jumped up and side-stepped down the row, carefully avoiding the brush of people's knees.

Kay watched Mariah until she reached the aisle, then quickly snapped her attention back to the beautiful pictures in the pageant program. She couldn't bear to see Mariah join her other family. She stared intently at the program's pages but nothing she was looking at registered. Despite being surrounded by a stadium full of people, Kay suddenly felt completely and utterly alone.

I can't let them ruin this for me.

To her great relief, the first band took the field and she was glad to have something pleasant to focus her attention on. Kay checked the program and saw it was an entry from one of the smaller high schools in the district. The band was correspondingly-small but they were putting on a big show.

Kay wondered what kind of magic they used to get all these kids to walk and play so precisely, when she couldn't get Cory to carry her laundry downstairs without dropping half the items on the way. Their deft footwork was mesmerizing to watch. Back, forward, sideways, diagonal. circular - all on the beat to a fabulous medley of Latin music. Unfortunately, someone in the drum line, carrying a set of four drums (that Cory later told Kay was called a "quad") lost his footing during their performance of "Turn the Beat Around" and tumbled head-first over his drums, knocking everyone down in the line in front of him.

Kay felt really bad for the kids who had probably been practicing for months, but giggled at the hilarious tangle of arms, legs and band instruments. She decided it might be better if she took her laughing self to the concession stand lest she offend any band member's parents who might be sitting nearby.

She searched the crowd for Mariah to let her know where she was going and to see if she wanted anything. Kay spotted her several aisles away, supervising Little Dave as he climbed up and down the steps of the stands. The resentful look on her face said it all.

She's missing the show.

227

Kay waved and called to Mariah, but there was just too much going on to get the little girl's attention. Kay decided she'd get Mariah something to eat and drink and then rescue her from her banishment to Babysitterville.

I'll probably be back before she even notices I'm gone.

As Kay entered the tunnel that led to the concession court, she was greeted by a deliciously-cool breeze offering penance for the unrelenting intensity of the morning sun. She slowed her pace and moved to one side so she could stop and relish the pleasant flow of soft air without blocking traffic. It turned out to be the perfect spot to get in some long, overdue people-watching.

Kay relaxed and allowed herself to become carried away by all the lively comings and goings. At first it seemed to be a mish mash of chaotic activity. But then Kay noticed the people seem to organize themselves into recognizable categories.

First, were the losers in the "short straw draw" game to designate the food go-fer. They all had the same, put-upon looks on their faces and a large box cradled in their arms. The box consolidated a sizable order of drinks, popcorn, candy, nachos, fries, hot dogs and, the occasional, giant dill pickle.

Then there were the harried moms trying to bribe tired, bored, thirsty, hungry little children into behaving with the promise of their favorite treat.

Next were the teenagers, who never bought anything, but used the food court as a safe place to congregate and feel less awkward in the company of

228

their equally-awkward peers.

Finally, there were the husbands who'd been dragged to the event against their will, escaping to the only place, besides the restroom, they could be alone. These guys walked extremely slowly, taking long, deliberate sips from their drink straws.

A couple of little girls suddenly streaked past, snapping Kay out of her diversion.

Mariah's probably at her wits end.

She was about to continue on her way to the concession stand when she someone behind her said, "How 'bout that pile-up? Let's just hope that doesn't happen to Cory. It'd be humiliating, don't you think?"

It was Sandy. A haughty smile and deep tan made Sandy's overly-whitened overbite look more prominent than it probably was. Her pompous demeanor clashed with the sweetness of the embroidered kitty cat sleeping on the bib of her denim jumper.

Kay had imagined this moment countless times. Over the years she had purposely avoided situations where they might have to meet face to face, knowing she'd be subjected to Sandy's attitude of entitled superiority. Well here it was and, so far, it wasn't all that terrible. Kay wondered why she'd been so afraid.

"Well, I guess anything can happen," Kay said with a nonchalant chuckle, "but Cory's band director has won this competition the last three years in a row, so I'm not too worried."

"Three years? You don't say. Isn't that

fascinating?" Sandy said.

The hairs on Kay's neck suddenly stood up and, instinctively, she knew she'd do well to bring their encounter to a quick conclusion. As casually as she could she said, "I was on my way to get something for Mariah and me to drink. I hope the lines aren't too long." Kay made her move, praying Sandy would turn left at the top of the ramp and proceed to the restrooms.

"I know what you mean," Sandy said, falling in step with Kay. "I was going to get some sodas for my little brood, but since you're taking care of Mariah, I'll just let you handle that one."

God forbid you spend an extra buck-twenty-five on her. She's watching your brat for you!

Kay tried to lose Sandy by jumping into the first short line she came to; Sandy remained close behind. Kay stared intently at the menu on the wall, trying to discourage any further conversation. The list of greasy, salty selections made her still-queasy stomach pitch in protest. Or was it the unsettling presence of her uninvited escort?

A cold lemon/lime soda ought to settle everything down.

Sandy, leaning uncomfortably close to Kay's backside, nevertheless, continued to prattle on. "I wish this line would move quicker. I hate the thought of my boys out in the hot sun. I told Dave to wear a hat, but you know how stubborn he can be. I had the same argument with him last week when we were in Maui."

Kay felt her feet go ice cold. Had she heard

230

right? They went to Maui?

Oh my god... the tan.

Kay felt sucker-punched, but held on to enough of her wits to hide her confusion from Sandy. She became acutely aware of the concrete surface pushing up hard against the bottom of her shoes.

The line moved, but Kay stood there frozen.

"Excuse me ma'am," an elderly gentleman leaning out from behind Sandy said to Kay. "I believe the line is moving up."

Kay forced herself to shuffle forward; the thought of refreshments at that moment piqued her fluctuating nausea. Rather than give in to her intense desire to collapse right there in a sick heap, she decided to confront the situation head-on.

Kay turned back to Sandy and, as dispassionately as she was able, said, "Ooh. You went to Maui. That's why Dave canceled Mariah's weekend."

I could've sworn he said he was going out of town for work. Or did he? Oh god, I can't remember.

Sandy treated herself to a wicked, self-satisfied smile. "That romantic husband of mine took me on a second honeymoon to Hawaii, complete with a gorgeous beach-front villa and our own private swimming pool." She punctuated her audacious statement with two, "take that" bats of her eyelashes.

But how? Dave - he - I - he CRIED for pity sake! His creditors...his mother...

Kay could feel the color drain from her face. She was beginning to lose her grip, but hung on by her fingernails.

Of course, Sandy being the cunning predator that she was, smelled blood. "Kay? Are you ok?" she asked, testing her suspicions.

Kay managed a weak smile. "I'm fine. I was just trying to remember something…"

Kay stood there desperately praying Sandy would just continue on with her mission to rescue her overheated "boys," and leave her alone. But once a beast smells blood, they have to go in for the kill.

"I guess I really should be thanking you. Dave would've never been able to take me on that trip if you hadn't agreed to wait for your back child support." Sandy turned up the evilness dial in her smile.

Kay's head was swimming. "Say what?" she said louder than she'd intended.

She can't possibly think I did it as a personal favor to Dave.

Sandy brought her face up close to Kay's and snarled. "Look, Kay. My husband worked hard for his bonus. It wasn't fair that the judge said he should give it to you."

Bonus? What bonus? There was never any mention of a bonus.

Kay's initial devastation was quickly turning to outrage. "I'm not sure what you mean about a bonus. Dave simply owed money - *to the girls* - and the judge ordered him to pay it."

Sandy moved back. "That stupid agreement you forced Dave to sign gave you everything you wanted. Why shouldn't he get a little something?

I got everything I wanted? Then why are you still here?

"Here you guys are," a familiar voice wailed. From out of the circulating throng of people, Mariah emerged with a crying Little Dave in tow.

"Little Dave won't stop crying for Sandy. Dad told me to come and look for her."

"My god, can't I have five minutes to myself without a search party being sent out?" Sandy said. She snatched Little Dave's hand from Mariah. "Go tell your dad I'll be right there," Sandy barked.

Kay wasn't going to allow Sandy to take up one more second of Mariah's morning. She was officially relieving her of duty. Kay put her hands on Mariah's shoulders and gently pulled her close. "I think it's best if Mariah stays with me now. It's almost time for Cory's band performance and I don't want her to miss it."

Sandy glared at Kay, then at Mariah, then back at Kay.

"Next!" came the cry from behind the concession stand counter.

With a big huff, pulling her little boy behind her, Sandy shoved past Kay and walked up to place her order. Normally, Kay didn't tolerate line-cutters, but she was still reeling from Sandy's stunning revelation. Cutting ahead in line paled in comparison to having your ex-husband take his new wife to the one place he had always promised to take you but never got around to it. And not only did he take her on *your* dream vacation, he tricked you into paying for it.

Try as she might, Kay couldn't get the picture

of Dave and Sandy lying on the white sand of a gorgeous Maui beach at sunset out of her head. She felt a jagged arrow rip through her heart as she imagined Sandy laughing up at Dave as he exclaims, "You're right. She really is an idiot."

Well, she'd have to be if they were able to slip a bonus past her and her attorney. For a brief moment she considered calling Judith and raising a stink. But then she remembered the notarized agreement, created without benefit of legal counsel. It would be too humiliating to admit to her lawyer she hadn't learned her lesson the first, second OR third time.

Her life, since last September, flashed before her eyes. The pain and humiliation were almost unbearable. But the more she thought about it, the more she realized it wasn't Dave's repeated offenses causing her anguish. It was the fact he'd succeeded in shattering her belief that she'd finally moved on and he couldn't get to her anymore.

"*Just when I thought I was out...they pull me back in.*"

For a moment, Kay thought the corners of her mouth might just turn up at the gangster movie quote that popped in her head. Unfortunately, the scene she had just played out with Sandy wasn't from a movie, and she wasn't Michael Corleone. The smile didn't come.

"Next!" *Exactly. What next?*

Kay felt as if she was drowning. She had no recourse. There was nowhere to turn. She was locked in. So she did the only thing available to her in that moment. She took Mariah's hand, pushed down another wave of nausea and ordered a large popcorn and two sodas.

17

New Old Friends

Kay kept her eyes peeled on the blinking tail lights of the motorcycle escort being forced to avoid oblivious, disrespectful drivers whizzing past their motorcade. The last thing she needed was to be the cause of a ten-car pile up. She sighed, dismayed that all the fun had gone out of driving the hearse.

Maybe a little "Stayin' Alive?"

She popped her Saturday Night Fever CD into the car's player but instead of resurrecting her customary funeral procession merriment, the pulsating, infectious beat only annoyed her. She hit the Stop button and drove in glum silence.

Probably more respectful to my passenger, anyway.

If there was one bright spot in this moment, it was the fact she was away from the office and didn't have to deal with the daily email from a guilty Dave. She could feel his desperation screaming to her from the Subject line. It usually said "I'm So Sorry" or "Can We Talk?" but she never bothered to open them; she already knew what he wanted - and it wasn't to beg her forgiveness for making a fool out of her. He was simply frantic to stop Kay from invoking Article 7, Section II of their agreement.

While he hadn't actually breached any of the stipulations, they were both aware the agreement was based on a pack of lies. To her way of thinking, that was enough to render the entire thing null and void. She just didn't know how binding their notarized document was or wasn't. But as long as he was unsure too, she was going to avoid him as long as possible. Her confidence had been completely shattered.

But those emails weren't the only reason she was happy to be away from the mortuary. She still loved her job but ever since (or maybe because of) her accursed run-in with Sandy the previous month, the mortuary had become an inhospitable place to be. Nothing seemed to be the way it once was - everything had gone out of focus and she was having trouble fitting back into the picture. She felt disconnected and lonely.

Kay was dying to reach out to Ruth but her usually-supportive friend seemed to be otherwise preoccupied and unavailable. And it just wasn't Ruth's distracted presence that had Kay flummoxed. Ruth's matronly appearance had undergone a surprising and unexplained transformation of late. Gone was the ever-present tight, gray bun and in its place sat a saucy, short do, colored in warm, light brown tones. And instead of drab, shapeless dresses and unattractive polyester pantsuits, Ruth was now sporting figure-flattering fashions in a variety of eye-pleasing colors. Something mysterious was going on.

Kay didn't feel comfortable butting into this new Ruth's personal business. She just sadly accepted the fact their friendship had, for whatever reason, returned to pre-marijuana intervention days.

Ruth's makeover wasn't the only puzzling change at Salinger's. Ed's attitude toward Kay had, inexplicably, gone cold and "all business." She couldn't be certain, but he even seemed to go out of his way to avoid her when possible.

At first she was hurt and disappointed. She kicked herself for entertaining the possibility that Dave's comment about Ed "having a thing" for her might be true. But then she figured it was probably best not to go down that path. Her dad's voice of experience echoed in her head. "Never shit where you eat."

Still, would it kill him to smile at me every now and then?

Then there was Uncle Owen. He had turned his humiliation at trying to buy Kay's silence into outright hostility. Kay found out that knowing people's secrets was a dicey situation to find yourself in. Now she understood why witnesses in murder trials so often turned up dead.

Oh my god. What would Owen do if he found out I knew about the limousine?

Leo was the only one who didn't treat Kay as if she was an alien from the planet Zeebo. He seemed to sense Kay's displaced state and went out of his way to draw her back in. His attempts were obvious and awkward, but Kay appreciated his effort.

After the morning's funeral service, Kay hid in the break room hoping for a quiet lunch. She didn't have much of an appetite so she sat there absentmindedly pulling little pieces of crust off her sandwich, and stacking them into small pyramids. When Leo arrived he took one look at Kay and debated whether or not to disturb her; she looked so forlorn he just couldn't resist.

"Hey, Kay," Leo said. "Guess who I saw the other day?"

Kay stared blankly at Leo, not really interested in playing along.

He pulled up a chair next to Kay, scooted in closer and lowered his voice. "It's someone with a juicy secret you and I have talked about before." He sounded like a game show contestant trying to get his partner to give the winning answer so they wouldn't go home with the consolation can of Simonize.

Awwww. How sweet. He's trying to bribe me with dirt about Uncle Owen.

She wasn't exactly in the mood to gossip but she couldn't leave Leo twisting in the wind. His puppy dog expression was just too pitiful.

"Ok, Leo." Kay said with a sigh. "I give up. Who did you see the other day?"

Leo sat up straight and smiled with satisfaction. Kay thought if he'd had a tail he would have wagged it.

"Lindy O'Malley."

At first, the name didn't register with Kay. Then it all came rushing back. The streaking dog. The immovable body. The ashen-faced police officer wilting to the ground before her eyes. Their disgraceful escape.

Kay shuddered. "Did she talk to you? What did she say? Did she bring up anything about that night?"

Leo laughed and shook his head. "She came into Gil's the other morning when Frank and I were having coffee. She walked over, real friendly-like and said hello."

"Hello? She just said hello?"

"Well, no. Not just hello," Leo said.

Kay could feel her heart racing. She didn't know how she'd ever explain her irresponsible behavior to Ed. If he was unhappy with her now, she could only imagine how he'd react if he knew she'd left the scene of an accident.

Well, I guess, technically it wasn't an accident.

"I got the feeling *she* was the one worried about being ratted out. I could tell by the way she was looking at my eyes. You know, kinda like she was waiting for me to say something." Leo said.

"And did you?"

"Did I what?

"SAY SOMETHING," Kay shouted.

"Of course I did. I had to." Leo said.

Kay's racing heart dropped to the floor.

"I said it was nice to see her again. Oh, yeah. I asked her about the drug bust that went down the other night on Sherwood."

Kay wondered how Leo could be so intuitive and yet so dense.

The sigh of relief Kay expelled felt good. She realized she must have been holding her breath for a while.

"You know, I forgot how pretty she is." Kay could hear the wistfulness in Leo's voice as it trailed off. It triggered alarm bells in her head.

"You can't possible be thinking of asking her out again," she snapped. The instant the words left her mouth Kay regretted making such a self-serving statement.

"I'm sorry, Leo. I had no business saying that. Its just that…"

It's just what? That I'm just an idiot who lets her selfishness get in the way of making good decisions?

Leo smiled sweetly at Kay. "Oh, forget about it. No harm done." He patted her on the shoulder. "I know you've been a little stressed out lately."

Kay choked up at Leo's display of kindness.

"Anyway, I think she already has a boyfriend." Leo said.

Kay wondered if that was really true or if Leo said that just to put her freaked-out mind at ease.

"Listen," Leo said standing and pushing his chair under the table. "You hang in there. Everything's bound to get better."

"Thanks, Leo," Kay said with a couple of sniffs. "Aren't you going to eat?"

"No time. I'm picking O up at his house. We're taking that ship-out to the airport."

Before he left the room, he grabbed a bottle of water and a can of root beer out of the fridge.

"Oh. In case Ed asks, I left twenty minutes

241

ago," Leo said.

Kay simply nodded, doubtful Ed would even acknowledge her, let alone ask about Leo's time of departure.

The remains of her sandwich were wrapped up and placed back in the fridge.

I might be hungry by afternoon break.

Kay had toyed with the idea of asking Ed for the afternoon off so she could finish getting Mariah packed for her summer visitation with Dave; with the mound of unfinished paperwork sitting on her desk, approaching him with such a request would be asking for trouble.

As she walked up the hallway towards her office she could hear the phone ringing unanswered. She looked back and saw that Ruth's chair was empty so she ran to her own desk to pick it up.

"Salinger's Mortuary. Kay Manning speaking."

"Kay! Just the person I wanted to talk to. Hello. This is Virginia Voorhees. How are you?"

Aaw jeez. Kill me now.

"Hello, Virginia. How nice to hear from you."

"Listen, I won't keep you. I know you're busy at work. I was just calling about the annual fundraiser for our local Boys and Girls club."

"Oh, yes," Kay said. "I remember reading something about it in your last newsletter."

Yes. I still read your newsletter, even though I don't come to your meetings.

Virginia explained she was on the board of directors for the organization and was contacting everyone she knew to ask for their participation in the giant flea market they were planning for the last Saturday in June.

"We need donations, so if there's anything around your house you'd like to get rid of, we'd be happy to take it off your hands."

For the second time that day, Kay felt as if she'd been brought to the brink, then rescued from disaster.

Dave is right. I am a drama queen.

"Well, I can't think of anything specific right off the top of my head. But I'm sure if I do a little rooting around I'm bound to find something you could sell."

Since Kay was being let off so easily, she vowed to herself to find (or buy) something of value to donate.

"That's just great," Virginia said. "We're asking donations be dropped off no later than Friday, the 21st."

"Where should I bring them? Kay asked.

"We have drop off locations at all the Boys and Girls clubs around town."

"Actually, there's one not too far from where I live," Kay said.

"Wonderful," Virginia said. There was a pause. "Kay, there's one more thing I wanted to ask you."

Oh boy. I knew it. Here it comes.

The intercom beeped and Kay politely asked

Virginia to go on hold for a moment.

"Yes?" Kay said through the speaker.

"It's your daughter on Line 2," Ruth announced.

"Will you tell her I'll call her back?" Kay said

"I'd be happy to." Ruth responded with her Kay's-friend voice. It gave her pang of longing for their friendship.

She took a deep breath before bringing Virginia back on the line.

"Sorry about that. You were going to ask me something?"

"Well, I was just wondering if you'd be willing to donate a couple of hours at the flea market? We have a shortage of volunteers to work the tables."

Kay was so relieved she wasn't going to be pressured to face (or smell) Delbert Schumacher at another meeting, she answered with a resounding, "Sure!"

"I just knew I could count on you," Virginia said. "Like I've said before, you have that positive energy people respond to."

There she goes with the energy thing again. I wish I knew what she was talking about.

Virginia wrapped up the conversation by saying she'd be in touch with the schedule for the flea market volunteers. Kay hung up, pleasantly surprised their conversation had left her feeling better than she had earlier in the day...or the last couple of weeks for that matter. Now she understood why Ed immersed himself in civic activities and causes. It felt good.

With a smile on her face and a warmth in her heart, she dialed her home number, happily anticipating the sweet voice of a daughter - it didn't matter which.

"Hi, Mommy." It was Mariah.

"Hi Stinker. What's goin' on?"

"Dad just called. He reminded me not to forget to pack my bathing suit." Mariah said.

"I didn't forget. It's already packed." Kay said.

"I know. I found it in the suitcase. But, Mommy, it looks really little. I don't think it fits anymore."

That's right. She's grown a lot this year.

Kay was tempted to tell Mariah just to have her dad buy her a new suit. Then she thought it might be nice to spend a little mother/daughter shopping time together before Mariah left for the summer.

"No problem. Why don't we go to Ocean Blue after dinner and see if we can find you something new and pretty." Kay said.

"Really, Mommy, really?" the little girl said with glee. "Can I get a two-piece this time?"

Kay thought how pissed Dave would be if his little girl showed up with a bikini.

"We'll see," Kay said, then quickly added, "but I'm not promising anything." She figured there'd be no harm in checking out the two-piece suits in Mariah's size.

"What time will you be home?" Mariah asked.

"The usual time. Make sure you and Cory have the house picked up by the time I get there. I want to fix dinner and eat right away so we'll have plenty of time to shop."

Kay had barely hung up the receiver when she heard it ring again, followed by a pause, then the buzz on the intercom.

"Telephone, Kay. Line 2."

It's probably Cory calling to complain about having to pick up the house.

"Hey, Sis. I hope I didn't catch you at a bad time," Leslie said.

Kay was delighted to hear her sister's voice, but felt twinge of guilt. Leslie still didn't know about the Dave and Sandy debacle. Kay knew she should have told her but in her current state she couldn't bear being the recipient of Leslie's inevitable (and justified) outrage.

"Hey, yourself," Kay said. "I'm glad you called. I wanted to remind you Mariah is leaving Friday for her summer visit with Dave."

"Is it that time already? Poor thing." Leslie said with a laugh. "So I guess it's just going to be you and Cory for the summer?"

"More like, just me. Cory has a jam-packed schedule with summer honors classes and all the things she's planned with her friends," Kay said.

"She's really growing up, isn't she?" Leslie said.

246

"Yeah, and I don't know how I feel about it. I mean, on the one hand it's great to see her blossoming into a young adult. But then it hits me I'm losing my baby." Kay said.

"Aaaaww. Don't kid yourself. She'll always be your baby," Leslie said.

Kay swallowed the lump that had swelled in her throat.

"So to what do I owe the honor of your call?" Kay said..

"Well, I don't know if you're aware, but it's been almost a year since you promised to come to a networking luncheon, and I've yet to see your pretty face grace one of our tables."

"I don't know if *you're* aware, but its been almost a year since you've invited me." Kay responded.

They both burst out laughing.

"Well, I'm calling to invite you now. Is there any way you can make it this Friday? That social networking guy is making a return appearance by popular demand."

Kay knew Leslie was expecting to hear the usual excuses from her, but she couldn't pass up the opportunity for a much-needed diversion. She hoped surrounding herself with enthusiastic, self-assured women might just work on her like a tonic. And given the topic, she knew it would be an easy sell to Ed.

"Sounds perfect," Kay said truthfully. "I'm sure Ed will let me off. We're still fumbling around with our own social networking. It'll be good to pick up some tips and pass out some business cards."

"Seriously?" Leslie said. "You're really coming?"

"Sure. Anyway, how else am I going to get to see my little sister?" Kay said.

"Ok. Great. We start at 11:30. Try to get there a little earlier so we can catch up." Leslie said.

"Will do. See you then."

"Hey, Kay," Leslie said before Kay could hang up. "I'm really looking forward to seeing you."

"Me too, Kiddo." Kay said softly. She was reminded how good it felt to be Leslie's sister.

Kay basked in the warmth of her familial comfort until the feelings were abruptly pushed away with Ed's hurried appearance in her office. He was taking a shortcut on his way to the break room. From the far away look on his face, Kay knew there was no plan to acknowledge her.

Even though she was scared, she knew she had to stop him before he sped out of the room; she might not get another chance.

"Excuse me, Ed. Can I talk to you a sec?" Kay asked. She tried to hide the fear in her voice.

Ed stopped, turned and looked at her as if she had just sprung up from out of the ground. His eyes retained their distant expression, but he gave her his practiced business-man smile and slowly approached her desk.

Leaning down to her he said, "Sure Kay. What can I do for you?"

He hadn't been this close since that Saturday at Percolatté. The scent of his cologne was intoxicating and she found herself having to clear her throat, not once, but twice.

Kay gave him a brief overview of her request to attend the luncheon and before she had a chance to sell him with all the beneficial details, Ed cut her off.

"That's fine. Just let Ruth know and make sure we can reach you on your cell." He ended with another brief perfunctory smile and quickly went on his way.

Kay was glad he'd given his permission for Leslie's lunch, but crestfallen because he'd been so impersonal. She wondered how or if she'd ever be back in his good graces again.

* * *

A sharp pain shot through Kay's twisting ankle as the spike of her heel found its way into a small hole in the pavement of the country club parking lot. She was late and Leslie was probably going to be pissed.

If I didn't know better, I'd think the Fates were trying to tell me something.

Thirty minutes earlier she had run out of gas and her attempt to coast into the station on fumes had failed right at the entrance. Fortunately, a guy filling up his truck took pity on her and ran over to help push the car to the first available pump. With a sigh of relief, Kay slid her credit card in and out of the processor only to hear a loud beep along with a message that read "See Cashier Inside."

Kay got in back of a long line slowly inching up to pay the lone cashier for their gas. Some of these people were so happy to finally get their turn at the counter they greedily hung on to the coveted spot, taking their time ordering nasty-looking burritos, cigarettes, gum, lottery tickets and scratchers. Kay looked at the time on her cell phone and knew her catching up session with Leslie would have to wait until after the luncheon.

Leslie, had been coordinating these business networking events for the last ten years and they'd turned out to be so successful Leslie had added two more groups.

Ankle throbbing, Kay hobbled up the stairs to the dining room, just happy to finally be at the venue. As she neared the door she could hear the enthusiastic cackling of women as they swapped business cards and pitched each other whatever new line of skin care, jewelry, purses, cookware or mortgage loans they were currently in business to sell.

Kay signed in and pasted the "Hello I'm..." badge to her blouse and scanned the room in search of her sister. She spotted Leslie at the table-top podium preparing for the guest speaker. Kay started out for the safety of her familiar face. She had never been comfortable "schmoozing" with strangers.

She was inching through the clusters of gabbing women when she heard, "Kay...is that you?" Kay spun around to see her old friend, Tina Chalmers, standing there, both arms held out in astonishment.

"Oh. My. God!" Kay screamed just like a fifteen year old girl. She ran into Tina's outstretched arms. They alternated between hugging, pushing back, looking at each other, screaming and then resuming the embrace.

Tina Chalmers was a gorgeous, vivacious brunette with the bluest eyes Kay had ever seen. She had a sweet disposition and wicked sense of humor which had bonded them in friendship from the moment they'd met. Their relationship had thrived during and after Tina's employment as the receptionist at Dave's office. They had even been pregnant together, with her son Mark coming into the world only a couple of weeks ahead of Mariah. When Tina resigned to have her baby, Sandy was hired as her replacement.

Kay often teased Tina about being the cause of her divorce. "It's all your fault. If you hadn't gone and gotten yourself pregnant, Dave would've never met Sandy," But it was all said in fun. Kay and Tina would laugh, shake their heads and chalk everything up to the strange workings of the Fates.

It was exactly those workings that allowed the two friends to drift apart, lose touch, and now come together again almost ten years later. It felt as if no time had passed.

"You haven't changed one bit," Kay said. "It's not fair."

"How about you?" Tina countered. "You're as gorgeous as ever."

"Me? Have you looked in the mirror lately?" Kay said.

"Ok. Ok. We can be here all day. Let's just agree we're both fabulous and get on with it," Tina said.

They both laughed and the familiarity felt good. After inquiring about their respective kids and marital status, they filled each other in on what they were doing to earn a living.

"I'm a leasing agent for a property management company," Tina said. "The hours are crazy but I really love it. How 'bout you?"

Kay's face turned somber and she lowered her voice to a whisper. "I see dead people," she said.

The look of horror on Tina's face told Kay the "dead" joke had, once again, missed its mark.

She laughed and gave Tina a reassuring pat on the hand. "I'm kidding. I'm working as an apprentice funeral director."

"Oh, thank god," Tina said with sigh of relief. "I thought maybe you'd lost your marbles since the divorce."

"Well, if I had, it'd be all your fault." Kay retorted.

They giggled again.

"I'm dying to know more about your job...no pun intended. Sounds fascinating." Tina said. "I'd ask you to sit here but our table is filled. How about after?"

"No worries. My sister is holding a seat for me at her table anyway." Kay said.

They gave each other's shoulders one last squeeze and let out a delighted squeal. Any concerns about omens from the Fates had now completely evaporated.

The food was great, the speaker quite

informative and Kay was able to exchange numerous business cards with a minimum of weird reactions. One woman, delighted to receive Kay's card said she'd be calling to make an appointment to prearrange her father's funeral.

IF, Ed asks, I'll have something positive to report.

As it turned out, there wasn't going to be an opportunity for Kay and Leslie to do much visiting beyond their time together eating lunch. Leslie had to rush off for a dental appointment, but promised to call Kay that evening. Kay was disappointed but relieved she'd been spared (for the time being) having to answer any questions about the current status of her situation with Dave.

With Leslie's departure, Kay now had extra time to visit with Tina before getting back to work. The two sat happily chatting amid the noise of tables being cleared. When it was time to leave, they exchanged business cards and Tina made Kay promise to call for a lunch date as soon as possible. The two locked elbows as they walked together through the parking lot. Kay was so happy to be reunited with her old friend, she didn't even feel the throbbing pain in her ankle. The Fates had brought them back together, and Kay couldn't help but wonder, this time, where it would lead.

18

Intentional Hanky Panky?

The people walking up to the office building turned their heads and stared as Kay skipped to her car with big, carefree strides - like a child on their way to recess. She didn't care.

The next time I see Leslie, she's getting a big sloppy kiss.

A few days earlier, during their catching-up phone call, Kay had finally come clean to Leslie. She'd braced herself for a blistering lecture, but instead was consoled by an outpouring of tender sympathy and support. Kay was ashamed she hadn't given her sister the benefit of the doubt.

"I'm sorry. You must get tired of seeing this movie, over and over again," Kay cried.

"Sure. Don't you?" Leslie said, trying to make her bereft sister laugh. When she didn't get the response she was looking for Leslie said, "Look, you've got to admit you learn something new each time you see it. Anyway, this replay stopped in the middle. Have you forgotten where the story goes next?"

Kay blew her nose, thought for a minute. "Are you saying I should go back to the lawyer?"

That was all Leslie needed to hear. She let loose her bossy little sister side and told Kay it was time for the amateurs to get out of the way and allow the experts to put things right.

Kay vehemently protested on behalf of her pride and potential embarrassment; Leslie countered with a forceful reminder. "Judith Kline makes her living by dealing with the dirty details of divorce. I'd be willing to bet this isn't anything she hasn't seen a million times before - if not worse."

And with that, Leslie won the argument.

Kay felt compelled to be vague with Judith Kline's receptionist about the reason for requesting an appointment. She didn't know how she was going to explain her royal screw up. She needn't have worried. Once she saw the welcoming, non-judgmental expression on her attorney's face, the whole story came pouring out - Dave's tearful plea, her agonizing deliberations, and her ultimate decision to come up with a new agreement. When she finished she presented the signed, notarized copy of the agreement for Judith's review.

The lawyer respectfully studied it then smiled at Kay - but not in a condescending way. "You may have missed your calling, Kay. As far as legal documents go, this looks pretty good."

"Don't give me too much credit," Kay said. "The internet can be a pretty amazing resource."

"I said it *looked* good...I didn't say it *was* good." Judith said. "Remember, the official decree is already on file with the court."

Kay could feel her cheeks getting hot. She knew how ludicrous the whole thing must seem to a real attorney.

"I know, I know," Kay said. "It's just that I've been desperate to prove to myself and everyone else

255

I've moved on - that the only thing I'm interested in is having a good working relationship with the father of my children. All I really ended up proving is I'm the same patsy Dave's always been able to count on to give him what he wants. I'm just afraid if we continue to relate to each other on this disingenuous basis, we're going to be frozen forever in that moment when he left me."

Kay turned her head; she needed a moment to get hold of her emotions. She looked out the window and spotted a cat crouching on a retaining wall. It was wiggling its butt in greedy anticipation of the moment it would pounce on an unsuspecting bird pulling a worm from the grass. The cat made its move and the bird and its worm were history. Kay sighed and looked back at Judith.

"What it all comes down to, Judith, is I'm divorced and I need to start acting like it." She took a deep breath and declared, "It's been brought to my attention there was a substantial bonus left out of Dave's financial report to the court and I'm here to see what we can do about it."

Judith showed no visible reaction. It was almost as if she'd been expecting Kay's news. "I'm not surprised, Kay. It's very common for one spouse to conceal assets from the other. I see it in my practice all the time," Judith said. "It's good you came to see me when you did. In this state, there's a time limit within which we're able to seek post-judgment relief. I'm going to immediately petition the judge to set aside the decree until we can get verification of the bonus from Mr. Noland's employer."

"And the agreement? I'm sure Dave's going to

argue that it's binding."

"I wouldn't worry about that," Judith said. "Granted, it's likely the judge isn't going to be too happy about you taking matters into your own hands...again, but I think he's going to be more concerned with this new information."

Kay felt a zap of panic as she remembered the judge's contempt of court threat.

Judith went on. "The legal presumption will be that the undisclosed asset was deliberately concealed. In cases like this, it's not uncommon for 100% of the asset to be awarded to the injured party."

Well, if I'm thrown in jail, at least I'll be able to make bail.

"Of course, that is unless the presumption is overcome by the non-disclosing party," Judith added.

"What does that mean?" Kay asked.

Judith laughed. "That means Dave and his lawyer are going to have to tap dance really fast if they're going to convince the judge there was no intentional hanky panky."

But Kay couldn't laugh. She still had unanswered concerns.

"Would we be pushing it if we asked the judge to include the stipulations from my agreement into any new decree? I mean, with the exception of the deferment, of course," Kay said. As much as she wanted to win, she didn't want to lose Dave's parental assistance.

Judith shook her head. "The court deals, primarily, with equitable distribution of assets, debts and child support. They don't like to get in the middle of parenting issues. The judge will consider the matter of the bonus and anything else he'll expect you to work out in mediation."

"You mean he'll send us back?" Kay said, dismayed at the prospect of another face to face negotiation with Dave.

"He will if we request it." Judith said.

Kay looked out the window again. The cat was back on the wall, licking its chops.

"Fine," Kay said. "If that's what it takes to get something Dave won't dare to screw with, then let's do it."

Judith stood and extended her hand to Kay. "I'll get started on our petition straight away. You'll be hearing from me as soon as I know how the judge wants to proceed.

Kay took Judith's hand, hoping to impart her gratitude through a firm, but gentle, grasp. Judith seemed to understand. She gave Kay a look of reassurance. "Just know, Kay, you're not the first person to go through something like this." Then she chuckled. "If all divorcing couples were as reasonable as you, I'd probably be somewhere, bored out of my mind, practicing tax law."

* * *

Kay smiled at the small, colorful bouquet of fresh flowers she'd placed on the night stand next to Mariah's bed. She took a couple of steps back to check her work and bumped into Cory standing in the doorway.

"Really, Mom? Flowers?" Cory said. "She's just coming home for the weekend. She's not a guest at Kay's Bed and Breakfast."

Kay ignored her daughter's snippy remarks and adjusted the flower placement a couple-more times before she was satisfied.

Cory continued to poke. "Hey, we learned a cool fanfare in band this year. Sounds good on the trumpet. Want me to play it when she gets here?"

Kay refused to get pulled into Cory's immature display of sibling rivalry. Just for good measure she smoothed imaginary wrinkles from Mariah's comforter and fluffed her pillow one more time.

"You'd have had flowers by your bedside too, if you'd gone to your dad's like you were supposed to," Kay said, without turning around.

She bristled inside at Cory's sarcastic remarks, especially since Cory had barely spoken two words to her over the last two weeks. Summer school, fun with friends, and the radioactive perimeter around Cory's bedroom had kept mother and daughter at a distance. Nevertheless, Cory had had her mother all to herself and she wasn't happy about the upcoming change in her special circumstance.

Kay straightened up and turned to say something but realized Cory had already retreated to her bedroom. She sighed.

At least she didn't slam the door.

The display on Mariah's bedside Tinker Bell clock read 5:23. Kay had just enough time to freshen up and change her clothes before she had to jump in the car for a punctual 6:00 pick up at Dave's.

Sandy's probably champing at the bit to be rid of Mariah for the weekend.

Kay was tempted to drag her feet and arrive for Mariah at a time of her own choosing but she just couldn't bring herself to play those kinds of games. She often wished she was a person of more dubious character, but her mom and dad had been too diligent with her upbringing. Not to mention it would have been cruel to leave Mariah there one second longer than necessary.

Kay's pulled in front of Dave's house at precisely 5:57. This was her first visit to her ex-husband's home since his return to town the previous fall. She looked around the exterior premises, surprised to see it wasn't as elaborate as she'd imagined; it was a nondescript, brick tract home. However, the freshly-mowed lawn and well-tended flower beds soaking up gentle drops from a lazy sprinkler created a picture of sweet domesticity that made Kay's stomach clench.

Working on the yard had always been one of Kay's favorite things to do with Dave when they were married. He had even taught her how to start up and maintain the power mower. She pictured her own, previously-neglected, front yard and felt another twinge. It was looking pretty good these days. But the guy from Green Shovel Lawn Care worked alone.

Kay got out of the car and as soon as she spotted Mariah jumping up and down in the front window, her discomfort evaporated.

Mariah came flying out the door before Kay had a chance to make it up the walkway to properly call for her. Apparently, this was not a problem, as the front door was quickly closed (slammed?) behind her. Mariah sprinted into her mother's waiting arms and hung on for dear life.

"Where's your bag?" Kay asked.

The door opened. The bag magically appeared on the doorstep. The door closed.

Kay just shook her head. She thought it was a shame adults had to act like this in front of impressionable children. Mariah didn't notice. She was still clinging to her mother.

Kay finally got Mariah to let go long enough to get her in the car. It was a joyous ride home with Mariah full of exuberant tales of adventures with new friends at day camp. But nothing compared to the level of happiness Mariah expressed once they were back at home. Even Cory seemed to be glad to see her little sister. Of course, Cory's warm spirits could have been due to the fact she was leaving for a sleepover at Violet's.

"I'm hungry, Mommy. Do we have anything to eat?"

The request, which typically grated on Kay's nerves, was now music to her ears.

"How does spaghetti sound? It's already made. I just have to warm it up." Kay said.

"Did you make garlic bread too?" Mariah asked.

"Would I give you spaghetti without garlic bread?" Kay said with a laugh.

Kay sent Mariah upstairs to deposit her bag and get reacquainted with her room. She pre-heated the oven and then opened a bottle of Chianti. She was reaching into the drawer for the table place mats when she heard Mariah say, "Wow...flowers."

Suddenly Kay thought about Cory's bed and breakfast comment. She wanted Mariah to feel at home and not like a guest, so she called up to her and asked her to come down and set the table. The little girl cheerfully complied

They were just getting ready to sit at the table when Violet appeared at the door to collect Cory. Kay could tell Mariah was delighted about Cory's departure and her turn at having her mother all to herself.

"Mmmmmm. This is really good," Mariah said.

Kay enjoyed watching Mariah vacuum up the long noodles which left cute spaghetti sauce tracks on her chin. Kay was enjoying the simple meal as well, made even better by her glass of full-bodied wine. Kay relaxed back into her chair and finally asked the question she'd been holding back since they'd pulled away from Dave's house.

"So how are things going between you and Sandy?" Kay said, hoping the question wouldn't provoke a negative turn in the light-hearted mood at the table.

"Sandy's been in a really good mood, Mommy. She hasn't gotten mad at me, not even one time."

Yeah. I imagine Maui has that effect on people.

According to Mariah it seemed Sandy's magnanimous spirits even extended to the next door neighbor, Mr. Knash, whom she and Dave, reportedly, couldn't abide. Mariah told Kay that Dave and Sandy called him "Mr. Trash" and complained about him being "phony-nice" just so he could poke his nose into their business. Dave and Sandy's overt cold-shoulder behavior was enough to give the sensitive Mariah a stomach ache.

"Mr. Knash says hello in the drive way and Sandy and Dad answer kinda snotty and get in the car real quick."

But apparently, there had been a recent change of heart. Mariah told Kay that just the day before, Sandy had "been real friendly" to Mr. Knash when he talked to them over the fence separating their two backyards. "And I could tell she wasn't pretending, Mommy."

"Why do you say that, Honey?" Kay said.

Kay's mouth dropped to the floor when Mariah launched into an explanation complete with elaborate scene reenactment.

"Little Dave and I were playing in his pool and Sandy was getting a tan. She was on a towel reading her book like this." Mariah got up from the table and walked over to the living room where she laid on her stomach on the carpet. She propped herself up on her elbows, bent her legs at the knees and alternated them in slow, languid kicks. Her semi-cupped hands supported an invisible book.

"Mr. Knash walked over to the fence and said, "Well, hello, Neighbor." I think Sandy was real happy to see him, cuz she looked up and gave him a great big smile." The little girl stood up and as she walked back to the table a cloud passed over her face. She sat down and was ready to take another mouthful of spaghetti when she stopped. "She never smiles at Dad like that. I think he'd be mad if he knew Mr. Knash was looking at Sandy in her bikini," Mariah said.

What? No flouncy denim one-piece?

Kay could tell by the tone in Mariah's voice she was beginning to become aware of the lurid side of adult behavior. Kay hated to see her little girl lose her innocence. She struggled to come up with something that would soften the little girl's concern.

"Well, it's probably good they're getting along. There's nothing worse than feuding with your neighbors."

As for Mr. Knash ogling Sandy in her bikini…well Kay wasn't prepared to adequately address that issue. So, she plastered over the awkwardness by introducing a new subject.

"Hey guess what?" Kay said. "I'm going to be helping out at the Boys and Girls' Club flea market tomorrow morning. I thought you might like to come along and be my assistant."

"Oh, did Dad call you about it?" Mariah asked.

"What? No! Why would your father call me about it?" Kay said.

"He's gonna be there too," Mariah said.

Absolutely, flippin' fantastic.

"I don't get it. Since when did your dad become interested in the Boys and Girls Club?"

Dave had always been quite vocal about his aversion to participating in any kind of organization - youth, civic, religious or otherwise. If memory served her, it all stemmed from some mysterious, traumatic experience with the Cub Scouts.

Probably made fun of his macaroni sculptures.

"Since he put me in their summer day camp," Mariah said. "I told you, Mom. I go there everyday."

Did I miss her saying it was Boys and Girls Club?

"I heard him tell Sandy somebody squeezed him and he got stuck helping out," Mariah said.

Kay giggled. "Do you mean, somebody put the squeeze on him?

"Yeah. Somebody put the squeeze on him." Mariah said. She took another big bite of her dinner.

This was news Kay hadn't expected. Since that day his wife had exposed his dirty dealings, Kay had managed to avoid a month of Dave's imploring emails and frantic phone messages. As far as she was concerned there was no explanation, no apology, NOTHING that could induce her to reestablish communication with him. Even though his attempts to contact her had eventually stopped, she knew she was bound to be in for a new round of harassment once he found out she was taking him back to court.

The noodles in her mouth turned to rubber. She felt a panic coming on and was overcome by an intense impulse to call Virginia and say she'd contracted a horrible, disfiguring disease. The thought was forced out of her mind by a flashback of her avowed declaration of independence to her attorney.

An electrifying current of empowerment surged through Kay which, strangely enough, began to calm her down. The more she thought about it, the more she realized an encounter with Dave at the flea market would be the perfect opportunity to trot out her new "divorced" persona. And if, by chance, she faltered, she knew Mariah's presence would be the ideal deterrent to any unpleasant confrontation.

"So, whaddya say? Wanna go?" Kay said.

"Do I get paid?" Mariah said.

Kay laughed. "We're volunteers, Honey. But I'll tell you what. If you do a good job, I'll take you to the Cream Queen, afterward, for a banana split."

The buzzing vibration of an incoming text on the phone in Kay's pants pocket caused her to drop her fork and let out a startled yelp. Her comical spasm caused spaghetti to blow out from Mariah's lips.

Did u 4get me already?

It was Tina Chalmers. Kay cringed when she read the text; she *had* forgotten.

Yes But not on purpose

Kay was completely at ease being truthful with Tina.

Oh. So u did it on accident?

Kay laughed at Tina's playful tease. After all these years, Tina had remembered one of Kay's most annoying pet peeves - the increasingly-common, improper use of "accidentally."

LOL Let me make it up to u Lunch next week on me

God, I hate texting. Where's the punctuation

266

on this stupid thing? Kay struggled to tap out even the simplest message.

> I'll call you next week to confirm
>
> Sounds good

"I thought you said it's rude to text at the table," Mariah said

Kay quickly shoved her phone back in her pocket.

"It is rude. I apologize," Kay said.

"So who was it?" Mariah asked, still shoveling food into her mouth with gusto.

"Excuse me? Now who's being rude?" Kay said.

"Oh sorry," Mariah said, putting down her fork, chewing then swallowing. She took a sip of water and checked to make sure her mouth was empty. "So who was it?" she asked again.

Kay burst out laughing.

"I swear, Mariah. Sometimes you're just too cute for your own good. I meant it was rude to ask who I was talking too."

The little girl's cheeks turned as red as the spaghetti sauce on her chin.

Kay felt bad about embarrassing Mariah. "I'm sorry, Honey. I didn't mean to laugh at you. Anyway, it's not anyone you know. Just an old friend of mine." Kay said. Kay knew it had been too many years for Mariah to remember Tina.

A reassuring pat on the hand from her mom was all Mariah needed to return to her contented mood and the rest of her spaghetti.

"Hey mom? Can I stay up tonight and watch Friday Night Frights? They're playing Dead Zombies Society. Alisha Resnick says if I watch it I can be in her club."

Kay could tell Mariah was trying to act older and bolder in the face of an intimidating initiation from this Alisha Resnick. Kay was tempted to say yes, knowing the first few eerie bars of the opening music would probably send Mariah running for the safety of her mother's bed. She decided to let Mariah completely off the hook by reminding her of their upcoming community service assignment.

"We're going to have to be up by 6:30. If you stay up late, I know it'll be a fight to get you out of bed. Let's save the zombie movie for some other night. Ok?"

The look of relief on Mariah's face confirmed Kay's suspicion. She was still too young for frights on Friday - or any other night. And just in case Kay was right about Alisha Resnick too, she was happy to provide Mariah with a valid excuse.

After clearing the dishes, Kay poured herself another glass of wine and she and Mariah settled on the sofa for some non-flesh-eating TV entertainment. Thirty minutes later Mariah was sound asleep with her head in her mother's lap. Kay scooped Mariah up and smiled sweetly, but sadly, at the sight of her rapidly-maturing daughter. She knew it wouldn't be long before carrying Mariah upstairs to bed would become an impossibility.

19

What's the Scoop

"Watch your fingers, Mariah!" Kay shouted, as the little girl attempted to extend the legs on the plastic folding table. "You almost got pinched." Kay carefully locked the legs in place before she and Mariah righted the light-weight table. With their task finished, Mariah asked to be excused, saying she'd be right back.

Kay was beginning to question the wisdom of volunteering for the early shift at the flea market. When she'd first agreed to Virginia's request, she had pictured herself in the coolness of the June morning, standing behind a table of beautifully-arranged, reasonably priced treasures, sipping coffee, and smiling sweetly as she offered assistance to eager buyers.

Her intention had been to avoid the heat of the blazing afternoon sun and boredom of the, sure to be, slower stream of customers. It never occurred to her she'd be helping with the labor-intensive set up. Contrary to Virginia's complaint of a dearth of volunteers, there were plenty of enthusiastic helpers happy to be pitching in for a good cause, including several members of Executive Connections.

Kay was amazed to see everything come nearly all-together by the 8:00 am starting time. For the first half-hour a tiny trickle of people slowly made their way around the community garden grounds which had been transformed into a large area of commerce. They had managed to sell out almost every booth and table space. Nevertheless, Virginia paced back and forth, worried her advertising campaign might have fallen short. But it didn't take long before hoards of shoppers swarmed tables and booths. The competition was fierce to be first to grab some perceived prize which would likely show up at a yard or garage sale the following weekend.

Kay picked up the box containing the only two items she felt worthy of donation and placed it on the chair next to her. One was a kitchen clock with the face of a large orange slice sitting in an orange-painted wooden frame, and an old-fashioned ice cream churn. Both items had been purchased by Dave at the beginning of their marriage and were still in perfect working order. The personal treasures held wonderful memories for Kay. As much as it pained her, she told herself letting these things go would be an important symbolic gesture. So she wouldn't be tempted to keep them, Kay made sure to price them to sell.

With loving care she lifted each one out of the box and gently placed it on the table.

"Is that what I think it is? I haven't seen one of those things in years."

From out of nowhere, Delbert Schumacher appeared at Kay's side, dressed in the crazy houseboat outfit of her imagination. If she hadn't been so shocked at his sudden appearance, she would've laughed at the accuracy of her imagery.

He picked up the ice cream churn, turning it this way and that, and admiring it with just a little-too-much enthusiasm.

270

He took one look at the price sticker and blurted, "Two dollars?" He put the churn back down hard on the table and looked at Kay with that same menacing face she'd seen that night in Virginia's kitchen. "What's wrong with it?"

Kay snatched up the churn to inspect it for damage and move it away from Delbert. "Nothing. That is, 'til you slammed it on the table." Kay said. She wanted to kick him in his black socks-covered shins.

Kay was repositioning it back on the table when she heard a familiar voice say, "That ice cream churn sure does bring back a lot of memories."

Kay looked up to see Ed, standing on the other side of the table, wearing the smile he'd been withholding from her for such a long time. "We had one of those when I was growing up. I used to think my arm would fall off from cranking that handle."

Kay smiled back, too flustered to respond. Ed took pity on her and turned his attention to Delbert, who was staring daggers at him. Ed was unfazed. "Are you gonna buy it? If not, I'd like to have it," Ed said.

Delbert harrumphed. "Well, you know what they say. Caveat Emptor. Anyway, my doctor has restricted me from eating ice cream."

Ed shook his head. "What? No ice cream?" he said. "That's brutal."

It was obvious Ed was busting Delbert's chops, but because of his charming delivery, Delbert ate up the faux sincerity. Kay could tell by the encouraged look on his face, Delbert was getting ready to launch into his lactose-intolerant spiel, so she spoke first. "The churn works perfectly, Ed. I just don't have much occasion to use it anymore and I hate to see it going to waste sitting in the cabinet."

Delbert looked at Ed, then at Kay. In a tone that was borderline accusatory Delbert said, "Well. It's obvious you two know each other. Aren't you going to introduce us, Kay?"

The thought had already shot through Kay's manners-conscious mind, but she was embarrassed for Ed to know about Delbert and the Executive Connections connection.

"Where are my manners?" Kay feigned. "Delbert Schumacher, meet Ed Salinger. Mr. Salinger is my boss."

Delbert' eyes opened wide. "Oh. Right. I thought you looked familiar. You took care of the funeral services for my ex-wife's uncle."

Ed smiled and nodded as if he remembered exactly who Delbert was referring to.

Delbert leaned forward and narrowed his eyes. "Tell me something, Ed. I've always wondered what that bronze casket set the family back. Seems like such a waste of money just to bury it in the ground."

Ed had heard questions like these a thousand times and it never bothered him. But right now, Kay was the one who was bothered. She didn't want Ed to dignify Delbert' boorish question with a response and she didn't want to explain her association with Delbert. So she punted.

"I'm sorry I don't have a box for the churn. Is a

272

plastic bag ok?" she said.

There's that smile again.

"Sure, no problem. But you might want to double bag it since it is kind of heavy."

Kay was all thumbs as she fumbled with the balled-up nest of plastic grocery bags she'd pulled out from under the table.

"Why don't you let me help you with that." Ed said. He walked around the table.

I think he enjoys making me nervous.

Delbert wasn't hiding his annoyance at the chummy scene between Ed and Kay. "Kay, shouldn't you take the money before bagging up the merchandise? I mean, after all, that's why we're here."

Kay turned to Delbert with her own version of menace. "Delbert, shouldn't you…"

Ed knew she was about to say something hateful, and ever the diplomat, interjected. "You're absolutely right, Delbert. That was totally my fault. Here, Kay." He reached in his pants pocket, pulled out a thin, folded wad of bills, peeled off a couple of ones and handed them to Kay.

"That's what I love about participating in these events," Ed said. "We have such dedicated volunteers helping us out. I'm going to be sure to mention your name at our follow up board meeting. It's Schumacher, right?"

That's why Ed's here. Duh.

Delbert's chest puffed out and all traces of

disagreeableness disappeared.

"D e l b e r t," Virginia called and waved from several tables away. "If you're not busy, I could use your help over here."

Eager to confirm Ed's opinion of him as a dedicated volunteer, Delbert turned to Ed and Kay. "You'll have to excuse me. But as you can see, I'm needed elsewhere." He made a crisp, 180 degree turn and sped off to answer the call of duty.

Kay chuckled. "For a minute there, I thought he was going to salute."

"He seems like an O.K. guy to me," Ed said. "A little goofy, but ok."

Kay didn't want to talk about Delbert Schumacher any more. She wanted to know why Ed was being friendly to her again. She was about to pose a question to open up the topic when Mariah walked up, accompanied by a chubby little girl Kay didn't recognize.

"Hey, Mr. Salinger. I didn't know you were going to be here." Mariah said.

"Mariah! How nice to see you." Ed nodded in the direction of Mariah's companion. "Who's your little friend?"

Mariah's companion rolled her eyes at the "little" reference.

Kay was annoyed Mariah had been gone so long. "Mariah, where have you been? You said you'd be right back."

"I'm sorry. Mom. I saw Alicia over by the popcorn stand and I wanted to say hi." Then true to her mother's training she said, "Mom. Mr. Salinger. This is Alicia Resnick. Alisha, this is my mom and her boss, Mr. Salinger."

It was hard for Kay to stay mad at Mariah when she demonstrated such beautiful manners.

"Hu'lo," Alisha muttered, eyes on the ground, completely uninterested.

Mariah wasn't finished with her introduction. "Mr. Salinger owns a mortuary. He and my mom work with dead people all the time."

Kay immediately picked up on Mariah's attempt to impress the implacable Alisha. She winked at Ed and said, "Ah, yes. Alisha Resnick. Mariah tells me you know a lot about zombies. We've been trying to tap into that market for awhile, but there just doesn't seem to be any interest. Maybe you could give us some suggestions?"

Alisha gave Mariah a look of fury, then turned back to Kay and Ed.

"Uh…uh…I gottago." The little girl sped away and disappeared into the crowd.

"Wait, Alisha!" Mariah called after her friend. "My mom was kidding."

Mariah turned back to her mom with a look of dismay. "That wasn't funny."

"Neither was trying to get you to watch Dead Zombies Society," Kay said.

Ed turned his head and pretended to be busy with his newly-purchased package. He didn't want Mariah to detect his amusement. Kay couldn't understand why he was still hanging around. As one of the people in charge of the event, Kay assumed he'd be running around like Virginia and would have little, if any, time for socializing.

Could it be he wants to talk too?

Kay grabbed a handful of ones from her purse and handed them to Mariah. "Here. Go find Alisha. Tell her your mother has a weird sense of humor and then buy her a funnel cake."

Mariah was only too happy to comply. With a friendly wave to Ed the little girl went in search of her embarrassed friend.

"Heh, heh. Kids," Ed said. He was peering into the bag with the ice cream churn as if it might spontaneously produce ready-made cones.

"Yeah…they can be pretty funny," Kay said.

A chasm of awkward silence opened between them. After a few uncomfortable moments, Kay decided to dive across and close the gap by being the first to speak.

"Ed, can I ask you a question?" she began.

He responded in the affirmative but Kay could hear the apprehension in his voice.

"For a quite a while now, I've had the feeling I've done something to displease you. Up until this morning, you've barely even acknowledged my presence - unless you were absolutely forced to."

"That's not a question," Ed replied, his mood turning serious.

"I know." She cleared her throat and regrouped. "It just seems that ever since that morning when we saw each other at the coffee shop you've done everything in your power to avoid me."

Ed mumbled something Kay couldn't hear. "Sorry?" she said,

He finally turned and looked at her directly in the eye. "Look, Kay. When I hired you I saw the potential for an exceptional funeral director and I was excited about having you as my apprentice."

Kay could feel her heart hit the top of her feet. She was sure he was trying to find a way to tell her she was no longer measuring up.

"I love my job, Ed. I know I still have a lot to learn, but I've tried to apply everything you've taught me to the best of my ability."

Please, oh, please, don't let me cry.

"Excuse me." An elderly woman was holding up a vase with ugly red parrots hand painted on the side. "I don't see a price on this vase."

The timing of the interruption was perfect. Now Kay would have a chance to stave off the tears threatening to stream down her cheeks.

"Here. Let me see," Kay said, gently taking the vase from the woman's gnarled hands. She turned the item upside down, revealing a price tag adhered to the bottom. "It's 75 cents."

With the way the woman reacted you'd have thought Kay had said 75 dollars. "Oh my. That's much too expensive." She peered at Kay and said, "I'll give you 25 cents."

Kay pretended to mull over the offer.

"50 cents and it's yours," Kay countered.

Kay enjoyed haggling, even if it was only for pennies.

For a moment the woman continued to stare sternly at Kay. Then a big grin broke over her face. "You drive a hard bargain. I'll take it."

Kay stood patiently by as the old lady searched for the little coin purse hiding at the bottom of an over-stuffed purse. Then it took a few more minutes to fish out two quarters from within her small ocean of loose change. The two quarters clinked as Kay dropped them into the small metal tackle box substituting for a cash drawer. Kay unfurled a large piece of newspaper, carefully wrapped the vase, placed it into a grocery bag and handed it to the woman with a smile. "Pleasure doing business with you."

Kay turned back to Ed who'd been watching the entire transaction with a bemused grin. "See, Kay. You're a natural people person. I've seen it when you interact with families and I've seen it with everyone at the mortuary. I know for a fact that Ruth and Leo really value you as a co-worker."

Kay looked away. She was embarrassed by the compliment and still confused about where Ed was going with this conversation.

"And what about you, Ed? Do you still feel I'm a valued employee?"

But before he could answer, Mariah walked up looking defeated and forlorn. She slapped the wad of ones back in Kay's hand. "Here. Alisha had to go home." Mariah plopped into a plastic folding chair and pouted. "I'm bored. When do you think dad's gonna get here?"

Ed's posture stiffened. He pulled his cell phone out of his pocket and checked the screen. "Wow, look at the time. I should have been at the registration table 20 minutes ago." He picked up the bag with the churn and started to take his leave but Kay couldn't let him go without knowing where she stood with him.

"Wait!" Kay said, pulling Ed's arm, causing him to drop the plastic bag. It hit the ground with a dull thud. Kay and Ed dove to recover the churn, clunking their foreheads together with a force that knocked Kay back on her butt.

Ed held his throbbing head and scooted over to make sure Kay was alright, then offered his hand. "I'm so sorry. Are you hurt?" he said, as he pulled her up.

Kay was a little dazed - but not so much that she wasn't still concerned about Ed leaving.

"I'm fine," she said rubbing her forehead. "You?"

Ed checked across his forehead with a light touch of his finger tips. "It's probably just a concussion with a minor subdural hematoma. Nothing really to worry about."

In her semi-dazed condition, it took Kay a few beats before she realized Ed was teasing her. But she couldn't laugh. She was too worried about him getting away before she got her answer.

"Too soon?" Ed asked with chuckle.

"How much for this chess set?"

"Do you know where I can find any more of these plates?"

"Hey, Herb. Look at this clock. Wouldn't it go great with my lemon tea pot?"

Kay looked over and saw things were getting busy at the table. She looked back at Ed with pleading eyes. "Please. Can you hang back for just a minute?" she asked.

Kay was able to quickly dispense with all but one indecisive customer. The woman was trying to pick out a pair of earrings for her god-daughter's birthday. As the woman took turns holding up the earrings to her lobe while looking in the mirror Virginia had provided, Kay would look over at Ed, smile sheepishly and shrug. She could tell his patience was beginning to wane.

"How old is your god-daughter?" Mariah, tired of watching the never-ending earring rotation, jumped up to help.

The woman cocked her head and looked at Mariah. Kay thought she was going to admonish her for interrupting. "She's about your age."

"I don't think she'd like any of those earrings you're looking at. They're more for grown-ups, like you." Mariah said.

"So what do you think I should get her?"

"Does she play video games?" Mariah asked.

"I think so," the woman said.

Mariah gave the woman a big smile and

directed her to a box filled with donated, used video games.

"They're real expensive if you buy them new. It takes me a long time to save up just to buy one. But when I buy used ones, I can get more."

The woman was impressed with Mariah's salesmanship and asked her to help her pick out the best games. While the two sifted through the box, Kay edged back over to finish up with Ed.

"I need an answer to my question, Ed. Do you still feel I'm a valued employee?"

Now it was Ed's turn to be embarrassed. It took him several uncomfortable moments to respond.

"That's just it, Kay. I think I was beginning to value you a little too much. It hit me that morning I saw you through the window at the coffee shop. You looked so beautiful and you had the sweetest, most inviting expression on your face."

Once again, she felt those little sparkles of delight bursting from her heart.

"But I don't understand, Ed. When you came to talk to me you were so warm and friendly. I got to work on Monday and you'd turned cold and stony. And you've been that way ever since."

Ed sighed. "I know. I'm sorry. That's what happens when I go into self-protection mode. I was already in over my head when I realized you were getting back with your husband. I didn't think it was right for me to get in the way of your reconciliation. I had to find a way to put a rein on my feelings. I was keeping my distance, waiting for them to go away until I could resume a normal working relationship with

281

you."

Kay was stunned. "Getting back with my hus...? What in the world gave you the idea I was getting back with my EX-husband?"

Ed looked down. "You should have seen yourself that morning. I'd never seen you so strong, so self-assured. You were positively glowing. Then when your hus...ex-husband came to the table acting so annoyed and proprietary, I knew I had walked into the middle of something important. I guess you could call it a "guy thing.""

Kay shook her head and laughed. "Yeah...a guy thing. That's exactly what Dave called it when he said he could tell you were interested in me. But I just sloughed it off as Dave being his usual a-hole self."

"Well, Dave read the situation correctly." Ed said.

"You didn't," Kay snapped.

Ed was taken aback by Kay's sharp tone.

"I'm not reconciling with Dave. I was just there to work out a few left-over legal details. To tell you the truth I was mortified when I saw you."

Ed winced at Kay's comment.

"That didn't come out right. What I mean is I was embarrassed for you to see me with Dave. And I certainly didn't want to introduce him to you."

"For god sake, why not? Were you worried I might embarrass you or something? Ed said.

"Absolutely not! It was quite the other way around. I was afraid you'd judge me on my foolish choice of a husband." Kay replied.

As if he already knew Kay's answer to his next question, a self-satisfied smile crossed Ed lips. "Why in the world would you care what I thought? After all, I'm just the guy you work for."

Kay's heart sped up. She felt completely exposed. But since Ed had made his confession, she thought she might as well come clean too.

"Well, if you must know, you're not the only person here who's been having certain feelings."

Ed's smile grew wider.

"I just didn't think it was a good idea to do anything about them. I mean, we've got the whole work situation, and I've been trying to work through these things with Dave."

Ed turned to Kay and gently grasped her upper arm. The strong but gentle feel of Ed's fingers wrapped around her arm made her want to offer him the other one. She met his penetrating gaze and she felt her knees turn to liquid.

"As Rhett said to Scarlett when she, at long-last, declared her love, "It seems we've been at cross-purposes, doesn't it?" he said.

"*Ed Salinger, please report to the registration desk. Ed Salinger, please report to the registration desk*," the PA system blared across the garden grounds.

Ed dropped Kay's arm and he gave her an apologetic shrug. He reached down for the bag with the churn still on the ground. "I'm in for it now. Should have been there ages ago." He rushed off to answer the summons.

In her exhilarated mood, Kay felt compelled to finish the climactic scene, so she called after him, "Ed...if you leave, where shall I go, what shall I do?"

Ed threw his head back and laughed, not missing a hurried step. In typical Ed-fashion, he called over his shoulder, "Frankly, my dear, we'll have to talk about it some other time."

Kay stood there watching him go, thrilled, but not completely sure what had just happened between them. All she knew was the wait for "some other time" was going to be a long one. And she would relish every agonizing moment.

20

Opa!

Kay strained to see out her car windshield, cursing herself for not replacing the corroded wiper blades when she'd had the chance. The relentless, Monday morning downpour didn't help her dispirited mood. Saturday's exhilaration over her encounter with Ed had given way to worry and doubt. The more she thought about the prospect of starting something romantic with him the more she realized the complications involved would surely spell trouble. But then again, if she spurned him, things at work might become even more awkward than they'd already been.

With any luck, they would compare notes and come to the agreement the whole thing is just entirely too foolhardy. Kay let out a sigh of relief, remembering Ed had a funeral service at 9:00 am. She wouldn't have to face him for another couple of hours.

But it wasn't just the Ed situation that had Kay feeling downhearted. Taking Mariah back to Dave's the previous evening had turned out to be harder than she'd anticipated. Not just because Mariah was so delightful to have around, and Kay missed her terribly when she was gone, but because there were things happening in Mariah's summer world which were out of Kay's control. Once Mariah was swallowed up behind Dave's quickly opened and shut front door, she was out of Kay's maternal protective sphere. The little girl would be left to cope with the likes of Sandy's questionable behavior and Alicia Resnick's potential bullying. But Kay had to remind herself Mariah was growing up and would, undoubtedly, be exposed to much worse.

Fortunately, by the time Kay got to the mortuary, the clouds were clearing and in their place was a sunlit, sparkling fresh blue sky. Kay could feel her spirits lifting as well, and she decided to enter the mortuary through the front door so she could greet Ruth and maybe engage her in a friendly chat.

Kay still hadn't gotten used to Ruth's new chic appearance. She was startled by the vision of fashionable loveliness sitting in the chair once taken up by a drab, matronly presence. A bright ivory print, silk wrap dress hugged and flattered Ruth's still-trim figure and her hair and makeup were done to perfection. But it wasn't her stylish beauty that commanded attention. It was an aura of satisfied contentment that seemed to fill the entire space of the front office. Kay couldn't help but smile.

"You look happy this morning. Good weekend?" Ruth asked.

"I was just going to say the same thing about you," Kay said. "Nice dress by the way."

Ruth looked down at herself as if she'd forgotten what she'd worn that morning. "Thank you, Dear," Ruth said with a smile and a rosy blush. "I found it at this great little dress shop over on Dellyne. They have such pretty things and their prices are reasonable."

"I'll have to check it out," Kay said, wishing she had the courage to ask Ruth about her makeover.

With Ed and Uncle Owen out on a service and Leo running death certificates Kay and Ruth felt comfortable having a little catch-up visit. Kay fetched coffee for the two of them and then sat across from Ruth, eager to hear any and everything about the latest goings on in and around the mortuary.

Ruth reported an uneventful weekend. Ed had charged her with phone duty since he was busy with the fund-raising flea market.

"There were only two death calls and Owen took care of them both," Ruth said. But then she leaned forward and lowered her voice to add something indelicate to the end of her account. "Adelaide came to see me last week." She widened her eyes at Kay and nodded to indicate Kay should know what she meant.

"Oh, no. Is she ok?" Kay said.

Ruth pressed her lips together in a strained grimace. "She definitely knows something is going on with Owen. But at this point it's only suspicion. She said he's lost twenty pounds and is considering getting a face lift. I know she was feeling me out to see if I knew anything."

"You must have really felt backed into a corner. What did you say?" Kay said.

"It wasn't what I said. It was *how* I said it. I was tripping all over myself to reassure her he was just doing a little, mid-life self-improvement." Ruth reached for the back of her head in search of her long-gone bun and self-consciously chuckled. "I told her even I had made a few changes. You know…just to keep from getting bored."

Kay knew it was more than boredom behind Ruth's updated image, but she still didn't feel comfortable delving further.

Ruth grimaced again and shook her head. "I know she saw right through me. If I was truly a good friend, I'd have told her she'd do well to keep her eyes and ears open. But that would've just invited more questions, and I'm a terrible liar."

Kay reached over and patted Ruth's hand. "Don't beat yourself up. You were in a no-win situation."

Kay's heart went out to Aunt Adelaide. She knew all too well what it was like to be in Adelaide's shoes, pressing for answers from people who knew the truth but were reluctant to inflict more pain…or be a snitch.

"Take it from me, Ruth. Women say they want to know, but they really don't, Kay said. "The truth is, they *already* know and are desperate for someone - something to prove them wrong. I think you did Adelaide a kindness."

"I sure didn't feel kind." Ruth replied. "But that's not even the worst of it. You're not going to believe this, but while we were talking, Dot Dash unexpectedly showed up with a batch of okra. I was afraid she was going to ask me to page Owen; I snatched the container from her hand, mumbled something like we were very busy and dismissed her with a curt "thank you." Adelaide just stood there looking at me as if I'd lost my mind."

Kay gave Ruth a wry smile. "That doesn't surprise me. It just tells me Adelaide is almost ready to learn the truth. The Fates are putting things in motion so all Adelaide's questions will be answered. That's when she's really going to need your friendship.

Ruth smiled at Kay but there was sadness in her eyes. "You're speaking from experience, aren't you?"

Kay smiled back at Ruth, happy to be having another heart-to-heart with her friend. But she didn't want to talk about her past. There were things going on in her present that were more worthy of discussion.

Kay gestured toward Ruth with her coffee mug. "I'm going to get a warm up. How 'bout you?"

Ruth shook her head and Kay headed for the coffee pot in the break room. She was looking in the refrigerator for a piece of fruit when she heard the phone ring. She hoped it was a death call she'd have to go on, thereby avoiding Ed for a little while longer. She walked back to Ruth's office expecting to be greeted with the pick up information; instead, Ruth handed her a Call Back message from Judith Kline.

Kay's heart beat faster, but this time from excitement rather than fear. She couldn't believe she was actually looking forward to hearing what her lawyer had to say. The only thing that gave her slight pause was the prospect of going back to mediation.

But if that's what has to happen, so be it.

Kay wasn't in any hurry to return the call. She and Ruth had a few more minutes before they'd have to get serious about their day. Without going into too much gory detail, Kay casually filled Ruth in on what had been going on between her and Dave. She smoothly segued to the subject of Ed by telling Ruth about the comical head butting incident as a lead-in to the story of their quasi-romantic moment. But Kay just couldn't work up the courage. Anyway, she could tell Ruth's interest was beginning to wane; she kept trying to steal a glances at her wrist watch.

"Here I am monopolizing the conversation. I haven't even asked you about your weekend." Kay said

"Sure you have. There just wasn't much to tell. Remember?"

The phone rang and Ruth jumped as if she was hearing it for the first time. She snatched it from it's cradle, almost knocking over her floppy disk pen and pencil holder. With a breathlessness worthy of Marilyn Monroe she said, "Salinger's Mortuary. Ruth Linton speaking."

Whoever was on the other end was just the person Ruth was waiting to hear from and she, obviously, didn't want to talk in front of Kay. "Can you hold on a sec?" She put her hand over the mouthpiece and turned to Kay. "Was there anything else, Dear?"

Even though she knew Ruth hadn't meant to be dismissive, Kay couldn't help feeling a little hurt. She was enjoying her chat with her friend and hated to see it end. Nevertheless, it was now clear what was behind Ruth's startling exterior renovation - a new love interest.

Why not? Doesn't everyone deserve some excitement in their lives?

She walked back to her office, thinking about the gentle pressure of Ed's fingers enveloping her upper arm and a delighted giggled escaped from her lips. Other than the morning when she'd removed the dried shaving cream from his ear, she couldn't remember another occasion when their physical contact had given her such a thrill. But as easy as it would have been to become carried away, she cautioned herself not to get too excited until the situation was duly discussed and clarified.

"I have death certificates for you," Leo sang as Kay walked into her office. Of course, Kay startled and Leo laughed. He was slouched in a chair in front of Kay's desk, fanning his face with the manila folder.

"If you heard me coming why didn't you clear your throat or something, so I'd know you were there? Kay said.

"Cuz it's funnier to see you jump." Leo answered.

Kay thought it was funny too, but she wouldn't give Leo the satisfaction of knowing he'd gotten one over on her. She pretended to be angry and forcefully grabbed the folder from his hand. It was her job to sort the certificates and then call the families to let them know they were ready for pick-up.

"Hey…check this one out," Leo said, leaning over Kay's desk and pointing to the certificate on top. "Remember that young girl we had last week? The one you said looked like that old time movie star…the one whose name was a day of the week?"

"Tuesday Weld." Kay said.

"Yeah. Check out her cause of death. She drank too much water."

"Get outta here," Kay said. She looked down the page to the line that listed the official cause of death. "That's not possible."

Cause of Death: Water Intoxication

"Now I've seen everything," Kay said, looking up at Leo.

"I heard she entered some contest trying to win a Wii gaming system. You had to drink a bunch of water and not go to the bathroom. I think it was called, "Don't Pee and Get a Wii.""

"Oh my god," Kay said. "I wonder if they're going to hold the contest people responsible?"

"Well, you just know some lawyer's going to get a hold of the family and convince them to sue." Leo said.

Lawyer! I need to call Judith.

So she wouldn't forget, she taped the pink message Ruth had given her to the top of her phone receiver. She had to attend to the death certificates before she did anything else. Families were waiting for their copies to file insurance claims and close out important financial accounts.

"Well, I'm sure we'll be reading about it in the paper soon enough. Thanks, Leo."

"No problem." Leo said. "Hey. Have you heard I'm gonna be updating the website?"

"Really? I had no idea you were a techno-geek." Kay said.

"Yup. I have an associate's degree in computer science and a certification in web design. Ed was tough to convince, though. I think he couldn't see past me washing cars and running errands. But once I showed him some of my work, he was on board."

"That's fantastic, Leo," Kay said. "It's great Ed's giving you a chance to move up. By the way, I recently attended a presentation on social media and I could share some of the stuff I learned if you'd like."

"Sure," Leo said with a big smile. "That'd be fun." He jumped up from his chair. "Well, this computer genius has gotta put away a big delivery of embalming room supplies. Talk to you later."

Kay watched him leave thinking how surprising people can be once you get to know them. And so far, that seemed to be proving true of everyone at the mortuary.

Kay got busy with her death certificates chore. When she was finished, she reached over to set the file in the folder rack on the corner of her desk and noticed something peeking out from under the rack. She pinched it on its exposed corner and slid it out the rest of the way. Kay gasped when she saw it was Tina Chalmers' business card. She still hadn't called Tina like she'd promised.

Tina was her usual gracious self and dismissed Kay's effusive apologies. "Please don't worry about it. I'm just as busy and addle-brained as you are. I'm just happy to hear from you."

Kay was anxious to set a date for their lunch

293

and suggested the upcoming Friday, when things at work tended to be a little more relaxed. But Tina said she preferred a weekend when they wouldn't be pressed to get back to work. Kay agreed.

"The only thing is I won't be available until the Saturday after next. Will that work for you? Tina said.

Kay looked at her calendar and realized that would be Mariah's next weekend visit home. But she knew getting away for a couple of hours to have lunch with a friend wasn't going to be a problem. Cory would be home to supervise. (Cory banned the use of the word "babysit" whenever it was applied to Mariah).

"That'll be perfect. How about Kouzina over on Henson? Say 12:30? A refreshing Greek salad and copious amounts of wine?"

Tina giggled. "I don't know. Do you think we can be trusted to behave ourselves?"

"I certainly hope not," Kay said. "What would be the fun in that?"

They ended the conversation and Kay made sure to mark her calendar.

One down, one to go.

Kay peeled off the taped pink message that had been fluttering around with every call she'd previously made. As she waited on hold for Judith to come on the line, she marveled at how dramatically her mood had changed since her dreary drive to work a couple of hours earlier. And for some unknown reason, she felt sure Judith was about to give her some news which would launch her happy disposition into the stratosphere.

Kay arrived at Kouzina precisely at 12:30 to find the weekend lunch crowd bigger than she'd expected. She inched through the large group of people at the front waiting to be seated and scanned the dining room for a, possibly-early, Tina.

No such luck. Better get my name on the waiting list.

"Two - for Manning," Kay said to the hostess standing behind the podium.

Without looking up from the scribbled list on her yellow legal pad, the bored young woman announced, "The wait is 15 to 20 minutes."

Probably hoping I'll leave.

"That's fine," Kay said.

She turned to find a seat among the other hungry hopefuls and almost crashed into a radiant Tina.

"Boo!" Tina said, causing Kay to let out a startled yelp.

The two women burst out laughing and immediately fell into an enthusiastic embrace.

"Excuse me. You're blocking the way." The hostess had come around from behind her podium of power, cradling a stack of menus in her arm and glaring at Tina and Kay.

"Whatever happened to that sweet tiny old woman who used to seat the customers?" Tina asked, not bothering to lower her voice.

"That was the owner's grandma. She died last

year. I know cuz Salinger's handled the services. They shipped her body back to Greece for burial."

The hostess just rolled her eyes and called out, "Dumbass, party of five."

"It's pronounced DooMAH," the disgruntled gentleman heading the waiting party said as they got up and walked past the hostess. "It's French."

"Whatever," the disinterested girl muttered under her breath.

Kay and Tina wasted no time filling the vacated seats. Happily wiggling herself next to her friend on the bench, Kay patted Tina on the thigh. "Here we are. Finally! I was beginning to wonder if the Fates were messing with us again."

Tina didn't answer. She just looked at Kay with a big goofy grin that made her feel self-conscious.

"What?" Kay said. "Do I have a booger?" Kay lowered her head and discretely slid the back of her index finger back and forth under her nose.

Tina let out a deep-throated giggle and shoved her shoulder against Kay's. "Oh stop. You're fine."

"So why are you looking at me like that?" Kay said.

The grin came back on Tina's face.

"Ok. Now you're starting to freak me out. What's going on?"

"Well…funny you should mention the Fates. It's happened again." Tina said, grinning even wider.

"It's hap…? What are you talking about?"

"You'll never guess who I've just come from renting a townhouse to?" Tina said.

"Manning. Party of two."

"That was quick," Kay said, perturbed the hostess had chosen that particular moment to become efficient.

Tina and Kay stood and followed her to a table. As soon as they sat a waiter appeared, took their drink order (a bottle of their best Pinot Noir) and then left them to study the menu. But Kay wasn't interested in the daily special quite yet. She was anxious to find out the identity of the potential tenant making Tina act so squirrelly.

"So who is this person you rented a townhouse to? I'm assuming they've rented from you before." Kay asked.

"Rented before? No, no, no. That's not what I meant."

"I'm lost, Tina. What's happened again and what does it have to do with the Fates?"

The wine arrived, and with a display of grand oenophilic showmanship, the waiter removed the cork and poured.

Tina raised her glass in a toast. "To our friendship." They clinked their glasses together and tasted their wine.

"Ok. No more interruptions. Tell me what the hell is going on." Kay said.

"Remember how we used to talk about all the

weird chain of events that led up to your divorce?"

"Yes," Kay said. The suspense was beginning to get to her. She took a big gulp of wine.

"Well, imagine my astonishment when I get a call from, none other than, Sandy wanting to make an appointment to see one of our properties." Tina said. "I've just come from the showing."

A cold shiver traveled down Kay's spine. Tina's statement was so unexpected and weird, for a brief second Kay couldn't remember who Sandy even was.

"Did she recognize you?" Kay asked.

"If she did she didn't say. We've only met once - I think it was when I came to the office for my last check." Tina said. "I told her who I was thinking she might appreciate the coincidence, but she didn't seem interested. All she said was, "You don't say," and then asked me about the garbage disposal. I was going to ask after Dave, but I got the feeling it wouldn't be well-received."

"No doubt," Kay said. "Did she happen to mention why she was looking?" Kay wondered if there could be trouble in paradise.

"As a matter of fact she did," Tina replied. "She said Dave was doing a big remodel on their house and they needed a place to escape the mess."

"Major renovations AND a temporary residence?" Kay said. "That doesn't make sense."

"Sure it does. I have clients who do it all the time." Tina said.

"No. That's not what I mean."

298

Kay spent the next few minuets filling Tina in on all of Dave's financial machinations over the past year and her well-intentioned, but misplaced efforts to work with him. Her troublesome tale climaxed with Sandy accosting her at the band pageant with the news of Dave's bonus and their trip to Maui.

"Ouch! That had to hurt," Tina said.

"Yeah, but only from hitting my head against the wall for falling for his lies again. But do you know the thing about hitting your head against the wall? It feels so good when you stop. Once my head quit throbbing I marched right back to my lawyer and *demanded* we take that sorry S.O.B back to court."

Kay emphasized her defiant declaration with a crisp bob of her head and another drink from her wine glass. Of course, Kay knew she had conveniently left out the part where Leslie had to convinced her to consult with Judith. But her heroic telling of the story was being fueled by Tina's rapt expression, as well as, the pinot noir. If they didn't eat soon, Kay was going to be drunk.

"So what happened?" Tina said. She was thoroughly engrossed in the story.

"Can I tell you after we order? I'm really starting to feel this wine." Kay said.

Kay talked Tina into sharing an appetizer of feta fries. "…something to munch on 'till they bring our food." They also agreed to another bottle of wine. "So what if we have to take a taxi home? This reunion deserves a celebration." Kay said.

"Tell you what. I'll spring for your cab fare," Tina said.

"And I'll spring for yours." Kay replied.

They giggled at their inebriated silliness then tried to straighten up long enough to give their order to the waiter. As soon as he walked away, they dissolved into giggles again.

"Did you see his face when we ordered the wine? I think he disapproves." Tina said.

"Nah. He's just worried about is his tip. Let's make a note not to forget his tip." Kay said.

"Duly noted," Tina said. She pretended to write on the table with an invisible pen. "Now, if you please, continue with your story. When last we visited, you were about to take your sorry S.O.B. of an ex-husband to court."

"You make it sound like an episode of the Lone Ranger."

"Well, then, Hi-Oh, get on with it, Silver." Tina commanded, setting off another round of uncontrollable giggles. Their failed efforts to gain control of themselves, naturally, irritated some of the more uptight diners in the room - which only made them laugh even more. Fortunately the feta fries were delivered to the table, providing the diversion necessary to move things in a more restrained direction. The hungry women dug in.

"As I was saying," Kay said between bites, "We took Dave back to court for failing to report his bonus. And, as my attorney would say, we prevailed."

"And by prevailing you mean...?"

"The judge awarded me half the value of the bonus, and Dave's been ordered to pay all attorney

300

fees." Kay said.

Tina was grabbing fries and putting them in her mouth like she was eating popcorn at the suspenseful part of a movie. "How much was the bonus, if you don't mind me asking?" Tina said.

Kay smiled. "$80,000."

Tina's jaw dropped to the table.

"Keep in mind I'd already been awarded $10,000 in back child support at the previous hearing. When you add everything together it's hard to imagine how he can possibly afford this new expenditure."

Tina shook her head in disbelief. "Well, maybe Sandy has money," she offered.

"I don't see how," Kay said. "She hasn't worked since before Little Dave was born and no one in her family has died."

"Curiouser and curiouser," Tina said with a bemused smile. "And then out of all the leasing agents in town she ends up calling me and I find out their plans an hour before I have a lunch date with you. I wonder if she knows you and I are friends? Do you think if she tells Dave I'm the leasing agent he might just nix the deal...you know, to keep you from finding out." Tina said.

"Maybe. But that would be kinda dumb since the girls would be bound to tell me sooner or later. Right? Kay said.

"Oh. Right," Tina said with an embarrassed giggle.

"Anyway, at this point I don't think it matters how they're doing it or whether or not I know. My business with Dave has pretty much concluded."

Their food came and Kay dove in with abandon. The moussaka casserole was better than she'd remembered. She was about to insist Tina take a bite when she noticed her friend was just sitting there staring at her plate of pastichio.

"What's the matter? Did you change your mind about what you ordered?" Kay said.

Tina picked up her fork and sighed. "I don't know. I guess I'm a little disappointed. You're just so blasé. I thought you'd be as weirded-out as I am."

"Honey, I *am* weirded-out," Kay said. "I even got a little dizzy when you told me. But I don't see how this has anything to do with me. Like I told you, where Dave's concerned, I've already taken care of business."

Tina just shook her head. "I don't know, Kay. I just can't shake the feeling this is more than just some crazy coincidence."

Kay tried to make her friend feel better with a reassuring smile. "Well, I DO know. It's just left-over karma. Every time Dave has tried to get away with something, he's always been busted. His karma's been on such a roll, now it can't stop."

Kay burst out laughing at her impromptu analysis; Tina still looked downcast.

Kay couldn't let her reunion (or her lunch) with Tina be ruined just because Dave's escapades no longer interested her. She had to get them back to their silliness of a few minutes prior.

"Anyway, I think Elmer Fudd summed it up

best when he said, "oh whadda wangled web we weave."

Kay's impersonation of the cartoon "wascally wabbit hunter" was so terrible, Tina could no longer hold on to her dejected mood. Much to the aggravation of their table neighbors, the two women began another round of boisterous giggling.

"C'mon. We better pull it together and eat. Our food is going to get cold," Kay said. "Besides, I've got something a little more serious I want to talk to you about."

The two happily ate and drank and Kay confided in Tina about her dilemma with Ed. Kay had hoped talking about it would reveal some deep, hidden insight she'd overlooked. But when she was finished the impasse of the situation remained.

"Well, what's the worse that could happen?" Tina said. "You go on a date and you find out he's as boring as a stump. Or he leaves his socks on when he's having sex."

"If only it was that simple," Kay said. "Even if he's the most fascinating man on the planet and rocks in bed, I still have to go to work everyday with the guy. If we hook up, I worry Ruth and Leo are going to see favoritism around every corner, even if it doesn't exist. And if we don't, I just envision oceans of awkwardness between us every time we're together in a room. And I haven't even begun to consider what this would mean for the girls."

"Whoa, girl," Tina responded. "I think you're borrowing trouble. From what little you've told me about Ed, he seems like a reasonable guy. You two are just going to have to talk this through. And as far as the girls are concerned, they've got you no matter what. They'll be just fine."

Kay sighed. "I hope you're right...about everything."

"You know Kay, it's just as easy to imagine the good that could come from this as it is the bad. Have you thought about that?"

Kay allowed a wistful smile to slowly inch across her lips.

"Did I tell you he said I was beautiful?...And that he was in over his head?"

"Yes, yes. You told me. You should see your face. Ed's not the only one in over his head." Tina said.

The waiter came by and offered dessert, but the well-fed women opted for coffee only.

"Instead of fighting over the bill, which you know we will do, why don't we just agree to split it." Tina said.

"Sounds like a plan to me," Kay said. "And what do you say, just to be on the safe side, we split a cab ride home? I feel fine to drive, but I don't want to take any chances."

"Ok." Tina said. "But do you mind if we have the driver run us by the post office? I have to mail the copy of the signed lease and extra keys to Sandy." Tina said, holding up a manila envelope she'd pulled from her purse."

"Fine by me," Kay said.

Tina used her cell phone to call for a cab and while they waited, they took care of the bill, put a generous tip on the table, sipped their coffee and made plans to get together again. A short time later a new, friendlier hostess came to tell them their cab had arrived.

They gathered up their things and headed for the door. "My god," Tina said. "We've stayed through a shift change. I'm surprised Tim hasn't called looking for me."

"Yeah. I'm going to have some explaining to do myself when I get home. But I've decided to turn it into one of those teachable moments. You know…never drink and drive. And if all else fails, I can just say it was your fault."

Kay and Tina laughed again and as was their habit, they locked elbows and walked to their waiting cab.

Tina lived closer to the restaurant than Kay, so she was dropped off first. Kay asked the cab driver to wait until Tina was safely in the door.

Kay smiled all the way to her house. Her lunch with Tina had been delightful. She promised herself to make these lunches a regular part of her social schedule.

The cab arrived at her driveway and Kay reached for her purse on her seat. There sat the manila envelope Tina was supposed to mail at the post office.

"We forgot to go to the Post Office," Kay giggled. She was still feeling the effects of the wine.

"Sorry, Ma'am. I only go where I'm told," the

305

driver said. "I'd be happy to drive you there now if you'd like."

Kay declined his offer. She only had enough cash for her fare and a tip.

Once in the house, she let the girls know she was home and then immediately put in a call to Tina to let her know about the forgotten envelope. Tina told Kay not to worry. She was fine with Kay putting it in the mail on Monday.

The next evening when Dave came to pick up Mariah Kay spotted the envelope sitting on the desk in the entry.

Why wait for the mail tomorrow?

Kay put the envelope in Mariah's bag and instructed her to give it to Dave when they got home. She figured there'd likely be some backlash for getting involved in his business, insignificant as it was. Kay didn't care. She was doing a favor for a friend

21

Poe is Spinning in His Grave

Kay's morning trip to OMI had been much less eventful than the last time she'd been sent to retrieve a deceased. Even though the mortuary van had all the modern automobile conveniences, it wasn't as much fun to drive as the old Country Squire. Kay backed up to the embalming room door and Leo appeared, ready to roll the well-secured body out from the van. At moments like this, Kay and Leo still shared guilty, knowing glances, but they never discussed the night of the flying fat man.

Back at her desk, Kay started a new file and filled it with the necessary forms Ed would need when the family came in to make arrangements later in the afternoon.

So far, she and Ed were doing well at maintaining a professional working relationship. Of course, their mutual decision to try a couple of "let's see" dates, hadn't gone much past their initial discussion. They had been swamped with cases at the mortuary, and Ed's outside jam-packed schedule had prevented them from making solid plans. Nevertheless, Kay was enjoying the anticipation of an evening out with the handsome man who thought she was beautiful.

A couple of loud growls from her empty stomach told Kay it was getting near lunch. But the clock didn't agree. It would be at least an hour and a half before she could leave to go eat.

Kay went to the break room for some small edible morsel that would, hopefully tide her over. She looked at the almost-empty plastic container with the remnants of Mrs. Dash's dehydrated chili okra and decided she'd be disloyal to Aunt Adelaide if she finished them off. Instead she chose a banana that was in desperate need of being eaten before it turned into soup.

Kay had made a good start on the obituary; all she'd need to finish it were the service times. Of course, the family would get final editorial say-so, but she seldom, if ever, had one sent back to her for a re-write. She was giving it one more read-through for typos when she was interrupted by Ruth who had rushed into her office visibly distraught.

"Oh thank god, you're back," Ruth said. "Mr. Noland is on the phone and he's every upset. He demanded that I put him through to you immediately. When I told him I had to check to make sure you were here, he said some very unkind things."

Kay panicked. *Maybe something has happened to one of the girls.*

"I'm sorry, Ruth. That's usually not like him. There must be something wrong." Kay said.

With her heart in her throat, Kay picked up the receiver and pushed Line 1.

"Dave, this is Kay. Listen, I don't think it's necessary to badger our recep…"

"I don't give a rat's ass what you think," Dave said. His nose sounded plugged up, like he'd been crying. "I should have known you'd find a way to get back at me. Well, you've won. I just never thought

308

you'd sink so low. You women are all alike and I just pray Cory and Mariah don't end up like you."

Dave slammed the phone down hard without waiting for Kay's response. She slowly lowered the receiver and stood there holding it in both hands shocked by the level of Dave's uncharacteristic fury.

"Is everything ok?" Ruth said. The concerned expression belonged to the old Ruth.

"Apparently not," Kay said. "I can't imagine he's just now hearing about the judge's decision. Maybe it's beginning to sink in."

"Well, are you ok? Did he threaten you?"

"No. No threats. Just angry bluster," Kay said. She gently placed the receiver back on its cradle. She was ok...surprisingly so. "I'm fine."

Ruth went back to her office and Kay returned to her obituary. It was wonderful not to be left all shook up after a conversation with Dave. A smile flashed across her face.

So this is what it feels like to know you've truly moved on.

Kay knew there might be a few uncomfortable moments still to come with Dave. She also knew they - *she* would get past them. She had taken full responsibility for her life and it was unfortunate Dave couldn't do the same. He had gotten exactly what he wanted. His mistake was expecting Kay to pay for it.

The phone rang again, and Kay prepared herself, lest it be Dave calling to continue his tirade. The intercom buzzed and Ruth said, "Kay, Line 1. The caller said her name is Tina Chalmers."

Kay was hoping Tina was calling to invite her for lunch. *Just a quick sandwich and soda this time.*

"Hey, girl. You're timing is excellent. I'm free for lunch," Kay said.

Tina ignored Kay's indirect hint. "I just got a call from a hysterical Sandy," said a breathless Tina. "She wanted to know how Mariah came to have the lease in her possession. Frankly, I'd like to know myself. I thought you were going to put it in the mail."

Tina's angry tone let Kay know something had gone terribly wrong with her good deed.

"I was, Kay said. "But when Dave came to pick up Mariah last night I thought it would be quicker to give it to Mariah to deliver. I didn't think it would be a problem."

"Well, from the way Sandy screamed at me, it's clear there is a problem. She called me a stupid bitch and said I'd ruined her life."

"Oh, Tina. I am so sorry. I should have checked with you first."

"Listen. They're telling me I have an urgent call on the other line," Tina said. "It's probably Sandy calling back to cancel the deal. Crap! I just hope she doesn't complain to my boss. I'll call you later."

Kay had expected some repercussion to the tiny part she'd played in the handover of the lease, but not to this degree.

It was just a sealed manila envelope for god sake.

Then Kay remembered what Tina had said about Sandy's appearance being more than just a coincidence. Kay had made up the whole thing about "left-over karma" and now was wondering if her silly interpretation might be closer to the truth.

The sound of screeching tires snapped Kay out of her musings. She thought she saw the tail end of the limousine flying past the window. She jumped up to see if she was right but the cloud of dust raised by the speeding vehicle obscured her view.

"Did you hear that?" Ruth said, running into Kay's office.

"I think it was the limousine." Kay said. Ruth joined Kay at the window and arrived just in time to see an older model sedan recklessly careen into the parking lot in hot pursuit.

They both started for the door and by the time they got outside they could hear angry shouts coming from behind the garage.

"Get outta that car, Salinger," said an enraged voice Kay didn't recognize.

Ruth came to an abrupt halt. She grabbed Kay's arm. "Oh, no. Owen."

Ed had also heard the ruckus from the embalming room and came running to catch up with the women.

"What in the hell is going on?" Ed said. "It sounded like a freight train barreling through here."

As they rounded the corner of the garage, the three gasped in unison to see Tony Burleigh, flushed with rage, beating on the driver's side window.

"Get out motherfucker. You're gonna be sorry if I have to pull you out."

311

"Knock it off," Ed shouted, striding up to Tony.

The sight of the tall, authoritative Ed was all it took for Tony to wither back from the car. He stood there breathing hard and pulling up his filthy blue sweat pants which had slipped down below his bloated belly. Ed yanked the limousine door open. "Get out here, now, O. I wanna know what's going on."

Kay stood there watching the heated confrontation when she thought she saw something out of the corner of her eye. She turned to catch a glimpse of a head and pair of eyes inching up in the back limo door window trying to get a peek.

Tony saw it too and began to wail. "Mother, how could you? How will I ever be able to show my face in public again?"

The head quickly disappeared.

"Just stand there," Ed ordered Owen. He walked over to the back limousine door and pulled it open. The space appeared empty. "Come out, Mrs. Burleigh. We know you're in there."

From the farthest reaches of the back seat, a small voice squeaked out, "I can't. I'm not decent."

Tony charged for the door. "You get your clothes on NOW. I'm taking you home."

Owen stepped in front of Tony to block his path. "Leave her alone, you big waste of space," Owen yelled.

Tony looked at Owen with a smoldering hatred. "So, Mr. Salinger. What does your wife think about your special limousine service?" he said. "Oh, that's right. SHE HATES IT. She told me so when she called me this morning."

In a move that would have impressed any NFL coach, Owen rushed Tony and tackled him to the ground. The women screamed while Ed ran back and forth around the tumbling tangle of arms and legs looking for an in to put a stop to the fight. Surprisingly, Tony was able to roll his substantial heft on top of Owen where he wasted no time landing a few well-aimed punches to the older man's face.

"Get your fat, lazy ass off of me," Owen grunted.

"Not until you promise to leave my mother alone," Tony said

Taking advantage of his parked position, Ed, Kay and Ruth charged Tony, each grabbing something pullable. In his adrenaline-infused state, Tony was able to fight them off for several more moments. Eventually they were able to free Owen from his assailant. With Tony on his feet again Ed pushed him up against the front fender of the limousine and held him there with the full weight of his body.

Ruth and Kay helped a humiliated Owen stand up. He shook their arms away and began brushing the dust from his suit. Ed offered Owen his handkerchief to stem the blood streaming from his nose. Owen took it while avoiding Ed's piercing glare.

"Now, let's everyone calm down and try to act like civilized human beings." Ed said. He turned to Tony. "If I let you go, do you promise to control yourself?

Tony, who couldn't stop crying, simply nodded. Ed released his hold.

"Now, will someone please tell me what's going on." Ed said.

Keeping his eyes on his shoes, Owen cleared his throat. "Evelyn is a fine woman. She's just lonely and needs a little companionship," he said. He looked up at Tony. "Lord knows YOU never pay attention to her unless you want her to shovel something into that hole in your face."

Tony lunged at Otis and they were back on the ground. This time, total chaos was averted by the sound of an approaching police siren. The squad car came to a stop and out jumped Officer Lindy O'Malley. Kay shrunk behind Ruth to avoid being recognized.

Without the slightest hint of a faint, the trained officer adeptly pulled the two men apart and got them to their feet. "Do I need to handcuff you, or can you two be trusted to behave yourselves?

They both muttered, "yes," and she guided them to neutral corners.

Officer O'Malley walked over to Ed who was gaping in amazement at the command of the petite policewoman.

"We received a call of a 10-16 at Salinger's Mortuary," she said. "There were also several reports of two cars speeding and driving recklessly through the middle of town. One of the vehicles was purported to be your limousine."

"Oh good, the cops are here." Leo said, running up to the scene. He blushed and tried to hide

314

his delight when he realized Lindy O'Malley was the responding officer. He inched up next to Ed.

"Did you call the cops?" Ed said from the side of his mouth.

Leo nodded and Ed smiled. "Good call," he said.

"I'll need to take statements," Officer O'Malley said to Ed, pulling a small notebook from her back pocket.

"I'm afraid it's all my fault."

Everyone turned to see Evelyn Burleigh emerge from the back of the limousine. She was fully dressed, including her signature black hat and sunglasses. In her best Black Dahlia sashay, Evelyn glided over and positioned herself halfway between her son and her lover.

She turned to her son whose tears continued to stream down his face. "Dahling, you mustn't make Mr. Salinger the escaped-goat. I'm the one who pursued his affections."

"But why, Mother, why?" Tony pleaded. "I thought you and I were happy together, just the two of us."

Evelyn smiled sympathetically at her distraught son. "Dahling, it isn't rocket surgery. I'm still a vibrant, full-blooded woman who, every now and then, needs the attentions of a man. It's important for my self of steam. But that can never take away the special bondage between mother and son."

If the scene hadn't been so heart-breaking, Kay would have taken Owen's place rolling on the

315

ground with laughter. She looked around to see if anyone else was having trouble keeping it together. Ruth and Leo seemed to be oblivious; they were eagerly waiting to provide their personal, official eye-witness account of the incident.

Oh well, their loss.

"Don't blame your mother, Tony. I was the one being promiscuous." Owen said.

Evelyn nodded. "And you know how much I love Greek mythology, Son."

Tony refused to be appeased. "But Mother, he's married," Tony whined. "It isn't like you to deliberately hurt another human being."

Evelyn cupped Tony's face in her hand. "Everyone makes mistakes, Dahling. Even me."

Owen took a tentative step toward the mother and son. "You're mother is trying to fix her mistake, Tony. That's why she broke up with me this morning."

Tony sneered at Owen. "So she fixes it by sleeping with you again? "

Evelyn looked at Owen with a bittersweet smile. "I had to say thank you…and goodbye."

"Mother, I want your solemn promise, here and now, you're never going to see him again."

Evelyn turned back to her son. In a dramatic move reminiscent of Scarlett O'Hara, the disgraced woman raised a defiant fist to the heavens and declared, "quote the raisin - nevermore!"

She brought her hand down, covered her face and began to quietly weep. Tony put his arm around her and she buried her face in his shoulder. The two waited for their turn to talk to Officer O'Malley.

When everyone's play-by-play had been duly recorded, Officer O'Malley addressed Owen. "Mr. Salinger, from all accounts it appears Mr. Burleigh was the aggressor. Do you wish to press charges?"

Head tipped back with blood-soaked handkerchief still pressed up against his nostrils, Owen simply shook his head no.

"Well, based on the frantic calls that came into the station, I'm issuing warnings to both you and Mr. Burleigh for speeding and reckless driving. I can't ticket you because there was no official police witness."

She completed the forms, tore them off her ticket pad and handed them to both men. "You two got off easy today. I'm sure I don't need to tell you endangering the lives of other drivers and pedestrians is serious business. Things could have been much worse than a bloody nose."

Ruth nudged Kay with her elbow and signaled with her head in Leo's direction. Leo was beaming at Officer O'Malley. "What's with him?" Ruth asked quietly.

"Isn't it obvious?" Kay said with a giggle.

What wasn't obvious was whether Lindy O'Malley returned Leo's affections. Her professional demeanor never wavered - even as Leo escorted her back to the squad car with a lovesick-puppy eagerness. He chatted her up, trying to think of things to say which would delay her departure.

Back at the Burleigh car, Tony was gently

317

helping his mother into the passenger seat. The tender sight sent a pang of guilt through Kay for thinking of Tony as a spoiled bully. Clearly, the two of them had one of those mysterious relationships that was difficult for someone on the outside to understand.

Before he closed his mother's door Kay heard Tony invite her to lunch. "What do you say we go to Carl's Crab Cove? They're having a two-for-one special."

"But, Dahling, you know I can't stomach the thought of eating crushed Asians."

"I don't care. That's what I want, and that's where we're going. You can have the fish," Tony said before slamming the door.

As they drove away, Kay couldn't help feeling a little sad. In light of today's events, it was likely Kay had seen her last Black Dahlia Cavalcade of Comedy show.

Oh well. It was good run.

"Ok, everyone. Back to work," Ed said. "Leo, let's finish up in the embalming room. Owen, put the limousine away and then come to my office. And ladies…well, carry on with whatever you were doing."

"So what do you think is gonna happen to Owen?" Kay asked Ruth as they walked to the back door of the mortuary.

Ruth sighed. "I'm not sure. I couldn't read Ed's face. It has to be difficult when something like this involves close relatives. I know he feels an obligation to Owen - you know, being his father's brother and all. And I'm sure he wants to protect Adelaide, AND the

318

mortuary. No matter which way you look at it, it's gotta be a bear for Ed."

"What in the world could Owen have been thinking?" Kay said.

"I don't know," Ruth said. "The heart wants what the heart wants and, unfortunately, thinking just doesn't come into play."

Kay wanted to disagree. Thinking was the only thing she and Ed seemed to be doing.

"I just feel bad for everyone involved," Ruth went on. "Love can sometimes be a messy business. But everyone needs it. Even those you least likely expect."

Ruth's far-away voice made Kay wonder if she was referring to herself. Then Ruth seemed to snap to and she let out a little chuckle. "Well, I definitely owe Mrs. Dash an apology. Of course she won't know the full extent of my regret, but I'm definitely going to ask her to forgive my rudeness of the other day."

"Are you going to talk to Aunt Adelaide?" Kay asked. She held the back door open for Ruth

"Probably. But I think it best if I wait for her to call me."

Kay followed Ruth into the building, tempted to offer her services as a person with experience in these matters. But then she figured Adelaide would be more comfortable talking to someone closer to her own age. Not only that, older couples were much less quick to resort to divorce. Given the way her own marriage had turned out, Kay realized she wasn't exactly the best person to offer Adelaide hope for a happy ending.

The loud grumbling in Kay stomach returned and she looked at the clock hoping it was finally time to go eat.

Yay! 12 noon.

"Kay, would you mind if I went to lunch first?" Ruth said.

Ruth and Kay usually alternated lunch times so there'd always be someone at the front desk. Today was supposed to be Kay's turn to go first. In spite of her protesting stomach, Kay couldn't refuse a visibly-excited Ruth. It was clear Ruth had a special lunch date; Kay was happy to put her hunger on hold for the cause of love.

For the next hour Kay fielded incessant phone calls from nosy townspeople wanting to know if everything was ok at the mortuary, or if the limousine had been totaled, or if it was true the police had shot someone in the parking lot. The rumor mill was as fast as it was incorrect. Fortunately, no one seemed to be clued-in to the salacious basis of the incident. Nevertheless, Kay felt extremely uncomfortable since she wasn't in a position to give an official statement. She just told callers she was a temp, didn't know what happened, and suggested they call back tomorrow. Knowing people's short attention spans, Kay figured it was unlikely anyone would follow up on her suggestion.

Kay was checking the restaurant app on her cell phone when Uncle Owen walked past on his way to Ed's office. Sad eyes kept straight ahead, he pretended not to see her. Kay knew whatever awaited him behind Ed's closed office door was nothing compared to what awaited him at home.

Kay braced herself for muffled shouts sure to come from the direction of Ed's office. But everything remained eerily quiet. When the door finally opened she heard Ed say, "Go ahead and go on home. I think you should take the rest of the week off. Addie needs you right now and we've got everything covered here."

Owen walked past Kay again, using the bloody hanky to wipe away tears. This time he stopped in front of the desk.

"I guess I just love too easily," he said, voice breaking. He searched Kay's eyes for absolution.

"Do yourself a favor, O," Kay said, as kindly as she could. "Whatever you do, make sure you don't say that to Adelaide."

Owen walked away, muffling a sob.

Kay wanted to feel sorry for him, but she couldn't. Choices come with consequences - especially when those choices affect other people.

"Where's Ruth?" Ed asked, suddenly coming into the front office. Kay could see he had been crying too. It was completely foreign for Kay to see him this way, and it broke her heart.

"Are you o…? Kay started.

"I'm fine" Ed said. "Did Ruth go to lunch?" He avoided looking directly at Kay.

"Yes. We traded today. But I expect her back in about ten minutes or so."

"Ok. I'm late for an appearance at the Chamber of Commerce lunch. Then I'm supposed to be at St. Mary's rectory for a meeting with the cemetery committee. Tell her I should be back in time to make arrangements."

He turned to hurry down the hall, but Kay stopped him. "Hang on a sec, Ed."

"Yes?" he said.

She walked up to him and without a thought, put her arms around him in a supportive embrace. For a brief moment he stood there rigid, not sure how to respond. But he couldn't hold out for long. He surrendered to her kind concern and the two maintained the embrace for an extended moment.

"I know dealing with Owen had to be difficult," Kay said. "No one would blame you if you told him not to come back."

Ed spoke softly into Kay's ear. "All I could think about was how my father would have handled this. Owen is his brother and my uncle. He's just as much a part of Salinger's as I am. How can I banish him?"

Kay pulled away and looked into Ed's distressed face. "Well, they say you shouldn't make important decisions when emotions are running high. Things will eventually settle down and then you'll know what to do."

Ed's expression relaxed and for a moment Kay thought he was going to kiss her. But he broke their embrace and combed his fingers through his hair. "You're probably right. I better get going."

Before he turned and sped away he took

Kay's hand and smiled. "Thank you," he said in a near-whisper. He leaned in and, to Kay's disappointment, kissed her on the forehead.

As she watched him sprint down the hall, she wondered if she had the patience for a slow courtship.

21

Meeting Your Fate on the Road You Took to Avoid It

"Cory," Kay called upstairs. "Come down and talk to me." She pulled two cans of soda from the fridge.

"Can it wait? I'm in the middle of my French practice drills." Cory called back.

"Je veux que vous me parler," Kay hollered in her best college French.

Kay didn't like to bother the girls when they were doing their homework, but the calamity at the mortuary earlier in the day had been so unsettling, she needed to anchor herself to something familiar. She told herself she'd only keep Cory long enough to transition back to her real life.

Kay pulled out a chair for Cory at the table, set down one of the sodas, then took a seat herself.

Cory was chuckling as she descended the stairs. "I didn't know you could speak French," she said.

"I can't. Not really. Took four years of French in college."

Cory was impressed. "Were you any good?"

Kay shrugged. "I was OK. I got B's. My dream was to go to Paris after college and live there for a year."

Cory sat and popped open the soda. "Why

didn't you?"

"Oh, I don't know. I guess Life got in the way," Kay said. "I met your father and suddenly going to Paris didn't seem very important."

Cory propped her elbows on the table and rested her face in both hands. "A year in Paris..." she said with a dreamy sigh. "I could never let some guy ruin my plans to do something that wonderful."

Kay smiled. "Your dad wasn't just "some guy."

Despite everything she'd gone through over the last eight years, nothing would ever rob Kay of her happy memories of her early years with Dave.

Cory stiffened. Listening to Kay's reminiscences about her father always made her uncomfortable.

"Speaking of Dad, are you taking him back to court again?"

Ever since their interview with the mediator, the girls had been aware of the legal goings-on between Kay and Dave - but only in the vaguest of terms. Kay had told them Dave's return after seven years had made it necessary to bring the divorce decree up to date. Mariah had been satisfied with the explanation, but Kay suspected Cory knew there was more to it than a simple update.

"No. All that's done," Kay replied. "Why do you ask?"

"There was a big manila envelope on the seat next to Dad in the truck. He said Mariah told him it was from you. Then he muttered under his breath about it probably being more crap from your ball-busting lawyer."

"You mean he hadn't opened it?"

Cory shook her head. "He said he was waiting 'til he got to work. He didn't want Sandy getting upset."

Kay got up to get some cheese crackers to go with her soda. She poured them in a bowl to share with Cory.

Cory grabbed a small handful of crackers and jammed them in her mouth. "So, if you don't mind me asking, what was in the envelope?"

"Please don't talk with your mouth full. And no, I don't mind. It was a lease for a townhouse your dad's renting while he remodels his house. The leasing agent is a friend and I just passed it along as a favor to her."

Cory stopped chewing. She swallowed hard. "Mom. Dad finished that remodel six months ago."

"Are you sure? Sandy told my friend they needed to rent a place while the remodel was going on."

"Unless he's planning to tear down the house and start all over again, I'm pretty sure."

Kay was totally confused. "Well, he must not have opened the envelope, because he called me this morning very upset and…"

Cory didn't want to hear any more. She jumped up from the table, grabbed one more handful of crackers and headed for the stairs. "I'm sorry, Mom. I really need to get back to my French. I have a test in the morning."

Kay knew she shouldn't have, but she just couldn't leave it alone. "How was he when he brought you home this afternoon?" she called after Cory.

"He didn't. I had to catch a ride with Gina Delroy. Dad was tied up with something."

"Something" is right. Something is definitely going on.

Kay poured the left over soda down the sink and threw the empty cans in the trash. The uneaten crackers went back in the box. She stood in the middle of the kitchen not sure what she should do next.

Watch the news? No.

Do a load of laundry? No.

Empty the trash? No

Water the lawn out front? That sounded good.

There was still at least three more hours of sunlight left and at this time of day the east-facing yard was in full shade. Kay knew mindlessly spraying water on the grass would be the perfect way to relax and recalibrate on this warm summer evening.

Some of her neighbors were out, too, and Kay felt comfortable smiling and waving - her yard was no longer a disgrace. As she stood there watering she surveyed her very basic landscaping. It wasn't long before she had identified several potential areas for improvement. In her mind's eye she could see trim, low hedges and attractive layouts of plants and flowers.

I wonder where my gardening stuff is?

Kay felt a burning itch on her ankle and realized the mosquitoes were out in full force. With the lawn sufficiently watered she hurried to turn off the faucet and re-coil the hose. She took off her wet shoes before going into the house to look for the anti-itch ointment.

She was rifling through the drawers in the downstairs bathroom cabinet when the phone rang. Cory's muffled steps thundered across the ceiling above Kay as she sped to answer it.

"There you are," Kay said to the wrinkled tube hiding behind bottles of nail polish, disposable razors and old eye shadow compacts. She put the lid to the toilet seat down and took a seat to apply some relief.

Cory called, "Mom, it's for you."

"I'll be right there," Kay yelled back. She squeezed what she could from the near-empty tube and rubbed it in frantic circles on the itching, swelling welt on her ankle. She hurried to wipe the excess cream off her finger and went in the living room to pick up the phone.

"I got it," Kay yelled one last time.

"Kay. It's Tina. I hope I haven't caught you at a bad time."

There was an ominous tone in Tina's voice that made Kay instinctively lower herself on to the couch.

Tina must have had read Kay's mind. "Are you sitting?" she said.

Tina picked up where she'd left off on her earlier call concerning a furious Sandy. She poured

328

out an astonishing tale of intrigue, intimidation, deceit and betrayal. The most astonishing of all was the small, but pivotal role Kay had unwittingly played in the plot line.

Tina began her story by confirming Kay's passing suspicion of trouble in Dave and Sandy's marriage. According to Tina, the problems went all the way back to the court order granting Kay her back child support.

Sandy suspected the courts might not go easy on Dave, so she'd convinced him to keep mum about his bonus. When Sandy's hunch came true she became enraged at what she considered cruel and unjust treatment from the judge. As far as she was concerned Dave had made his spousal choice clear, and it wasn't fair she should be punished just because Dave no longer loved Kay.

Sandy's hate and resentment had to be appeased. She demanded Dave find a way to get some kind - *any kind* - of concession from Kay. Sandy was hell-bent on preventing Kay from enjoying the full benefit of the court's decision.

Dave knew his life would be hell unless he did what his wife wanted. But he also knew convincing Kay to concede a second time was going to be an even bigger challenge. Nevertheless, he reassured Sandy that Kay was an easy-sell, pointing to his success with his initial child support reduction snow job.

Enter Dave's tearful, post-mediation performance in the truck.

When Kay responded to Dave's deferment

request with her written agreement he was caught completely off guard. He struggled to convince Sandy it was in their best interest to sign it.

Ultimately, Sandy relented, but only on condition Dave take her to Maui - the one place she knew Kay had always wanted to go with Dave. Running into Kay at the band pageant was a heaven-sent opportunity for Sandy to gloat. Unfortunately, Sandy's contempt for Kay got the best of her and she ended up spilling the beans about the bonus.

Now, a new, even-harsher judgment from the courts, coupled with Sandy's uncontrollable jealousy piled more stress on the marriage. Dave was weary of feeling like ping-pong ball between Sandy and Kay; Sandy resented Dave's growing indifference to her expectations for attention and reassurance.

Things finally came to a head when on a trip to the grocery store, Sandy spotted Dave driving in the opposite direction with an unidentified female passenger in the front seat of his truck. A quick u-turn and stealthy pursuit led Sandy to an apartment building where she watched Dave enter with the receptionist from his office.

A long, agonizing hour later the two emerged and were confronted by a berserk Sandy. Afraid Sandy might become violent, the woman hid behind a high fence and listened as Dave vehemently denied she was of any importance to him. The woman ran back into her apartment crying and cursing at Dave's disavowal.

Dave pleaded with Sandy, saying anything that might dissuade her from leaving him. He was terrified she'd make good on her long-held threat to "pick his bones clean," if she ever caught him with another woman.

Despite her deep hurt and betrayal, Sandy wasn't sure she wanted to divorce Dave; she knew a separation was necessary. Her rash decisions had gotten her into trouble in the past, so she vowed to do things more slowly and well-thought out.

First, she'd make sure the receptionist lost her job. Next, she'd find a place for her and Little Dave to live. Finally, she would tell Dave they needed time apart if there was going to be a chance for their marriage to work.

The morning of the townhouse showing, Sandy had immediately recognized Tina. Sandy panicked. She remembered Dave mentioning something about Tina and Kay being friends.

Her intuition screamed at her to turn and walk out, but she really liked the townhouse and was tired of touring properties. So she made up the story of the remodel, just in case Tina and Kay were still in contact. At the very least, she figured she could delay Kay learning about her true intentions.

But the Fates had already lined up the dominoes. Bringing Tina and Kay back together was the trigger that set off the chain reaction of colliding individuals and circumstances:

Against her loudly-nagging doubts, Sandy signed the lease.

Tina promised to put a copy of the lease in the mail with the extra keys.

Tina and Kay met for lunch, drank a lot of wine and called a cab to take them home.

Tina forgot to tell the driver to take her to the Post Office.

The envelope with the lease and keys was left on the seat of the cab.

Kay called Tina to tell her she had the envelope.

Tina told Kay to mail the envelope on Monday.

Dave came to pick up Mariah on Sunday, and Kay gave the envelope to Mariah to give to him.

Dave assumed the envelope contained more bad legal news and hid it from Sandy.

Dave opened the envelope and found the copy of the lease and the extra keys.

Dave raced to the townhouse.

Using the extra key, Dave unlocked the door and discovered his neighbor, "Mr. Trash," consoling Sandy with a passionate embrace that had them writhing in passion on the living room carpet.

Tina finished her story by saying, "Didn't I tell you the Fates were at it again? Whenever you and I get together, watch out!

"But how in the world did you find all this out?" Kay said.

The last thing Kay expected to hear Tina say was, "Ellen Cleary." Kay winced at the name of the bookkeeper at Dave's former office, remembering her snickering solidarity with Sandy that day at the pizza parlor. What Kay had forgotten, however, was Tina and Ellen had been good friends, before and after, Sandy arrived on the scene.

"You know, Kay, Ellen never approved of Dave and Sandy's affair," Tina said.

Kay scoffed. "She gave a pretty good imitation of it from where I was sitting."

Tina defended her old co-worker. She said Ellen had made a true effort to keep her distance from Sandy. She confessed to Tina she was very relieved when Dave and Sandy moved away.

"When they moved back to town, Sandy got in touch with Ellen again and it wasn't a happy surprise." Tina said.

Over the months Ellen did everything she could to discourage Sandy from calling her. And it had worked until this past Saturday when Sandy recognized Tina at the townhouse. Sandy immediately called Ellen, and in a highly-agitated state, relentlessly quizzed her about Tina's professional integrity.

Ellen was happy to vouch for Tina. She validated Sandy's decision to sign with Tina and her property management company. Then she dispensed with Sandy as quickly as she could, hoping it would be the last time she'd hear from her. But on Monday, a hysterical Sandy called again accusing Ellen of purposely misleading her. Sandy worked herself up into such a frenzy she finally broke down and the whole story came pouring out.

"Ellen called me immediately afterward," Tina said. "And now I'm calling you."

Kay felt drained after hearing Tina's story. Her

emotions had been drug across the gamut from stunned, to validated, to angry, to giddy, to avenged, and finally to a little sad. She was about to ask Tina if Dave had beaten Mr. Knash to a pulp when the doorbell rang.

"Let me call you back," Kay said.

She opened the door to an ashen-faced Dave. Next to him was a smiling Mariah, delighted to be at her mother's doorstep.

"I need to leave Mariah here for couple days," Dave said. "I've got some urgent personal business to take care of and I think it'll be better if she's here with you."

Mariah crossed the threshold with her customary skip, seemingly unaware of her dad's distress. Kay was thrilled to see her, relieved she was out of the middle of Dave's domestic mess.

Dave wasted no time walking back to his truck where Kay noticed Little Dave strapped in his car seat.

"Do you have anyone to help you with Little Dave?" Kay called to Dave.

He turned and leaned slightly forward. "No. Not really," he said.

"Bummer," Kay said, and slammed the door.

"I'm hungry, Mom. Do we have anything to eat?" Mariah said.

"I was just about to call Cory down to help me make some spaghetti," Kay said with a smile. "How about helping me with the garlic bread?"

Kay put her arm around her little girl and they walked into the kitchen.

Epilogue

Leo held his palm over the top of the cold barbecue grill. "The coals haven't even been lit yet," Leo said, as walked back to the patio lounger. He plunked into the chair and the lightweight mesh and aluminum structure threatened to fold like a Venus flytrap. "At this rate we won't be eating for at least another hour." Leo was pouting.

"Shhh," Lindy O'Malley said. "Ed's gonna hear you."

Lindy was stretched out next to Leo on a comfy lounge chair of her own. She lifted her sunglasses to the top of her head and gave Leo a look of disapproval. "You don't want him to think you're an ungrateful guest."

Ed emerged from the sliding glass doors of his kitchen balancing a large platter of steaks, burgers and bratwursts on the palm of his hand. He carefully transferred the platter to his other palm, slid the door shut, then hurried toward the built-in brick barbecue grill stationed at the far end of his flagstone patio.

"I didn't expect you two so early," Ed said. "You do know the party was scheduled for two o'clock?

Lindy nudged Leo's arm with her elbow, knocking it off the arm rest. "I told you we were too early," she whispered.

"I thought we'd get here ahead of everyone and see if you needed any help," Leo said. His overly-relaxed position in the chair belied his magnanimous explanation.

Lindy glared at him. Helping out was never mentioned as a reason for showing up thirty minutes early. She knew Leo was simply hoping to get a head start on all the party food.

"Well, now that you mention it, I could use your help carrying a couple of coolers from the garage," Ed said. He was busy preparing to light the grill.

Leo didn't respond to the request. "You'll never get those coals started without lighter fluid," he called to Ed from his stretched out, comfortable perch.

"It's a gas grill, Leo," Ed called back. He opened two small doors underneath the grill, and gestured toward the large white propane tank.

"Leo, go get the coolers," Lindy said. "Ed knows what he's doing."

With a disgusted sigh, Leo swung his long legs over to one side and reluctantly rose from his lounger. "Some party," he mumbled to himself. "I might as well be at work."

Lindy shrugged and smiled at Ed. He gave her a wink and pushed the red ignition button on the grill.

The sliding glass doors opened again and out walked Kay rubbing her arm. "I can't crank the churn any more, Ed. Can we switch up for awhile?" Kay had been in the kitchen, hard at work on her old ice cream churn.

"I'd be happy to give it try," Lindy said, jumping up from her chair.

Kay had missed the arrival of Lindy and Leo,

who had let themselves in through the side gate of Ed's home. As the unofficial hostess of Ed's bi-annual employee appreciation party, Kay felt obligated to greet the guests and get them comfortably situated. However, Kay wasn't prepared to see Officer O'Malley leap up in front of her and couldn't help reacting with a knee-jerk alarm. But Lindy's welcoming smile quickly put Kay at ease.

"Wow. Are you making fresh butter?" Leo said. He joined the scene carrying a large, and seemingly heavy, red cooler. Leo's wide-eyed excitement never failed to amuse Kay.

"Home made strawberry ice cream," Kay said with a laugh.

Lindy relieved Leo of one end of the cooler and guided him over to a table sitting under the shade of the patio cover. Ed watched, ever amazed at the level of strength packed into Lindy's diminutive structure.

Kay looked at her watch. "Aren't you guys here a little early?"

Lindy rolled her eyes. "Don't ask," she said.

Despite Lindy's annoyance, Kay knew she had a true affection for Leo. She thought it was great they'd decided to give dating another go.

Leo was about to lower himself back on his chair when Lindy stopped him short. "What about the other cooler?" she said.

He popped up straight again and let out another sigh. "I'm going. I'm going. But you better not say anything when I have to pig out to make up for all this energy you're making me burn."

Lindy playfully grabbed Leo's arm by the elbow. "Oh, come on, you big baby," Lindy said. "I'll go with you."

Leo yanked his arm away. "Don't come unless you're going to help," Leo said.

"I swear, Leo. Sometimes you can be so…"

The two disappeared through the back door to the garage before Kay could hear Lindy finish her sentence.

"I've got the burgers and the brats going," Ed said, walking up behind Kay. "You keep an eye on them and I'll go work on the ice cream." He smiled at Kay and gave her a quick peck on the cheek.

"We'll wait on the steaks 'til everyone is here," he said over his shoulder. This time he wasn't in a hurry.

* * *

It was a perfect day for a party. Mariah and her guest, Alisha Resnick, splashed in the pool, while Cory and Violet talked quietly in a far corner of the back yard. The scene around the large patio table was both lively and relaxed, courtesy of plenty of cold beer and a bottomless pitcher of margaritas. Guests feasted on Ed's expertly grilled selections and delicious side dishes pot-lucked by the party guests.

"What happened to the container of Mrs. Dash's okra that was sitting here a second ago?" Leo asked, on an urgent quest to fill his plate for the third time. "They're better than potato chips."

"Check in the kitchen, Leo," Ruth said. "There should be another bag sitting on the counter next to

339

the sink." Ruth turned to Ed. "That reminds me, Ed. How are Addie and Owen doing?" she asked. "Have you heard from them lately?"

"As a matter of fact, I got a call from Uncle O day before yesterday." Ed said. "He and Adelaide really like Miami." Ed went on to report their counseling sessions were going well and that O was feeling confident Addie would soon be moving out of their daughter's home and back in with him.

"That's wonderful news," Ruth said. "If there were ever two people who truly belong together, it's Owen and Adelaide."

"What's this about two people belonging together?" George McNab said, swinging his leg over the picnic bench, cozying in next to Ruth. He carefully set a hot casserole dish on the pot holder sitting on the table in front of him. He turned to Ruth and flashed her a dazzling smile. Ruth's responded with a look of utter delight such as Kay had never seen.

Kay's heart squeezed at the tender scene. She knew Mr. McNab had probably once smiled at Emily the same way, knowing *they* had belonged together. But Emily was gone and Kay marveled at George's willingness to open himself to belonging to someone else - especially when it was her lovely friend, Ruth.

"You all have to try this amazing chicken casserole," Mr. McNab said. "I hate to think what I would've missed if Ruth hadn't insisted on showing me how to make it." He scooped out a portion and served Ruth before taking some for himself.

Kay excused herself from the table to check

on the ice cream hardening in Ed's freezer. The home-made strawberry recipe had turned out so well, she looked forward to trying a more-challenging flavor next time.

What in the world ever possessed me to sell that churn?

"I'd say the ice cream is going to be perfect by the time we're all ready for desert," Kay said, returning to the table. She took her place next to Ed and he patted her on the thigh.

Ting, ting, ting. Ed tapped his water glass with the end of a butter knife.

"I know you didn't come here to listen to me give a speech. But I want to thank you all for allowing me to express my appreciation for all your dedication and hard work. It was always my grandfather's dream to keep Salinger's a family business. 70 years later, I'm the only Salinger left at the mortuary, but because of you, it still remains a family business."

He blinked back tears and cleared his throat a couple of times before he continued. "I'd like to make a toast," he said, raising his beer can.

Everyone at the table raised their glasses.

"To...."

Briiiing

The ringer on Ed's phone went off. It was the mortuary line forwarded to his cell.

"Salinger's Mortuary. Ed Salinger speaking." He walked away from the table to give the caller professional privacy.

"I'll take some of your chicken casserole, Mr. McNab," Kay said.

"Please call me George," he said, smiling and taking Kay's plate.

"Thank you…George."

That's definitely going to take some getting used to.

"Death call," Ed announced, coming back to the table. "It's at Memorial so I should be back in an hour or so. Everyone, please stay and enjoy yourselves."

Leo jumped up from his half-eaten plate. "I'll go with you Ed. It'll go faster with two of us."

"Thanks, Leo. I appreciate that." Ed started to leave, but changed his mind and came back to the table. "I want to finish my toast."

Once again everyone raised their glasses.

"To family!" he said.

"To family," everyone heartily replied.

Ed threw back the last of his beer, crushed the can with his hand, leaned over and planted a long, unabashed kiss on Kay's lips.

Thank you for purchasing **Same Old Truths**, the second in the Reluctant Avenger series.

Indie stories like this one rely on good word of mouth to find readers. If you enjoyed this book please consider letting others know by leaving a review on the book's Amazon page, or Goodreads, or wherever you discovered **Same Old Truths**. (Even a sentence or two would be greatly appreciated.)

The next story in the Reluctant Avenger series is Delora Dennis' short story, **Code for Karma**. Delora wrote this as a sequel to **Same Old Truths** and it finds Kay's girls, Cory and Mariah, all grown up, but still dealing with their less-than-decent dad, Dave.

Enter Kay and her old ally, karma. Together they make sure Dave isn't able to get away with his old tricks.

Get Book One

It's Free!

Code for Karma

Go to http://deloradennis.com, enter your email address

and you will receive **Code for Karma** RIGHT NOW!

Acknowledgments

This book could have never been completed without the love and support of the patient, loving, insightful individuals whom I'm blessed to have in my life.

To Juliane Romero for reading and critiquing each and every chapter as they came off the assembly line, and for so graciously allowing me to use her "fainting cop" story.

To Angela Dumas for allowing me to read aloud to her and laughing at all the right parts.

To Dicky Romero for enthusiastically reading the book and being my expert consultant on all matters mortuary.

To Sam Moya for allowing me to interrupt his busy day with all my questions.

To Barbara Romero, my biggest cheerleader and supporter who made it possible for me to devote thirteen months to writing this book.

And last and foremost, to my "Cory" and "Mariah" for being so gracious to have me as their mother.

About the Author

Delora Dennis launched her writing career in 1965, at the tender age of nine, with the production of her play (with a long-since forgotten title) by her elementary school's Home and School Association.

Of course, the trajectory of said launch didn't exactly follow a straight path. Detours along the way included stints as a human resources manager, assistant funeral director, legislative analyst, speech writer, state fair exhibit manager, and independent video producer.

Delora returned to the path in 1993 and since then has been writing in one form or another - video scripts, website content, how-to books, product reviews, informative articles, blog posts, press releases, etc. Looking back now it's clear all of this was preparation for the type of writing she knew she had to try, but resisted like crazy.

"I've discovered writing fiction is like playing with a new toy. Once you've mastered the basics, the real fun comes from finding new ways to play with it. I'm having a ball."

Learn more about Delora and her books at http://deloradennis.com

Like her on Facebook at https://www.facebook.com/deloradennisbooks

and follow her on Twitter @deloradennis and

https://plus.google.com/+DeloraDennis/posts

www.ingramcontent.com/pod-product-compliance
Lightning Source LLC
Chambersburg PA
CBHW030141200626
46812CB00015B/101